Praise for *Day of the Assassins*:

"Time travel mixed with warfare, what more could
a boy want!"
– Nat, aged 10

"When you see the front cover you know this
is going to be exciting. Lots of different fonts
and pictures inside but most of all, a really
action-packed story where there are things
happening all the time and you never get bored."
– Harry, aged 12

For Sally, Tom, Peter and Anna – J. O'B.

THE YEAR: 1914

THE PLACE: SARAJEVO

THE MISSION: ASSASSINATION OF ARCHDUKE FRANZ FERDINAND –
HEIR TO AN EMPIRE

Jack Christie and his friend Angus are caught up in a major event that will dramatically change the future. Should they intervene? And, more importantly, will they survive?

Join Jack on a dangerous chase across pre-war Europe to the rain-sodden trenches of World War I, as the future of mankind hangs in the balance.

A TEMPLAR BOOK

First published in the UK in 2009 by Templar Publishing,
This softback edition published in 2010 by Templar Publishing,
an imprint of The Templar Company Limited,
The Granary, North Street, Dorking, Surrey, RH41DN, UK
www.templarco.co.uk

First edition

ISBN 978-1-84877-091-1

Cover design by Butterworthdesign.com and Jonathan Lambert
Map and Timeline design by Leonard le Rolland
Editorial by Anne Finnis, Helen Greathead, Ruth Martin and Rachel Williams

Printed and bound in Great Britain by
MPG Books Ltd, Bodmin, Cornwall

Picture Credits: P.31: Archduke Franz Ferdinand © Mary Evans Picture Library; P.33: Gavrilo Princip ©

ullsteinbild / Topfoto; P.196: Archduke Franz Ferdinand and the Duchess Sophie of Austria moments before their death

© Illustrated London News Ltd / Mary Evans Picture Library; P.216: The five ringleaders of the assassination © Daily

Herald Collection / Science & Society Picture Library.

A JACK CHRISTIE ADVENTURE

DAY OF THE
ASSASSINS

JOHNNY O'BRIEN

templar publishing

Choices

A Word from the Author

A few years ago my dad showed me some medals that his dad (my grandfather) had received during the First World War. He explained that my grandfather had been injured in the war and had later lost part of his leg. Apparently, my grandfather was reluctant to speak about how he got the injuries or how he won the medals. I don't really know why. But I know what he did was brave – because I have a citation at home signed by the 'Minister of War', Winston Churchill.

Anyway, unlike millions of others, my grandfather survived the war and went on to have children and live to a ripe old age – although I never knew him. It got me thinking though. He made important choices in his life – he chose to fight in the war. It seems he chose to do something brave. Later he chose to have a family. If he had made different choices, of course, I might not be here and you would not have picked up this book.

The war he fought in was also caused by people making choices. Lots of choices over many years – some important, some seemingly trivial. The war was horrific and led to many other tragic events in the twentieth century. I wonder if people who made those choices would have chosen differently had they known what would happen?

So I suppose this book is about choices. Some of the events described really happened and some of the people really existed. Other people you will meet here are, of course, made up. But they all have to make choices.

You're probably going to make some choices today as well. Some will seem important and some not – although sometimes you don't really know which are the important ones until afterwards – perhaps a long time afterwards. Nevertheless, you need to try to choose well – because whatever you do, it could change the future.

Contents

Europe–1914

Front Line

The shock wave from the air burst caught Jack full on, lifted him up and threw him backwards a full six metres, his body twisting in mid air as he flew. Gravity pulled him back to earth, but where there should have been churned-up mud to cushion his landing, there was nothing. Instead, he was propelled into a huge empty space on the ground. With a crunching thud, his face, and then the rest of his body, hit the sloping inner wall of a large hole. As he slid down, mud filled his ears, nostrils and mouth.

His helmet had already been blown free, as had everything else: webbing, gas mask and, of course, his Lee Enfield rifle. He'd only fired the stupid thing once, and that had been a mistake – one that had nearly got him court-martialled. He continued his headlong slide down the sharply sloping hole, mud gathering around his collar and easing itself inside his uniform. He finally came to rest, head first, in a pool of putrid water that had settled at the bottom of the hole. He lifted his head from the pool, spitting and coughing, and peered upwards at the lip of the crater from where he had just fallen. Just then, the noxious mix of smoke and grey mist above the crater lip flashed a dirty orange and the concussion from another explosion ripped through the air. Instinctively, he dunked his head back into the cold water, seeking protection from the fury above. He waited a few seconds until the icy chill started to seep through him, then scrambled his way up, so only his boots rested in the pool. He was breathing hard, but the explosions had stopped, although he could still hear the chatter of at least one machine gun in the distance.

Day of the Assassins

He had been lucky. The rest of the company had been wiped out – spattered about this godforsaken landscape of mud by the sudden barrage. They had only arrived at the front the night before. He cast his eye over the inside of the crater. Bizarrely, it had saved his life. But he realised that no one was going to come and get him. Somehow, he would have to crawl back to the trench.

Suddenly, on the other side of the mud puddle, he saw two bright blue eyes staring straight back at him. They shone piercingly from a mud-freckled face and were locked onto him, trancelike. Like Jack, the figure opposite was prostrate, and caked in mud. Across the thigh of one leg, Jack could make out a large dark patch. The soldier had kept his helmet and Jack could see the familiar spike that indicated that his companion was a soldier of His Imperial Majesty's Grand Army of the German Second Reich. He quickly scanned the other details – the *feldgrau* uniform, the black boots. But there was something strange about the uniform: it seemed loose, the cuffs were too long and the collar rose round the soldier's thin neck uncomfortably. Jack studied the face peering back at him; his German friend could not even be sixteen years old. He was white and he was trembling. It was then that Jack realised, with dismay, that within his white, fragile, boy-fingers, the soldier held a large black pistol – and the pistol was trained on him.

The heavy lump of black metal was comically out of proportion with the rest of the boy's frame – like when you see a child wearing his dad's boots. Jack felt a new wave of panic start to build, sickeningly, from the pit of his stomach. The boy was as terrified as Jack was, but even at that distance, Jack could see a pendulous index finger slowly squeezing the trigger of the pistol. Jack pushed out a hand in a vain gesture of protection and started to scream, but it was too late. There was an orange flash as the chamber of the pistol emptied. Jack shut his eyes and braced himself, pushing back hard into the dirt, hoping it would somehow enfold him in its thick, sticky blanket and insulate him from the impact.

But the impact didn't come. He opened his eyes and looked at the boy who was now shaking even more, a look of incredulity on his face. He held the pistol up again, this time both index fingers wrapped round the trigger and squeezed... Jack braced himself again. But nothing happened. There was a click: the gun was empty. Jack felt a wave of euphoria wash over him. The boy fumbled furiously at his belt, but the dark patch on his leg had started to grow ominously, and he was finding movement difficult. Jack had no weapon. Everything had been blown from him in the blast. Should he stay put or scramble free from the crater... and run?

It wasn't his decision. At that moment a second figure loomed from behind the lip of the crater and peered in. Even at that distance, Jack could see that this new figure was stockier and heavier than the boy opposite. He moved with a confidence that came with the professional soldier's greatest gift – survival. The soldier's helmet had the same distinctive spiked silhouette as the boy's. It signified only one thing: Jack was about to die.

Despite his stocky build the soldier descended the side of the crater with ease, assessed the situation and made his decision. He muttered something gruffly in German to the boy and without breaking step marched directly through the puddle to where Jack lay with his back pressed into the damp earth. The soldier reached down to something on his belt, which glistened in what remained of the daylight above. He fastened the object to the end of his rifle: a serrated-steel bayonet.

The soldier raised the barrel of the Mauser Gewehr rifle and moved the bayonet slowly towards him. Jack caught the soldier's eyes, but they showed no excitement, no fear, no emotion. His humanity had been drained from him through months of attrition. The soldier pinned the bayonet under Jack's chin, and rested it momentarily on his throat. Jack felt the prick on his skin and prayed for death to come quickly. The soldier looked down at him, steadied his boots in the mud and, with a grunt, pushed the steel 'hard into Jack's neck.

Point-of-Departure

Jack groaned in frustration, turning to Angus. "I'm dead – again. This level's impossible."

"You're rubbish." Angus put both hands behind his head and leaned back in the moth-eaten armchair, grinning smugly.

Jack rolled his eyes and tossed the controller over to his friend. "So why don't you try?"

"Nah… this level's too much for me. Get it all the time from Dad…"

"Get what?"

Angus yawned. "Can't be bothered to tell you…"

"Tell me what?"

"Great Grandfather Ludwig…" Angus rolled his 'Rs' mockingly.

"Who's he?"

"I'll tell you – but don't say I didn't warn you. My Great Grandfather Ludwig, as we are all sick of hearing, was a German soldier – he fought in the war," Angus pointed at the screen, where Jack had paused *Point-of-Departure*, "that war – the First World War."

Jack was impressed. "You're joking?"

"No. And I know that 'cos he's still on the mantelpiece back home… In a jar."

"A what?"

"A jar. Not all of him, you plonker, just a bit of him. A piece of his left tibia… whatever that is."

"A bone in his leg."

"Whatever. We've got an old photo of him as well. Part of his ear is missing."

"Why have you got that on your mantelpiece? You lot are mad."

"Dad likes talking about it – Great Grandfather Ludwig and Great

Gran Dot." Angus looked across at Jack with a pained expression. "I'm going to have to tell you the whole story, aren't I?"

Jack nodded.

"Great Grandfather Ludwig was a German infantryman." Angus tipped his head at the screen again, "Like that guy who just owned you in the last level… Anyway, he fought in the war. He got medals and all sorts. Then one day there was a big British offensive. Ludwig's trench was about to be overrun. Apparently, he refused to budge, even though all his mates were about to retreat. In fact, he did the opposite – he went over the top to search for German survivors in no-man's-land. Apparently, he saved at least one young lad who would have died from his injuries otherwise."

"Amazing."

"Before he got back to his lines, the Brits attacked and he was captured, although he was wounded in the process – in his leg…"

"…the bone in the jar on your mantelpiece?"

"Right. They patched him up and he recovered. In fact, it seems he developed a bit of a soft spot for the British. There is some story about how he'd met some guys, some lost British soldiers or something, out there in no-man's-land when he was searching around. Apparently, they were going to kill him but decided to let him go… I think so he could rescue his injured friend or something… I'm not sure… it's a bit hazy."

"What happened to him?"

"Met Dorothy. Great Gran Dot. She was a nurse in the field hospital. She was Scottish. They hitched up. The war ended. They got married and he never went home. Moved to Scotland with Dot and took over the old sheep farm when Dot's old man died."

"What – your house up at Rachan?"

"Very same."

"So you're German, Angus?"

"S'pose – eighth German or something… My surname, Jud, is a German name. I think. It's pronounced 'Yood' – but no one knows that so everyone just says 'Jud'. It's easier."

Jack smiled. "You never said anything before. It's a good story."

"Maybe – Dad just goes on about it a bit. I think Dad was close to his grandfather when he was a lad. I'll bring the photo in tomorrow, if I remember, but maybe leave the jar at home…" Angus suddenly remembered something and looked at his watch. "I'm late!" He jumped to his feet and grabbed his coat, which had been discarded on the dusty cellar floor. "Sorry mate, I'll have to leave you to it. I've got Pendelshape first thing tomorrow – and I haven't started my essay. You know what the Pendelino's like… he'll go ape. I'm in his bad books anyway. He confiscated my iPod yesterday."

Angus was already disappearing back up the cellar stairs to the kitchen.

Jack shrugged. "See you then…" He picked up the controller, which was still moist from his sweaty palms, and turned back to the computer game. Underneath, the console's piercing light winked back at him, challenging him to try just one more time. Angus's story had suddenly somehow made it much more real. He felt the adrenaline in his veins and, while holding the controller with one hand, instinctively fumbled in his trouser pocket with the other for his puffer. He felt a rush of comfort as his fingers located and then encircled its familiar plastic outline.

He muttered to himself, "Captain Jack Christie's ready – I hope you are."

Cairnfield

It was four pm. Jack stood by the imposing wrought iron gates as school dispersed. He turned the collar of his blazer up and stamped his feet to thwart the biting autumn wind that whistled round the Victorian buildings. Until ten years ago the buildings had been empty; they had only been revived by an endowment from a reclusive benefactor. The local community was grateful that the secluded site and its surrounding parkland had been redeveloped – it brought in much needed money. A lot of the local kids now attended the school and its reputation was growing.

Jack's hands were turning pink with the cold. He rubbed them together.

"Where is he?"

His head was still buzzing from double history, which had just ended. They were doing the First World War. Dr Pendelshape, the history teacher, had become even more animated than usual. The man was obsessed. Even though it was a world away, Jack could not help being caught up in Pendelshape's story. Maybe it was because he had seen some of it in *Point-of-Departure*… or because of Angus's story yesterday about Ludwig. He remembered the opening titles from *Point-of-Departure* with its black-and-white pictures of the crusty, moustached generals of the great European imperial powers and their paraphernalia of office – medals, uniforms – all the grandeur of empire.

Pendelshape had explained about the new military hardware of that time. Apparently, there were howitzers that could belch a shell of Jack's size thirty kilometres away. They were launched way out of sight and would land in a maelstrom of shrapnel and fire that would create a hole bigger than a house. There were new guns that could fire six hundred rounds in one minute, dismembering anything in sight. How had Pendelshape put it? That's right, he had said, "It all lay amassed and untried in that beautiful European summer of 1914 that was poised, unknowingly, for the bloodiest war that mankind had ever unleashed upon itself." When he had said it, Jack had thought that Pendelshape was about to burst into tears.

Despite his interest, Jack hadn't hung about after school to chat like he sometimes did. He got on well with Pendelshape. But he reckoned today he should really be thinking about, well, about happier things. After all, today was his birthday.

He didn't want to wait any longer. He stamped his feet again and shivered. Suddenly he heard the pop and whine of a motorbike buzzing up the hill from the lower car park, trailing a plume of blue smoke from its 125cc two-stroke engine. Jack's heart sank. Angus had brought the bike to school again.

The blue and yellow Husqvarna WRE trail machine skidded to a halt, but Angus had misjudged the kerb, and Jack jumped back to avoid being squashed by the front tyre.

"Idiot!"

Angus cut the engine and the air was suddenly still. He removed the full face helmet, revealing a mop of straight black hair. At sixteen, Angus was a year older than Jack and at one metre seventy-seven, he was also fifteen centimetres taller. With all the sport he did, plus helping his dad out on the farm, Angus was strong and broad shouldered. He had a wide face that always seemed to be flushed from physical exertion or from being outside. Jack still had the slender frame of a boy. He had messy blonde hair that could never decide whether it wanted to be curly or straight. Jack and Angus were bit of an unlikely pair.

"Are you trying to kill me?"

"Keep your hair on, Jackster…"

"You're not supposed to be riding that thing, you've only got a provisional…"

"Well, test is only a few months away. Anyway, how else am I supposed to get to school?"

"The bus?"

Angus shrugged. "It was early this morning."

"You were late, you mean."

"Who cares. We're going to your place aren't we? Let's stop farting around…" Angus unclipped the spare helmet and tossed it to Jack. He grinned. "Climb aboard, big man."

Jack remembered the last time he'd been on Angus's bike. It was at his folks' who had the sheep farm up the valley in Rachan. The family was machine mad and Angus had grown up with bikes. Trouble was, Jack hadn't. He'd had a go, but lost his balance, the bike had spun off in one direction, and Jack in another, and he had ended up with a face full of mud. Angus had laughed so much he'd nearly fallen over.

"You're joking?"

Angus shrugged, "Well you can walk if you like." He snapped down on the kick-start and the engine burst into life. Jack rolled his eyes, reluctantly donned the spare helmet, climbed behind Angus and clenched his eyes firmly shut. Angus turned back the throttle and the engine wailed; he dropped the clutch and the machine jerked forward. The front wheel immediately lifted off the ground in a spectacular but completely unnecessary wheelie. Jack was taken by surprise and just avoided slipping right off the back and onto the tarmac. Once the bike had two wheels back on the road, it was too late for Jack to complain.

They soon reached the main bridge out of town, which crossed the river that was starting to swell from the extra rain in the hills. As they crossed it, Jack could feel the temperature drop. The river acted like the cold element of a freezer as it snaked through the fading light of the border hill country. In two minutes they would be turning into the long drive at Cairnfield. A journey which usually took him twenty-five minutes on foot had been completed in only five.

*

They had moved to Cairnfield with his grandparents when his mum and dad came back from Geneva, Switzerland – just before they had split up. Jack had been only six. Jack's mum had kept the Cairnfield estate when first, Jack's grandfather and then, later his grandmother, had died. This had left him and his mum on their own rattling round in the big old house together. His mum didn't talk much about their life in Geneva or why they had left. Nor did she explain why she had split up from his dad soon after they'd moved to Scotland. She had just said he was "too obsessed with work" or "there wasn't room for us and his work". Jack sometimes tried to find out more, but his mum would become all buttoned up and quickly change the subject.

Jack prodded Angus as they made their way down the drive. "Stop!"

Angus pulled the bike to one side, and the engine puttered away in neutral.

"Put it somewhere, we'll walk from here. Mum'll go berserk if she sees me on the back of this thing."

"If you say so."

Angus pulled the WRE behind the thicket of yews that flanked one side of the drive. They left their helmets and pressed on down the track. Soon the big white house loomed into view.

*

Jack's mum was making tea and looked up as they came through the back door into the kitchen. Her hands wet, she blew her hair from her face. Carole Christie looked a lot like Jack. She had the same grey-blue eyes and blonde hair. She was still slim, although her figure had thickened a little with her forty-three years.

"You're back early…"

Jack looked at Angus nervously. Angus avoided the subject and attempted his most winning smile, displaying a mouthful of uneven teeth in the process. It was a sight that would have traumatised a small child.

"Hello Mrs C. My cake ready?"

Carole Christie looked at Angus with mock affront. "So it's *your* birthday now, is it?"

Angus started to move towards a large bowl of chocolate cake mix.

"Looks tasty." He brought a large, dirty-nailed index finger dangerously close to the sugary mixture. But Mrs Christie was too quick.

She whipped out a wooden spoon and landed a swift blow expertly on Angus's knuckles. He yelped.

Jack approved. "Nice one, Mum."

"You'll just have to wait," she said. "Go and do something for an hour."

"Mum – has it arrived?" Jack asked.

His Mum's smile quickly vanished and she gave him the look – a sort of grimace that passed over her face whenever the subject of his father came up.

"It's in your bedroom." She turned back to the worktop. In his excitement, Jack did not notice the hint of satisfaction in her voice, when she said, "But I don't think it's much to get excited about, love… definitely smaller than usual."

He ignored the comment and rushed out of the kitchen.

Soon they were in his bedroom, and there it was sitting on his desk, just like all his other birthdays: a parcel wrapped in brown paper and string. He flipped it over and instantly recognised the italic writing. His heart beat faster.

"Come on… open it." Angus said impatiently.

But his mum was right. Based on size, the parcel looked disappointing – compared to earlier birthdays, anyway. He placed the precious package on the floor and stared at it, inspecting it from each side in turn. His mind flicked through the presents from previous years. The year before, there had been the remote controlled aeroplane and before that, all the fly fishing stuff. Every year, a present had arrived, like clockwork, and it had always exceeded his expectations. These birthday presents were his only connection with his father now.

Jack could no longer resist and, egged on by Angus, tore open the wrapping paper. Then his jaw dropped in disappointment as the contents were revealed.

"It's a book." Angus was alarmed.

Jack picked it up and shook it. Maybe something would drop out – like a cheque for a thousand pounds or an airline ticket to some exotic holiday destination. But no. It was a book. And, worst of all, it was a textbook.

"It's a school book," Angus said with growing horror.

Jack's heart sank. He read the title: *The First World War*.

"It's called, *The First World War*," Angus said. "Dull-arama."

"I can read."

This present did not have the 'wow' factor of those from previous years, but maybe it was better than nothing.

Angus had already lost interest and busied himself with a particularly annoying wooden pyramid puzzle that rested on the mantelpiece and which he had failed to master even after several months of trying. It had taken Jack four minutes and twenty-eight seconds.

Jack scanned the front cover and then opened the book to inspect the crisp, sharp-edged photographs arranged in three sections. They showed trenches, ships, barbed wire, 'over the top' howitzers, aeroplanes, tanks, maps, women in factories, leaders, soldiers, medals, observation balloons, trains and more... Some pages were blurred and sepia, others were crystal clear, but together they gave Jack an instant insight into the four years of brutal war.

"Weird."

"What?" said Angus, without raising his head from the puzzle.

"I get this history book from Dad, right, and yesterday you talked about your Great Grandfather Ludwig who was in the war, and then Pendelshape was on about the same stuff today in class."

"What stuff?"

"You know – the First World War – all that..."

Angus shrugged, "So?"

"Quite interesting – don't you think?"

"For a boffin like you. Doesn't do it for me."

He looked up at Jack with a piece of the puzzle in each hand. "How do you do this stupid thing, again?"

Jack leaned over, took the pieces and manipulated them expertly. In under a minute the puzzle had been done and Jack handed it back. Angus stared at it in awe.

"See – easy."

"You're really annoying sometimes."

"Pendelshape was saying today that millions of people died in the war. Millions. And that if things had been slightly different it might not even have happened."

Angus yawned. "If you say so. For me, it's all in the past. Gone, dead, finished."

"What about *Point-of-Departure*? That's based in the past. You like that, don't you?"

"That's different – it's a game. It's real."

It's what Jack would have expected Angus to say. But something about the images and the clear black text on each page of the book stirred a distant but strong emotion in Jack. He couldn't quite put his finger on it. He sometimes got a similar feeling when he played *Point-of-Departure*. A sort of flashback – a connection to somewhere else, somewhere different. He was transported back to a time, he was not quite sure exactly when, but he had been very young – maybe only four years old.

He remembered that they had been on a family holiday. He had been vaguely aware that Dad had not had a day off from the lab for months and had been working very late. This was to be his first break in a long time. They had gone to France or Belgium and had visited Cambrai or some such place – a monument to the First World War. He had been aware that his father was interested in history and, he supposed, this period of history in particular.

What had happened and in what sequence had remained a disconnected patchwork in his head – sometimes fragments came into greater focus when he thought back but they would evaporate, chimera-like, as he struggled to make sense of it all. He remembered visiting graves – an endless sea of white crosses – and also the grassed outline of old trench networks. He recalled a voice describing "how it was". Maybe it had been his father's voice, or maybe a tour guide's, or maybe some audio-visual show. He had not understood the words, or if he had, he no longer remembered them, but the serious, gravelled voice conjured up a strong image of the war and the plight of its young victims.

There had also been one of those short but violent summer

thunderstorms. Jack remembered it being very hot and then getting wet and running along for shelter. He had heard thunder and seen lightning and remembered thinking that the raindrops were huge – big pea-sized blobs that exploded on the tarmac. He hadn't been frightened; more curious. The images of the thunder and lightning combined in his head with what his young mind imagined the soldiers must have endured. This had made it real to him – for a moment it was as if he had become one of them, but because he was from another time somehow he wouldn't be harmed; he would always be able to escape.

But the strongest memory of that time was waking up in the hotel or guest house or wherever they had been. He'd had his own room and the closeness of the night had woken him. He had pottered along the short corridor to his parents' room, opened the door and seen his mum and dad standing there. He remembered feeling it was strange that they were not in bed and that the bedside light was on. They were quite far apart and he would never forget the pleading expression on his mum's face. Both his mum and dad had red eyes and he felt uneasy when he realised that they were both crying. He had never seen an adult cry. Then his mum swivelled round to the open door, saw Jack there staring up at them and, with alarm, whisked him back off to his bedroom.

He saw even less of his father when they finally returned after the holiday – he was hard at work at the lab. Always working. Then the move back to Scotland had come and suddenly one day his mum told him that his father had left, and that "it would just be us now".

*

"Hey, what's this?" Angus had finally tossed the pyramid puzzle onto the floor in disgust and it had shattered back into separate pieces. Next to the puzzle, there was a piece of folded paper that must have dropped from the parcel when Jack had ripped it open. It was a letter.

Jack,

I am so sorry that once again I can't be with you on your birthday, just as I have been sorry to miss so many important events in your life. I hope that one day I will have a chance to redeem myself and that I can make it up to you. Fifteen already! I hope you enjoy your day. This year I have sent a gift of a more cerebral nature. I hope you are not too disappointed. In time, I think you will appreciate its significance. I know that you are a great student and are destined for a great future, so I think you will enjoy it.

Love,

Dad

Jack stared at the page blankly. Suddenly a wave of sadness welled up from deep within him. For a moment his eyes moistened. He bit his lip hard. He didn't like to show emotion. Especially in front of Angus.

"What does he say?"

"It's just a letter," Jack said quietly.

Angus shrugged. "Whatever. Least your dad sends you presents. My dad only ever sends me to the farm – to work."

Jack looked at his friend and put all thoughts of his father out of his head. "Food. Let's go."

*

They sat round the kitchen table. There was a smear of chocolate on Angus's top lip and on the table, there were a few crumbs where the cake had been. It looked as though the kitchen had been visited by a swarm of locusts.

Mrs Christie looked at Angus.

"Any more?"

"Sorry Mrs C, I couldn't eat another thing."

"But you've only had five slices…" Her eyes twinkled.

"It was very nice, thank you, Mrs C." Angus groaned. "But I think I need to lie down."

Jack leaned over and poked Angus in the ribs. "Don't they feed you at yours or something?"

Angus grunted.

Mrs Christie said, "On you go Angus – Jack can you just help me clear away?"

With some difficulty Angus rose from the table and waddled his way towards the cellar door.

Jack called after him, "Try the first level again – *The Archduke and the Assassin*."

But Angus could only offer a weary nod of his head in response.

*

"So, come on then, what was the present?" His mum looked at him expectantly as they started to clear the table.

Jack shrugged. "Just some book," he squeezed out a smile, "I think you were right Mum, Dad's presents are going downhill."

"Sorry about that love – that happens when you get older."

"Suppose."

Jack stared into the open dishwasher.

Suddenly he blurted out, "Mum, what happened to Dad – where is he now – " he immediately regretted the question, " – exactly?" The words hung uncomfortably in the air. His mum sat down, holding a plate, a sad look in her eye.

"I don't know, love. We just kind of grew apart. That sort of thing just… happens."

"But why do we never see him… I mean most people who are separated or whatever, well… they still see their kids… right?"

She shrugged. "Not necessarily. I don't think it's that easy for him."

"Why did he leave?"

"It was… complicated." She put a gentle hand on Jack's shoulder, "He was always working. He was a bit of a machine, truth be told." She sighed. "Soon there was nothing left… for us, I suppose."

"But I thought that all ended when we left Geneva and came here?"

His mum snorted. "What? It got worse! More work, more pressure, more stress. I loved him… and he loved me… and you, of course, but after a while, I figured…" her cheeks flushed, "he felt what he was doing was more important."

"And then he left – just like that. Where is he now?"

"I have no idea," she shrugged. "But whatever he's doing – he thinks it's important... and more important than us. And that's the problem – always was."

"But people always have problems... shouldn't you have patched it up? Shouldn't you have tried, I don't know... harder?"

This time she was defensive. "We did try... I tried, anyway, it's not easy to explain."

Jack knew he was about to reach the limit in this line of questioning. He didn't want a row, but he pressed on, more boldly than before. "Well I don't think you tried hard enough... I never hear from him. I get a present once a year – and that's it. Is that normal?"

"I know it's not a great explanation, Jack, but it's the only one I have. I'm sorry."

The Archduke and the Assassin

"**I**t's Europe, 1914 and the continent is on a knife-edge. An alliance system of great powers has been created. Germany and Austria-Hungary on one side; Russia and France on the other. Britain has moved closer to the Russian and French camp…"

They sat in the cellar – Angus perched up on the edge of the moth-eaten armchair and Jack on a beanbag. The screen went dark and the title of the level popped up in the game's distinctive gothic font:

The Archduke and the Assassin

Jack studied two images that had appeared on the screen in front of them: old photographs from before the First World War. In the left-hand photo stood a man who looked like royalty. He had on the full dress uniform of a cavalry officer – a dark tunic with a high collar and cuffs, a golden sash, light trousers and a hat adorned with ribbon and plumes. The other photo, on the right, was quite different. Dark shifty eyes peered away from the camera from an unshaven face with a defiant stare. The man looked like a peasant.

The bass voice-over of *Point-of-Departure* explained who the men were.

"On your left is Archduke Franz Ferdinand, the nephew of Franz Joseph I – Emperor of the Austro-Hungarian Empire. Franz Ferdinand is the heir to his throne… a mighty sprawling empire that covers a quarter of Europe."

There was a pause before the narrator continued.

Archduke Franz Ferdinand

Day of the Assassins

"To your right, is Gavrilo Princip – student, freedom fighter… or terrorist, depending on your point of view. Princip is a Serbian who grew up in Bosnia in a very poor family."

Angus glanced at Jack. "Looks thin and pale – a bit like you."

Jack ignored him.

"…Princip and his co-conspirators of the 'Black Hand' are planning to assassinate the man on the left, the Archduke, in Sarajevo, a town in Bosnia – part of the Austro-Hungarian Empire… By shooting the Archduke, Princip will set in motion a chain of events that will lead to the outbreak of the First World War. Eight million people will die in this war."

The boys both gripped their controllers tightly.

The narrator completed the introduction, "Your mission is to infiltrate the Bosnian Serb assassination cell, prevent the killing of the Archduke and thereby stop the countdown to war. In this way you will change the course of world history. Good luck."

*

They spent the next hour working their way through the level, taking turns. It was compulsive gaming. They travelled across 1914 Austria in a train to Vienna. From there, they journeyed by horse, cart and even a pre-1914 motorbike to Belgrade. They dodged Austro-Hungarian imperial lifeguards, secret police and a range of other unsavoury characters. On more than one occasion their cover was blown and they were thrown back to the start of the level. Finally, they infiltrated the 'Black Hand' in a dusty café in Belgrade and learned of the plans for the assassination in Sarajevo, which would take place at the end of the level. If they could stop Princip before he pulled the trigger of his pistol, history would be changed forever. Much more importantly, they would move on to the next level.

The great thing about *Point-of-Departure* was that depending on how you played the early levels, the subsequent levels would change – sometimes subtly, sometimes drastically. Sometimes the diplomatic intrigue would take a different course or the war, triggered by the assassination in Sarajevo, would be delayed or possibly even averted (although they hadn't managed to work out how to do that yet).

Gavrilo Princip

Day of the Assassins

In other scenarios, apparently, the war was successfully postponed only to turn into a much longer and even bloodier affair. It was all down to how you played the first levels and the choices you made.

Now it was Jack's turn. He held the controller in two sweaty palms. In the game, he was standing on the Appel Quay in Sarajevo next to the Lateiner Bridge. He knew that Princip was near him in the crowd – but he couldn't see exactly where. Suddenly, a car passed in front of the crowd, then a second. There were a few muted cheers as a third car passed. He caught a fleeting glance of hat feathers and finery over the heads in front of him… and then the Archduke Ferdinand and Sophie, his wife, and the pursuing motorcade were gone.

Suddenly, out of the corner of his eye, he saw the unmistakable figure of Princip furtively crossing the Appel Quay in front of him and then disappearing into Moritz Schiller's delicatessen. Beside him, in the cellar, Angus was on tenterhooks, staring intently at the images on the screen.

"There he is!" he shouted. He jumped up and down in excitement as Jack expertly fingered the controller to manoeuvre himself towards Princip.

"Yes, I can see him," Jack said sarcastically.

"You've got to get him!"

"I know."

The tension mounted. In a few minutes Jack knew that the motorcade would be returning from the Town Hall and Princip would have his final chance to shoot the Archduke – and strike a devastating blow for the Bosnian Serbs against their oppressors, the Austro-Hungarian Empire. Instinctively, he followed Princip and took up position next to the shop. History was about to happen before his eyes.

At that moment they saw the big headlamps and fender of the *Graf und Stift* lumbering round the bend. The car was slowing down. He could see all the occupants including, perched up high in the rear, the Archduke and, to his left, Sophie. A man was leaning over to the driver to tell him something. Suddenly only two and a half metres away, Princip appeared. He had emerged from the delicatessen and had a sandwich in one hand. He had a look of amazement on his face as the Archduke's car ground to a halt, right in front of him. Princip dropped his sandwich and reached into his jacket pocket.

Angus was standing on the armchair. "There! Get him!"

But Jack kept his nerve. "Wait for it…"

He reached into his own coat and pulled out the pistol that he had been given earlier in the game. He held it in both hands and levelled it directly at Princip, who was by now pointing his own gun into the large car.

Angus was apoplectic. "Shoot him!"

Jack pressed the button on his controller once. The pistol jerked in his hands on the screen and Princip collapsed to the ground.

"You got him! You got him!"

They had completed the level. They had foiled the assassination and thereby stopped the countdown to the First World War. They had changed history, but they would not know exactly how they had changed it until the next level. In his excitement, Angus leaped onto the armchair. The big old springs inside the chair absorbed his weight, but then unexpectedly rebounded. Angus suddenly found himself flying over the back of the armchair and towards an old bookcase that stood against one wall of the cellar. Jack turned away from the game just in time to see Angus's large frame crash headlong into the bookcase. There was an explosion of splintering wood and collapsing shelves as he made contact. Then, the entire structure started to move. With a huge crash, the bookcase, its contents and Angus landed in a heap of rubble, wood and dust.

Missing Sim

As the air cleared, Jack peered into the gloom over his friend's prostrate body. The bookcase had fallen backwards through a thin partition into… Jack was not quite sure what.

Angus groaned and pulled himself to his feet. "What happened?"

"I got him, like you said, but…"

Jack had put down his controller and had already stepped over Angus and the bookcase and into the opening next to the cellar.

Gingerly, Angus got to his feet wiping off the dust from his shirt and trousers. As the air cleared, a mysterious annex to the cellar took shape. It looked like a… library. The hole in the cellar wall had opened up onto a narrow balcony, which housed an upper section that swept completely around a small oval room. From this upper section you could reach the lower room by a spiral staircase. The lower floor was well below the level of the adjoining cellar where they had been battling with *Point-of-Departure*.

The upper level of the library was packed with books from floor to ceiling – although it looked like there were gaps where some books were missing. In the lower level of the library, there were papers and journals stacked haphazardly. The walls of the lower level were also plastered with large panels of brown paper to which an extraordinary array of photographs, diagrams and stapled notes were attached. In some places, large felt-tipped arrows were scrawled, connecting one section to another. There were scribbles and crossings out everywhere. In some cases, different-coloured string had been used to interconnect various items and above each main panel of paper there was a large label. These labels were the only things that seemed to exercise any kind of order on the messy workings pinned on the wallcharts beneath. From right to left along the wall, the labels for each wallchart could be read in sequence: 'Timeline Simulation 0103', 'Timeline Simulation 0104', 'Timeline Simulation 0105', and so on, all the way up to 'Timeline Simulation 0109'.

"What is this place?"

"Looks like a kind of control room..." Jack replied.

"Or something out of *Crime Scene Investigation*."

"Yeah – all those weird maps, pictures, photos, notes... kind of linked together..."

"And what the hell is a Timeline Simulation?"

"No clue..." Jack looked along the wall at the various sheets. About halfway down the room he noticed that there seemed to be a whole wallchart missing – just the bare wall and plaster remained behind, pockmarked by the Blu-Tack that had been used to attach the sheet to the wall.

"Funny..." Jack said. "Simulation 0107 seems to be missing..."

Angus shrugged. "Come on – let's take a closer look."

They rushed down the spiral staircase to the lower level. They had not noticed that a dim light had automatically come on as they entered the library. Soon they were in the midst of the lower room and it felt like they were drowning in a sea of paper, books, diagrams, pictures and notes. It was as if they had entered the brain of some ghostly intellect and caught it in the midst of solving some mind-bendingly difficult puzzle.

Opposite the wallcharts, there was a series of floor-to-ceiling shelves and glass cabinets.

"Look at all this stuff..."

Each shelf and each cabinet seemed to be stuffed full of all sorts of historical paraphernalia. Jack had done enough history with Pendelshape to realise that much of it was military in nature – possibly from the world wars. He spotted a trench telescope, some medals, old maps, at least five different sorts of shell casings, uniforms, plus an array of rusty-looking revolvers and other equipment.

"Amazing, do you think any of it can still be used?" Angus said, hopefully.

Between two of the glass cabinets there was a large easel to which was pinned a map. Jack recognised it immediately from one of Pendelshape's recent lessons – an old map of the Balkans. Just like the wallcharts opposite, various notes, photographs and diagrams were pinned to it. Some were connected to specific points by hand-drawn lines. The cities of Sarajevo and Belgrade were marked, but most of the other names he could neither recognise nor pronounce. The pictures pinned around the map included some sort of fortress in a town called 'Doboj' quite near Sarajevo and a picture of a country church or monastery.

"What about that?" Angus was staring towards the far end of the library, his eyes on sticks. There, in the shadows, was a low steel platform set at about waist height. It was perhaps half a metre across and surrounded by eight curved pieces of metal that looped up from the floor, bulged out around the central platform and then rejoined at the top. The whole thing was encased in a canopy of thick green glass. Around the platform there was an intricate arrangement of metal pipework, cabling and wires. There were two main work areas next to the platform, housing an array of oscilloscopes, tools and old computer equipment, but in terms of the overall arrangement of all this technology, the platform was at the centre of things and therefore seemed in some way important.

They moved over to the laboratory area at the far end of the library. As with the other objects, it was clear that a number of pieces of equipment had been removed. There were large spaces in the control panels where multicoloured wires hung loose, spaghetti-like, from empty metal framing.

"Look at this thing." Jack was examining the steel platform inside the thick glass canopy. He suddenly realised that a strange metal object had been left on the platform between a set of symmetrical markings etched into the steel surface of the platform. As he peered closer, Jack put out a finger to touch the glass. Suddenly the whole casing swung silently back from the platform. He snatched back his hand.

"Help! It's moving!"

Soon the canopy had rolled back completely and the boys had a chance to study the object before them. It was a piece of flat shiny metal. One end was pointed. It looked incredibly sharp. The other end was clasped around a narrower splintered piece of cylindrical wood. Angus picked up the object. It was very much heavier than it looked.

"Kind of a spike?" Angus said.

"Here, look, it's got an inscription…" Jack said.

"What does it say?"

"No idea – the metal has a sort of brown stain on it, too."

"Lots of history stuff in here – maybe it's another antique?"

"We should take it to Pendelshape. He'll know." Jack placed the object in his pocket.

After a while, Angus said, "Maybe all this is to do with your father, don't you think? You said he was some sort of scientist, didn't you? And into history."

"Yes. But I don't know why it's all hidden away down here… And such a mess." Then he added resentfully, "I don't know why Mum hasn't said anything about it before. I'll go and get her."

But he didn't have to. Having heard the commotion, Mrs Christie had arrived on the scene and was on the balcony looking down at them.

"Looks like you've made a bit of a discovery."

"What is all this Mum?" Jack looked up at her expectantly.

His mum shrugged. "It's your father's old workshop. When he left he took some things with him, but he wanted the rest left alone and… well, we closed it off."

"But…"

There was a pause. "Sorry I didn't say anything," she sighed. "With your father's work, it was best not to get involved."

A Message

Dr Neil Pendelshape slurped from a mug of tea as he inspected the artefact. The mug had a slogan on it that read, 'Historians do it after the event'. Nobody quite knew how old the head of the history department was – but judging by the crow's feet around his deep-set eyes and the cropped grey hair, he had to be well into his fifties. He wore a tweed jacket, which struggled to cover a squat, portly frame. Pendelshape didn't go in for the open neck fashion of the younger teachers. Jack had never seen him without a tie. He would march around the History department as if it was his personal property – always in control. Jack had never heard him raise his voice, let alone lose his temper, yet discipline was never a problem.

Jack proudly presented the artefact to Pendelshape after school. He and Angus had spent quite a bit of time the previous evening exploring his father's extraordinary library and workshop. To Jack's dismay, his mum had continued to be coy about the discovery. She had said that she had been "meaning to clear it all out" for some time; and that she "had always meant to tell him that it was there", but over time, and being so busy, had "kind of forgotten". Jack did not understand this at all. But as he and Angus had inspected each of the artefacts and the mysterious wallcharts and all the strange equipment in turn, he'd begun to feel a sneaking sense of pride that all of this had once belonged to his own dad.

Pendelshape listened to the boys' revelations with quiet interest. But as the story unfolded, his brow furrowed. He nodded thoughtfully and looked at the lump of steel more closely, with a magnifying glass taken from his desk. He studied the stem of splintered wood first and then carefully worked his way up to the arrow-shaped tip. He was staring intently, his nose millimetres from the object. His face flushed momentarily and a small bead of sweat slowly formed on his forehead. They had expected Pendelshape to be excited. But instead he looked increasingly... worried.

"So what is it, sir?" Angus asked.

"It's the tip of a lance."

Pendelshape thrust the magnifying glass over to Jack and pointed a finger at some lettering on one edge of the arrow-shaped lance head.

"I can see the letters, sir. But I don't know what they mean."

"Let me translate. It reads, 'By God's Grace – F.J.'"

Jack stared blankly at Pendelshape. "F.J.?"

"Franz Joseph."

Jack remembered the name but Angus shrugged, none the wiser.

Pendelshape rolled his eyes. "It means, boys, that we have here the ceremonial lance tip of one of the life guards of the Emperor of Austria." His voice trailed off thoughtfully. "Or, to give him his proper name: Emperor of Austria, King of Jerusalem, Apostolic King of Hungary, King of Bohemia, Galicia, Lodomeria, Illyria and Croatia, Archduke of Austria, and Duke, Markgraf, Prince or Count of some thirty other places in the Austro-Hungarian Dual Monarchy... indeed." He smiled grimly and snorted, "They don't give them titles like that any more!"

"Indeed." Angus said. Pendelshape narrowed his eyes and looked back at him sharply, trying to decide whether Angus was taking the mickey. Jack pressed on before he could make up his mind.

"Sorry, sir, I didn't think there were any empires left; I mean Austria is not an empire... do they even have a king?"

Pendelshape was impressed, "Very good Jack. You're absolutely right, but of course, this artefact is not modern. In fact, it is at least ninety years old..."

"And what's that funny brown staining on the metal, sir?" Angus asked.

Pendelshape delayed his response, rubbed the back of his neck, and then said, matter-of-factly, "It's blood."

Jack's heart jumped and he glanced at Angus.

Pendelshape stared out towards the window, deep in thought. A sparkling autumn day had gradually been enveloped by clouds that had rolled down from the hills. Suddenly, Pendelshape seemed to come to a decision about something. He stood up and kicked a rusty fan heater – it rumbled into life and reluctantly started to exhale tepid air into the classroom.

"The Schönbrunn raid," Pendelshape finally muttered. "It might well be…"

"Sorry, sir – what's that?" Jack asked.

"Little is known about it – some people think it did not happen at all – that it is just a myth. Apparently, there was some sort of raid on the Palace of Schönbrunn in Vienna – a few days before the assassination of Franz Ferdinand in 1914. The Austro-Hungarian government was very embarrassed about an attack at the very heart of the empire. They tried to erase any evidence that it took place. The story goes that Austrian lancers took on a group of Serbian rebels in the gardens of Schönbrunn itself. There were a number of casualties."

"You think this lance could somehow be linked to this… raid?"

Pendelshape shrugged. "Well, the design is distinctive and places it quite accurately at that time… and…"

"What?"

"It would certainly be an important historical find if we could place the lance to that date… it might even be evidence that the raid did indeed happen."

"Wonder how Dad came to have it in his workshop…" Jack said.

"Yes – Jack…" Pendelshape said thoughtfully, "I would be interested to know that too."

The room fell silent for a moment. Finally, Pendelshape announced, "Well, school's finished for today. I suggest you two stay around for an hour or so. Maybe do your homework in the library. I will go to the staffroom and phone a few colleagues, make some enquiries. Let's see if we can find out exactly what the piece is and perhaps discover its value – maybe even test my theory. That might be interesting, don't you think?" He looked at his watch, "Why don't you come back at, say, five or so?"

Jack looked at Angus with an enthusiastic nod. Angus shrugged.

"Great. Thanks, sir. If you're sure." And with that they left Pendelshape as he picked up his magnifying glass and looked at the lance head.

*

As they left the classroom, Jack turned to Angus, "Pretty cool, eh? What do you want to do, then?"

"Not go to the library for a start."

"Agreed. Gino's?"

"Nah. Boyle will be there – remember – four o'clock, Friday... and it's Friday 13th – unlucky – I can't face that lot."

They walked slowly down the austere Victorian corridor past the old classrooms, wondering how to kill an hour.

"Watch out. Trouble ahead." Angus suddenly said, and nodded in the direction of the far corridor as two burly uniformed figures approached.

"The terrible twins. What have we done to deserve this?"

Sure enough, the two school janitors, Tony Smith and Gordon MacFarlane, approached as they checked each of the empty classrooms before locking up for the evening. Tony was tall, with a ramrod back and puffed-out chest and, as ever, he was immaculately turned out. Gordon was shorter and stockier, but also strode around with the authority of an ex-army officer. Both men were feared and to be avoided due to the pleasure they took in enforcing the pettiest of school rules and their habit of dispensing discipline with the maximum level of sarcasm. There was a rumour in the school that Tony and Gordon were ex-SAS – a notion that neither janitor made any effort to dispel. There was another rumour, too, that they were actually ex-traffic wardens. This was the story that Jack and Angus thought more likely.

The boys looked for some way to avoid the two men. But it was too late. Soon the two large figures were looming over them, Tony peering down at Jack over a carefully trimmed moustache, an eager twinkle in his eye.

"Well now, what do we have here?" Tony said.

"One waif and one stray," Gordon chimed.

"It's Mr Christie and Mr Jud, is it not?"

"Yes Mr Smith," Jack said.

Tony turned to Gordon and impersonated Jack's voice mockingly, "Yes Mr Smith."

Gordon laughed and repeated in a squeaky voice, "Yes Mr Smith…"

Tony said, "Remind me, Mr MacFarlane, what is the penalty for loitering in school grounds twenty minutes after the final bell, outside the designated zones?"

Gordon turned back to Tony taking his time to consider the answer. "Mmm… I don't know, Mr Smith. Outside the designated zones, I think the penalty might be a detention… but actually, we could make up any penalty we want."

Tony looked back down at Jack. "Shall we do that boys… shall we make up a penalty?"

"But… we were going to the library…"

Gordon exhaled sceptically making a sort of drawn-out 'psshht' sound as he did so. Thankfully, just at that moment, Pendelshape emerged from his classroom and marched down the corridor towards them.

"Good afternoon, gentlemen, anything I can help you with?"

Tony and Gordon's manner changed instantly. It was as if the sergeant major had appeared and they snapped to attention.

"Good afternoon, Dr Pendelshape. I believe these are your pupils?" Tony said obsequiously.

"Yes, Tony, they're with me. They were just off to the library – weren't you?"

"No problem, sir – we were just closing down for the night. You know the rules, sir."

"Very good – you can leave my room open for a little longer… I have the keys."

"Sir." And with that Tony and Gordon slunk off in disappointment.

"Right lads – along to the library – and I'll make those calls."

*

Five minutes after reaching the library, Angus was already fidgeting with boredom.

"Stop it," Jack said, trying to focus on his maths homework.

"I can't. I've got an idea."

"Great. Not another of your 'good' ideas…"

"Yes," Angus said. "One of those." He lowered his voice and looked up and down the silent aisles of the old library furtively. "It's our big chance."

"What is?" Jack was getting worried.

"Well – Pendelshape is in the staffroom, making calls. The terrible twins are out of the way… and…"

"And what?" Jack asked.

"And, well, we know that Pendelshape has left his door open."

Jack hissed at Angus across the table, "No way!"

The prim librarian, still sorting returns, briefly raised her eyes above her reading glasses.

"Angus – I'm not standing guard while you sneak in and rummage through Pendelshape's cupboard to get back all the stuff he's confiscated off you…"

Angus looked hurt. "I only care about the iPod… I can't do without that for a whole week. It's totally unacceptable."

Jack shook his head, "It's wrong and it's your own fault anyway. Pendelshape can be pretty severe, if he caught us, I don't know – maybe we could even get expelled." He considered this for a moment and then added, "Or something really bad."

Angus had an evil smile on his face. The kind he got when he knew he was about to get Jack to do something he really didn't want to.

"Come on… think about it."

"Think about what?" Jack said.

"It'll be fun."

Angus grinned inanely. Jack stared back at his friend across the table and shook his head. He looked over at the librarian who was ignoring them. For some reason, he could feel his chest tightening. He felt for his puffer in his pocket.

"You're a pain, Angus."

But Angus was already up, away and sneaking out of the library.

*

Strangely, when they re-entered the classroom, they spotted the lance head still lying on Pendelshape's desk. Jack had assumed that their teacher would have taken it with him to help in his enquiries, but it was still there. Without really thinking, he grabbed it and put it into his rucksack to keep it safe.

A quick search for Angus's precious iPod in Pendelshape's large store cupboard proved fruitless. Angus was disappointed.

"Right – so let's get out of here," Jack said. "Probably a good thing we can't find it."

But just as they were about to leave, Jack noticed that Pendelshape had left the computer in his store cupboard on. Jack could never resist computers and as he made his way through the store-cupboard door, he touched the keyboard absent-mindedly. The screensaver had not kicked in yet. Without warning, a window popped up on the computer screen. It caught Jack's eye, because of its unusual design. It was some sort of an email application, but compared to the slick applications he was used to, it looked very basic. Just simple black text on a white background.

"What's this?" Jack murmured, then his brow furrowed, "What the…?"

Angus turned back to look. They both stared at the screen. It was the title of the email that grabbed them:

> **Subject: Lance artefact at Cairnfield.**

Then they looked at the recipient and sender fields:

> **To: Neil Pendelshape. From: Benefactor.**

"Who is 'Benefactor'?" Angus said.

"No idea – what's this…?" They started to scan the strange email; it blinked back at them.

> Do not concern yourself with the Cairnfield workshop. Lance is artefact from early experiments into the pre-war period. A rare piece that helps confirm the Schönbrunn raid

did occur. Anyway – irrelevant as things have now moved on. I have momentous news! Our own Taurus is complete! Yes! A functioning, full-scale system. We can now complete execution of Sim 0107 for real! We will activate Zadok. And very soon we will be in a position to defeat VIGIL. You must do something urgently, before we start. I fear that when they find out, they may take Orion. There is nothing we can do about Lynx now – she has gone over to the other side. But we must protect Orion. You need to enact the plan and then contact me as we discussed. We are about to change the world!

Good luck!

Your loyal friend – the Benefactor

They stared at the extraordinary message on the screen.

"What the…?" Jack started to speak, but stopped mid-sentence, dumbfounded.

"What's Taurus…? VIGIL? Zadok?" Angus said. "What does it mean?"

Jack shook his head. "I don't know… but one thing's for sure…"

"What?"

"Something's going on… and it's more interesting than your damned iPod…"

"But I don't…"

Angus didn't finish his sentence.

In the doorway stood Dr Pendelshape.

The VIGIL
Imperative

They hadn't even heard a footstep.

"Find anything interesting, boys?"

We're stuffed, Jack thought. Then, without a word, Dr Pendelshape did something quite unexpected. He reached for his inside pocket and pulled out a thin piece of plastic – a bit like a large pocket calculator. The sleek gadget was rather out of place with the rest of Pendelshape's overflowing store cupboard of dusty books and papers. He gently pressed a button on the device and the cupboard door closed automatically.

He nodded towards the computer.

"Best encryption in the world… but it's no good if you forget to lock the screen."

Strangely, he did not seem angry. Instead, he peered at the message from 'the Benefactor'.

"It makes no difference now anyway." He spoke urgently, "But I will explain all that later. Come, we haven't got long. I hope you two don't mind… surprises. Step to the back, please." He ushered them to the rear of the small store cupboard.

Pendelshape pressed the calculator device in his hand a second time and then, without warning, a slight aperture appeared in the floor. Angus gasped. Jack just stood, gaping. A very narrow, steep spiral staircase led down from the aperture, dimly lit by a blue light, which produced an unearthly shimmer.

"You can't get out, so I'm afraid you will just have to follow me. But don't worry – you're perfectly safe. Please – on you go."

Jack and Angus didn't move.

With a little more firmness now, Pendelshape urged them forward. "Please – we have little time. Trust me."

Reluctantly, they stepped onto the spiral staircase, quickly followed by Pendelshape. It was some sort of escalator and the steps began to descend automatically. As they dropped beneath floor level, the aperture above them mysteriously closed and after a couple of minutes they came to a gentle halt. Ahead of them was a door. Pendelshape pressed the device again and the door opened. There was a short metal-clad corridor illuminated by the same dull blue light. At the end of the corridor was a large round door, like the entrance to a bank vault – it looked very heavy, maybe it was steel. It had five letters etched on it:

'V I G I L'.

The door opened silently and Jack noticed that it was at least seven centimetres thick. Next, they found themselves in an oval-shaped room. It was similar to his dad's workshop at Cairnfield – although there weren't quite as many books and there was no mess – in fact, it was spotless. Towards one side of the library were two large leather sofas between which a glass-topped table was positioned.

Pendelshape waved them forward. "Please take a seat, gentlemen. I think I have some explaining to do." He looked at his watch and then waved vaguely in the direction of a modern fireplace, which suddenly erupted into a roaring log fire. Jack and Angus jumped.

"Don't worry – it's not real…" Pendelshape snorted. "Just adds a bit of atmosphere. Otherwise it can be a bit grim all the way down here." He clapped his hands. "Now, first things first, would either of you like some tea?" But the two boys were still in shock. "I'm rather partial to Jaffa cakes… we usually keep a few goodies down here, you know, just in case…" Pendelshape moved over to what appeared to be an ante-room to the library. He talked over his shoulder.

"I should explain where we are. This is a facility of VIGIL. They oversee everything."

Jack finally found his voice. "What's VIGIL?"

Dr Pendelshape returned to the table with a pot of tea and a plate of biscuits on a large tray.

"Ah, apologies, of course, I will need to start at the beginning. One forgets how little is known…"

"Sir, I'm sorry, we didn't mean to look at your computer…" Jack blurted out. "We were just… waiting for you…"

"You're not in trouble," Pendelshape said firmly and then added… "But I'm afraid you might be, if you don't listen very carefully to what I have to say…"

"But, sir…"

Pendelshape put up a hand to quieten Jack, "Please… just listen."

Pendelshape bit into a Jaffa cake, and then rocked backwards and forwards as if weighing something up in his mind. "Indeed. I think you will find what I have to say quite surprising… shocking even." And with these words, their teacher launched into his story, which was quite unlike anything either of them had ever heard from him in a history lesson.

*

"VIGIL is the governing body of an elite network of physicists, engineers and computer scientists. However, VIGIL is not an institution that you will find listed in a library or on the Internet. It is secret." Pendelshape picked up another Jaffa cake and waved it around in the air as he spoke. "We are beneath the radar," he coughed, took a sip of his Earl Grey and swallowed. "Indeed. This is because VIGIL manages the most powerful technology ever invented."

Jack and Angus looked at each other – surely this was a joke?

"I am talking about the technology of time travel." He said it in a rather pedestrian way, as if it was something that he was quite familiar with and dealt with on a day-to-day basis – like switching on an electric light.

"The ideas have been around for many decades. I am sure you have heard of physicists such as Planck, Heisenberg and Schrödinger… and the concepts of quantum mechanics, parallel universes, wormholes and such…" He looked at the boys expectantly, but all he got back were blank stares.

Preliminary notes on the Tawru

Armageddon scenario?
Deep time limitations?

2.5m

2.5m

Formula →

1.5m

$$\left[\gamma \left(i \frac{\partial}{\partial x^{\mu}} - e A^{\mu} \right) + m \right] \psi(x) = 0$$

Schematic movement
of the Tawru

Day of the Assassins

He waved dismissively. "Never mind. All you need to know is that the world of subatomic physics is an extremely mysterious one, not one where our normal experience of everyday life applies at all. It has baffled some of the greatest minds... including Einstein..." Pendelshape frowned, "You have heard of Einstein, haven't you?" They nodded stupidly.

"That's a relief. More tea?" he asked matter-of-factly. But Jack and Angus had not touched the tea or the biscuits. "Come on, eat up, you'll need to line your stomachs for what you're about to hear, I can tell you."

Jack steadied himself. "Time travel – that's just theory, isn't it? Mumbo jumbo. It can't actually be done," his voice trembled, "can it?"

"Yes Jack – it can. Let me show you something."

He pressed the device he was holding and the room lightened. On the opposite wall, the shelves of books slowly moved apart revealing a solid wall of thick green glass that extended from the floor all the way up to the ceiling. The glass had the same hue and texture as the casing around the small platform back at Cairnfield, where they had discovered the lance head. Behind this glass screen was a flat metal platform surrounded by an array of scientific equipment – pipes, cables and steel. The platform itself was bounded by a semi-closed arrangement of hefty black girders. Jack counted eight of them. They rose from the ground and bulged out to surround the platform and then rejoined at the top of the structure. All together, it looked like a giant gyroscope. It was on a much larger scale, and looked more complex than the device back at Cairnfield, but the basic structure was similar – with one exception. Between two of the large metal girders, a gantry rose from the floor and up to the level of the platform. Whatever the thing was – it looked like you could go inside it. Through the thick glass, they could make out some lettering above a terminal. It spelled out one word:

'Taurus'.

Pendelshape gestured proudly towards the structure, "Gentlemen, here is where theory becomes reality. It's a far cry from H.G. Wells, I know, but Mr Taurus there will take you back in time."

All Angus could say was, "Will it bring you back again?"

Pendelshape smiled, "Yes it will." He paused. "Well, in general, it will." He shrugged. "Details, details."

Jack expected to wake up at any moment or, probably worse, find the host of some reality TV show jump out in front of some hidden cameras to reveal that the whole thing was a set-up and that they'd been humiliated in front of millions of viewers. Neither happened.

All he could say, lamely, was, "How does it work?"

Pendelshape laughed, "I'm afraid that would take a little while to explain... and you would need a PhD in theoretical physics or computer science and maybe genetics." He frowned, looked down at his shoes and paused. "In fact, probably all three... but, if you like, I can give you the ten-second version..." He looked at the boys expectantly; there was no response.

"The ten-second version it is then. You switch on the power. You might think that is just a question of pressing a big red button – but it is a little more complicated than that." He thought to himself again. "The button is green actually. Anyway, then you set the date and where you want to go, you stand on that platform," he pointed at the circular platform inside the 'Taurus' structure, "and you click this..."

From his pocket he pulled something similar to a mobile phone – maybe a bit fatter and longer. He flipped the phone open and a very faint blue light came on from the inside. It was similar to the light of the stairwell and access passage. The boys could see a small screen and a number of small buttons.

"The Taurus itself, over there, stays put – it focuses the energy. But to move through time and space, you need to have physical contact with this little chap. It's a time phone. You need it to go... and to get back." He looked at them, "And that's about it. Oh, except that while back in time, the time phone is controlled and tracked by the Taurus, and its console over there, using a set of codes – with a reasonable degree of accuracy..." A look of doubt ghosted across his face. "Most of the time, anyway."

"What do you mean?"

"Well, it will only work when the Taurus is at the right energy state, and also when there is a strong enough signal."

"What? Signal? Like a real mobile phone? Come on, sir, you're winding us up." Angus laughed. This couldn't be serious.

But Pendelshape pressed on. "It's a bit more complicated, but you're more or less right – look – that bar, there at the side," he held up the device so the boys could see and pointed to one corner of the display on the time phone. "It's greyed out at the moment, but when it turns yellow, you can exchange signals with the Taurus, text messages if you like: it means the Taurus here knows where you are… and it means you can time travel. When it's off, you can't do any of those things."

"Wow!" Angus exclaimed.

"It's off at the moment?" Jack asked.

"Of course."

"But…"

"This is all completely irrelevant. I'm afraid that none of it can be used… great tragedy."

"Why not?" asked Jack.

"Not allowed. It's known as 'The VIGIL Imperative.'" Pendelshape sighed. "Rules, gentlemen, rules… which we must follow on pain of death. Literally."

Taurus Class

Pendelshape sat back and clasped his hands behind his head while he continued his extraordinary story. "About fifteen years ago, a small group of physicists, associated with the nuclear research facility at CERN, near Geneva, conducted the first practical experiments in time travel. At first, very simple non-organic structures were transported backwards and forwards through space and time. Then, we started to experiment with more complex structures. We then moved on to the first organic material, then living creatures… and, finally, a human being. Up to this point the level of excitement among the group was incredible, as you can imagine. But then, one of the leaders of the group, Counsellor Inchquin, started to think seriously about the power of what they had created. Here was a technology that had the potential to change the past, and thereby change the future. In the wrong hands, or, even in the right hands, this could be catastrophic." He paused. "Think about it."

"You're right, you could go back and steal some money, no one would know…" Angus said, intrigued.

"Of course. But I'm afraid that's the least of it. Think about the pivotal moments of history, some of which have rested on small, even chance, events that have had huge consequences. These are the 'what ifs' of our history." Pendelshape's eyes opened wide in enthusiasm. "Think about it: what if Hitler had been killed in the First World War and had not become the leader of Germany? What if Gavrilo Princip had not assassinated Archduke Ferdinand? The list is of course endless – and fascinating. The consequences for us and for future generations, however, are difficult to comprehend."

Jack spoke slowly, trying to understand what he was hearing,

"So you're saying that these scientists created this thing... the power to time travel... but decided not to use it?"

Pendelshape replied sadly, "It was debated. Despite the computer simulations that we could create to model the consequences of any changes made in history, most felt that it was too risky and that no one should be given the chance to exercise such power. Counsellor Inchquin felt this most strongly and led the group with this point of view."

"Who won the argument?" Angus asked, engrossed.

"Who do you think?" Pendelshape said. "In the end it was decided that, although it was not possible to 'un-invent' the technology, it was possible to control it. VIGIL was formed and everyone agreed to abide by a strict set of rules. A code of conduct if you like. It came to be known as 'The VIGIL Imperative'. All those in the know were forced to abide by it. The early Taurus experimental facility was closed down and, outside of a select group, it was suggested that the project had been an abject failure."

Jack looked around, "What's this place then?"

"It's a replica Taurus made using components from the original machine. Although you don't know it, yours is a rather special school: it secretly houses a working Taurus. All members of VIGIL have moved on to rather mundane jobs. I, for example, am now your history teacher. Rather appropriate don't you think? And our Rector, himself a brilliant scientist, finds himself here as head teacher – during term time at least. But in fact he has a much weightier responsibility: to keep this facility permanently mothballed and secret, yet in working order so that the technology is preserved."

"Why not just destroy it altogether?"

"That was certainly an option – but in the end the people who had worked so hard could not quite bring themselves to go that far. It was also anticipated that in the future, there might possibly be scenarios where it could be necessary to use Taurus. We might not even know now what these scenarios could be, but science moves very fast. It seemed sensible at least to retain the option to use it. But that's not all..."

"There's more?"

"Yes. There was also a small group with a different point of view to

Inchquin and the others. They were led by the Benefactor and they believed that the technology could and should be used as a force for good." Pendelshape paused for a moment and eyed Jack with an odd, enquiring look. He seemed to be thinking about something and lost concentration for a moment.

"Benefactor – that was the name in your email," Jack said.

"Yes, Jack... and..." but before Pendelshape could continue, Angus butted in.

"OK, hold it right there, sir... I'm not sure what this place is, but I have to tell you I'm finding it difficult to believe all this..." he glanced at Jack. "Very difficult – it's a big joke – right?"

Pendelshape's eyes flashed in frustration. "Wrong. I know, Angus, it's a lot to take in. But I must ask you to try. It is quite important... for us all. As you are about to find out. However, I agree it is reasonable to ask for some proof..." He looked round the room, then stood up and walked over to one of the shelves and started leafing through a thin folder.

"Here. Maybe this will do it."

Pendelshape produced a small photograph and handed it to them.

"So, Jack, remember our lessons on the First World War, the assassination in Sarajevo, the Black Hand... Gavrilo Princip... and all that...?" He looked down at the photograph knowingly, "Well...?"

Jack suddenly realised what he was looking at. His heart jolted. It couldn't be. But the image was unmistakable.

It was an old black-and-white photo of four young men – grim faced and serious. One of them was the assassin from Sarajevo that Jack had seen in one of the early levels of *Point-of-Departure* – Gavrilo Princip. But on the other side of the photograph, to the far left, was a fifth man. Jack narrowed his eyes to be certain... he looked a little younger, but there was no mistaking him. The man staring out from the photograph was Dr Pendelshape.

Jack slowly raised his eyes to Pendelshape who smiled knowingly at him.

"So you see, boys, this photo was taken in Belgrade in the Balkans... in 1914. And no, it's not a fake or a digital enhancement. It's real.

There's me on the left. On the right is Gavrilo Princip, the man who shot Archduke Franz Ferdinand in Sarajevo and triggered the First World War. To the left of Princip are two of the other assassins – Grabež and Čabrinović."

"And what about him?" Angus pointed to the fourth man standing next to Pendelshape.

"Dani Matronovic. Lesser known – was killed before the assassination. History does not relate what happened to him. His sister took the photo," his eyes glossed over for a moment. "Pretty girl… Anna."

Pendelshape flipped over the photo. "Their names are on the back – look."

Sure enough on the back of the photo, in Pendelshape's distinctive scrawl, were scribbled the words – 'Belgrade, Serbia, 1914', followed by the names: 'Princip, Grabež, Čabrinović, Matronovic.'

Angus just couldn't believe it, "So you've gone back in time using that… thing?" He looked over at the Taurus brooding silently behind the green glass of the blast screen.

"Yes, Angus. Even though the purpose of VIGIL is to preserve the technology – and not to use it – everything still had to be fully tested. No point in deciding to keep the technology – unless you know it will work."

"But why did you go back then, you know, to 1914?" Jack asked.

Pendelshape shrugged, "It was a pivotal point in history."

"Why you? Why did they choose you?"

"I'm the historian, anyway, I thought it would be interesting…" Pendelshape's eyes glazed over as he added, dreamily, "and I was right. It was incredible, to see even a tiny piece of what you had learned from a textbook, to see it, to smell it…" He smiled. "Keep the photo if you like."

Jack took it gingerly, as if handling a precious jewel, and stared at it silently for a moment longer, before putting it carefully in his bag.

*

Pendelshape pressed on more quickly now, trying to bypass interruptions from his bewildered pupils. He revealed more about

VIGIL. He explained how the idea of hiding the Taurus in a school had worked well – the initial refurbishment of the school had been a good front for the early building work, with holiday periods providing quiet time for research and maintenance, and, of course, it was easy to maintain a staff of teachers, who were, in reality, scientists from the original Taurus team. It had taken them some time to identify an appropriate home for the Taurus – until they had finally found the quiet and secluded site near the hamlet of Soonhope in the upper Tweed Valley. The local community had been grateful for the sudden injection of cash that the endowment had provided and the creation of a new school on a rundown site. After a while, an increasing number of local pupils began to attend, assisted by generous subsidies. Pupil numbers had been kept low, ostensibly to preserve academic standards, but in reality, to free up faculty time for more important matters.

As Pendelshape talked, Jack saw the expression on Angus's face gradually change. His mouth was morphing into that warped, toothy grin that meant only one thing. Trouble. Sure enough, as Pendelshape paused for breath, Angus seized his chance.

"So, sir... er, it all sounds great, but are you going to show us how it really works?"

To Jack's utter amazement Pendelshape replied, "Yes, Angus, in fact I am."

Jack nearly fell off his chair. Pendelshape looked at his watch nervously. "We've spent far too much time talking already. The truth is that unforeseen circumstances have arisen. This is why I have brought you here. I will explain why in a minute. I and, er, well, we have a kind of... mission to complete. But first, I would like you both to understand how it all works..." he smiled, "you know, just in case..."

*

A crack in the floor stretched from one side of the library to the other. A green glass barrier rose up from it, extending to the ceiling. They stood in front of it.

"This is the blast screen. Press this..." Pendelshape clicked the device in his hand, "and down it comes." Jack and Angus jumped back as, with alarming speed, the blast screen descended into the narrow aperture in the floor and the whole Taurus structure was revealed to them in its full glory.

"Awesome," Angus whispered reverentially.

"Be careful. You don't want to be standing over that blast screen when it goes up again. It could give you a nasty bruise in your nether regions."

Pendelshape moved over to one of the control panels and began typing at a keyboard. Soon they heard a slight rising hum. Pendelshape explained the basics of how the machine was operated. It was surprisingly simple. He showed them how you synchronised the time phone with the Taurus console by placing it in a special recessed pod. He showed them how you entered the Taurus through the surrounding girders from the gantry, and how you then positioned yourself on the steel platform by placing your feet between the etchings drawn into the metal. He reminded them of the limitations of the Taurus and its umbilical linkage to the time phone.

"As you said Angus, its a bit like a mobile phone – you can only use the time phone when you have a signal. Remember that bar?" he indicated the little greyed-out display on the time phone. "When it's yellow – you're good to go – you can communicate, we know where you are and the Taurus can send you back and forth through time. When there's no signal, you're stuck – although the phone's energy source will continue to tell you where and when you are."

"And if you lose the phone?" Angus asked.

Pendelshape looked back at Angus with steel in his eyes, "Lose that time phone, Mr Jud, and you're not only *in* history... you *are* history. No way back."

Jack was engrossed. "Can you go anywhere?"

"There are constraints. The variability of the time signals through the space-time continuum is a major one. It's like shifting sands. Periods of time open up and then close. It's not as if all periods of time and all locations are accessible all the time. Then there's 'deep time'."

"Deep time?"

"A specific constraint that exists along the lines I just mentioned. It seems that the Taurus is only effective at transportation from when you depart to more than about thirty years or so in the past. We call it 'deep time'. Anything sooner is a sort of no-go zone. This also means you can't travel back from the past to just before you left." Pendelshape's brow furrowed, "And there's one more thing. We call it the 'Armageddon Scenario'." Pendelshape said the words quickly – as if he was hoping the boys might not even notice he had said them.

"Well that sounds pretty harmless," Angus said.

Jack frowned, "What is it?"

Pendelshape shrugged his shoulders nonchalantly, "Another part of time theory. It postulates that if you revisit the same point of space-time more than once, you dramatically increase the risk of a continuum meltdown. At worst, the possible destruction of the universe – but in reality, probably not as bad at that – probably only the destruction of some bit of it."

"Oh – that's OK then. Presumably it's the bit we're in?" Angus said.

"Yes. Think of a bit of tissue paper. It's like putting holes in it with your finger. These are like visits to the past using Taurus to particular points in time. The tissue will hold together for a while but too many holes and the whole lot will disintegrate. So best not to risk repeat trips in and around the same point. The precise parameters of this constraint are not known – and of course have not been tested."

Suddenly the pitch of the humming from the control room rose an octave. A number of lights around the console flashed on.

Pendelshape smiled in satisfaction. "We're in business! Right, gentlemen, before we go any further, I have to explain to you what we must do next and why we have decided to show you all this. It's not a step we have taken lightly. You're going to have to trust me one more time. I assure you, it is in all of our interests."

The boys glanced at each other nervously.

Pendelshape marched over to the table and was joined by Angus, who wandered backwards slowly, still staring up, mesmerised by the Taurus and its surrounding apparatus of cables and pipes. Jack waited by the quietly humming machine, still trying to absorb everything that Pendelshape had said.

"Jack, please, if you would come back over here, quickly..." Pendelshape gestured impatiently for him to move away from the structure. He took a deep breath, "The Taurus is already set so that we can travel back in time to somewhere I know and where we will be safe, before being picked up. The truth is..."

But he did not finish his sentence.

Armed Response

The heavy door at the far end of the control room swung open and through it marched Tony and Gordon. Over their usual uniforms, each was wearing an army flak jacket. From his position next to the Taurus, Jack could just make out some small silver lettering on each of the jackets. The lettering read: VIGIL Response.

Behind Tony and Gordon were two other men – Mr Belstaff and Mr Johnstone – the games teachers. They wore the same get-up as the two janitors and moved with the same imposing power. But what alarmed Jack most was that, quite extraordinarily, all the men were… armed. If he had been an expert on military matters, he might have recognised the weapons that they carried to be Corner Shot APRs – one of the most advanced automatic weapons in the world. With their laser sights, video screens and swivelling gun-mounts, the machine pistols also had a special feature – they could shoot round corners. What on earth they were doing in the hands of the school janitors and the games teachers, Jack had no idea.

The four men were followed by a tall slim figure with a bald head, poorly disguised with thinning wisps of silver hair. With his trademark black gown flowing from a pair of hunched shoulders he looked a bit like a carrion crow. Jack recognised him immediately. It was the school's head: the Rector.

He advanced towards Pendelshape and Angus, his face purple with rage.

Pendelshape jumped to his feet. He looked terrified, "John… I'm sorry… I…"

But the Rector shouted back, "Silence!"

Pendelshape sank to his knees; he seemed to be… begging.

"Please! I didn't mean…"

The Rector loomed over Pendelshape, "You idiot! I always had a sneaking suspicion about you. Didn't you think we'd find out?"

Pendelshape really was begging now, "Please, please. John… I didn't…"

"I should have guessed you might betray us. You and the Benefactor. A bad combination of hopeless romantic and dangerous lunatic…"

"I'm sorry…"

"MacFarlane. Deal with him."

From his position only five metres away Jack could not believe what he saw next. Gordon stepped forward. He had a sinister grin on his face – as if he was actually enjoying himself. He withdrew a large knife from a scabbard on his black belt. As he did so, he spun the serrated blade in one hand like a circus knife thrower. Suddenly Jack realised that he and Angus had been wrong. Tony and Gordon were not ex-traffic wardens. The theory that they'd been in the SAS was, in fact, the correct one.

With one hand Gordon reached down, pulled the whimpering Pendelshape to his feet and smacked him hard against one of the wooden bookcases. Pendelshape moaned in pain. With only one hand, Gordon held him a clear ten centimetres off the ground. With the other hand, he took the blade and plunged it into his neck. Jack felt the bile rise in his throat. He thought he was going to be sick. But then he realised that, expertly, Gordon had only nicked Pendelshape's neck, impaling him instead by both his shirt and jacket collars against the wooden frame of the bookcase. Blood oozed from the wound, but Pendelshape was not dead. Yet. Instead, he was starting to choke as his weight pulled him down and his collar – pinned to the wall by the knife – slowly tightened around his neck. His face was turning purple. The Rector nodded towards Angus who, like Jack, was staring slack-jawed at the violent assault.

"Smith. Please deal with this young man."

Tony stepped forward and grabbed Angus by the scruff of the neck, yanking him from the sofa with surprising ease. With no hesitation,

Tony landed a punch to Angus's solar plexus. For Tony, it was a light, controlled blow. But there was no doubt, if Tony had chosen to, he could have killed Angus on the spot. But Tony had held back, and instead Angus doubled over, badly winded, and retched like an old man. The Rector now directed his attention to Jack at the other end of the library, next to the Taurus.

"Bring Master Christie here. You know your orders – no damage."

Jack looked back across the library as Belstaff and Johnstone strode towards him. Pendelshape was slowly choking to death. Angus was on the floor clutching his stomach. It didn't look like Jack was going to get away any more lightly. His heart was in overdrive. He needed time... time to think. But in five seconds the two men would be on him... and then what?

He snatched the controller that Pendelshape had left by the console and stabbed the button. Just as Belstaff was in mid stride, the glass blast screen accelerated upwards from its housing under the floor. It caught him without warning clean between the legs. Belstaff screamed in pain and found himself powering on upwards, balanced precariously on the top edge of the thick glass. Two seconds later, with a dull thud and crunching bone, the rising panel crushed the unfortunate man right into the ceiling – like a fat finger caught in a car's electric window. The powerful motors beneath the floor continued to grind and push upwards as the glass blast screen failed to slot itself into its upper housing, now blocked by Belstaff, suspended five metres above. Johnstone, who had been behind his colleague, smashed into the opposite side of the blast screen and reeled backwards, clutching his head.

Cornered at one end of the control room next to the Taurus and behind the blast screen, Jack knew he didn't have long. He didn't know why these people were after him, but he knew he had to escape. It was a long shot – but there was only one way out. Through the blast screen, he could just make out the Rector, Tony and Gordon rushing around in alarm trying to find a way to lower the screen and get to Jack, who, though safe for the moment, now had a new fear. His breathing had intensified and he was starting to wheeze. His chest had that awful hollow feeling that usually preceded an asthma attack. He reached for his puffer and took a mighty suck. For a moment, it calmed him.

He leaned over the console that Pendelshape had shown them earlier. There, still nestling in its pod, was the time phone. Above it, a small digital read-out blinked invitingly. It said:

'Initiate synchronisation procedure'.

Jack looked back over his shoulder through the screen. In a few seconds they would have it lowered again and would be on him. He had no doubt what he must do. He snatched the time phone from its pod and flipped it open. Immediately, he saw the little bar to the side burning bright yellow. Just as Pendelshape had said it would. The read-out on the console flashed:

Synchronisation initiated.

To his surprise another message flashed up.

Are you feeling lucky? Yes/No?

"What the...?" He whispered in desperation as the commotion on the other side of the screen intensified. He stabbed an 'N' on the keypad underneath the console. He definitely was not feeling lucky. Another message immediately flashed up:

Would you like preset space-time fix? Yes/No?

"Come on... come on..." Jack, drenched in sweat, stared at the device. He stabbed a 'Y' on the keypad. There was a pause.

Thank you. Synchronisation complete.

The read-out changed again:

Board Taurus within thirty seconds.

And then a final message popped up:

Enjoy your time-travel experience.

"This is not for real…" some propeller-head programmer had a warped sense of humour. He grabbed the time phone and then his bag and, shaking with fear, mounted the gantry onto the steel platform in the heart of the Taurus. From his new position, he looked out between the black girders, through the green blast screen into the library, where he could see Pendelshape still pinned to the wall and Angus bent over on the sofa. Seeing Angus there, helpless, Jack felt a stab of guilt – but what could he do? The Rector, Tony and Gordon were fighting with a control panel to find some way to lower the blast screen. He suddenly spotted a small heads-up display that hung just outside the Taurus structure. His heart missed a beat when he realised what was happening. Taurus was counting down.

Preparing for transfer…
14… 13… 12…
Transfer initiating…

Suddenly, the glass blast screen started to lower. Belstaff, pinned to the ceiling, lost his balance as the pressure from the screen released and he tumbled back to the floor. He didn't move. Jack stared numbly at the body of his games teacher and felt bile rise in his throat as a terrifying thought suddenly occurred to him – Belstaff might be dead.

Jack saw Tony and Gordon look down at their injured colleague and then look back up at him in his vantage point inside the Taurus. When he saw their eyes, he knew he had made the right decision to board the Taurus. Tony and Gordon only had one thing on their mind as they rushed forward towards him.

3… 2… 1…

Dreadnought

Jack looked down at the time phone in his hand. The read-out had changed. It said:

Date: Saturday 20th June, 1914
Time: 7 a.m.
Location: Portsmouth, England

The read-out glinted back at him. Portsmouth…? He was in Portsmouth? On England's south coast? He looked around. The Taurus and library had vanished, the people in the control room – also gone. He had escaped. But had he really moved? And had he moved in time?

He was standing in the open on a flat concrete surface. There was a damp mist all around, but he could hear muffled voices. He was facing a giant wall – only about two metres away – extending upwards and sideways as far as he could see, although the mist limited his view. It looked like he was on the outside of a large building, maybe a warehouse. The building was not made of bricks, but had a dark, grey smooth surface. He took a step forward to touch it, hoping to find an opening and, in so doing, he nearly plummeted to his death. He jumped back, as if he had just touched an electric fence.

Five metres below, there was a channel of icy, black water lapping between the side of the wall that he had tried to touch and the platform on which he stood. He'd nearly plunged straight into it. He craned his neck up again. The mist peeled slowly back from the wall and way above his head. To his left, he could make out some letters:

T… H… G… U… O… N… D… A… E… R… D

What does that mean? The direction of the clearing mist had revealed the letters to him from right to left. But in the right order they spelled: '*DREADNOUGHT*'. The wall he was looking at was made of steel. Jack was not staring at a warehouse, but a ship, and he was standing on a quayside. Moreover, it was no ordinary ship. He had only spied part of the stern, but even by the proportion of this, the ship was a monster. In fact, Jack realised, this was *the* ship – the one that Pendelshape had said revolutionised naval warfare before the war. It had given Britain superiority at sea. *Dreadnought*. It was all the evidence Jack needed to prove that he had indeed been transported through time.

He moved back cautiously from the quayside. Nearby, was a series of large pallets. Some were stacked with crates, others with large sacks. On one pallet, there was a gap between two large piles of sacks and, seeking temporary refuge, Jack managed to squeeze himself between them. He tried to control a growing sense of panic. Once again, he took out his puffer, pressed the button and inhaled deeply. The tightness in his lungs relaxed. He crouched down. A hundred and one questions flew through his head. What on earth had he witnessed back at the control room? Why had the Rector been so angry? What had they done to Angus?

Having no answers, he tried to focus on an activity to distract himself. He checked what he had with him. First of all – the time phone. He still had it. So, in theory, he could go back... but to what? A bunch of thugs who wanted to beat him up... or worse? He flipped the phone open, just as Pendelshape had shown him. The bright yellow bar was flickering and starting to grey out. He racked his brains... what was it that Pendelshape had said? They could only use it when the bar was yellow.

But he had been more specific than that, hadn't he?

You can only use it when you have a signal and when the host Taurus is in the right energy state... when it turns yellow, you can exchange signals with the Taurus... it means the Taurus knows where you are... and it means you can time travel.

That was it. Now the bar was completely grey. So that meant even if he wanted to get back, or communicate with someone, he couldn't. He would have to wait. But it also meant, Jack suddenly realised, that if he started to move away from here, where the Taurus had deposited him, he could not be tracked until the signal was restored. The Rector, and his henchmen, would only know his landing point from the Taurus's space-time fix… as Pendelshape had called it. If he moved away from this spot while the signal was off, it would be more difficult for them to follow him.

He turned his school rucksack upside down to see what else he had. For a start, he took off his blazer and put on his fleece jacket. It was warmer – and probably less conspicuous. Then there was the usual rubbish – moth-eaten exercise book, sweet wrappers and a couple of textbooks. He could ditch those for a start. Then he noticed that he still had the history book – the present from his father. The irony was not lost on him and he briefly flicked through its pages. Could be useful, he thought to himself, and stuffed it back into his rucksack. As he did so, something dropped onto the wooden decking of the pallet. It was the lance head. He'd forgotten all about it, but of course it was this that had got them talking to Pendelshape in the first place. He dropped it into his trouser pocket and quickly checked over the rest of the rucksack. In a side pocket, he discovered some crumbly remains of his mum's chocolate cake wrapped up in cling film. He felt a lump forming in his throat.

Suddenly, the wooden pallet beneath his feet groaned. It was moving. Jack found himself rocking gently from side to side and had to steady himself with both hands between the two walls of sacks. He looked up. He could make out some cables and the hook of a large crane. The pallet and its heavy load, including Jack, were being hoisted into the air. Through the wooden slats of the pallet he could see that there was already clear air between him and the quayside. Then the crane stopped and he could feel the whole structure swaying gently. From his vantage point, Jack saw that both the ship and the quayside were throbbing with activity. Without warning, the massive load started to move again – sideways this time. With horror, Jack realised what was happening. *Dreadnought* was taking supplies on board – and the mighty battleship had an uninvited guest: Jack was about to be lowered deep into the hold.

The crane paused once more. Jack was helpless and peered desperately from his hiding place, scanning the edge of the ship and the quayside for some means of escape. Just as the massive crane started to lower its load into the ship, Jack spotted two figures standing further down the quayside – not ten metres away. The Taurus must have delivered a final spasm of energy, after transferring Jack, before losing the signal completely. They were after him already: Tony and Gordon.

*

He'd been lying in the dark hold for what seemed like ages with dusty smells wafting around him. He was well hidden and one thing was for sure, he wasn't going outside again, right into the hands of Tony and Gordon. He tried to make himself comfortable. After a little while, he detected a slight vibration as the ship's steam turbine engines gently pushed *Dreadnought* away from the dock.

They were going to sea.

Jack tried to think logically through the events of the last few hours. Most worrying were Tony and Gordon. They must have been sent to get him. They must have their own time phones – also connected to the Taurus. He wondered if he had made a clean getaway – or whether they had guessed he had boarded the ship and had followed him aboard to hunt him down like a rat in a steel maze.

Jack thought back to the strange conversation that he and Angus held with Pendelshape before the Rector had stormed in. Pendelshape had been about to tell them something. Something important – about the Benefactor – and this was linked to the strange email they had discovered. He tried to remember what the email had said. It had been from the Benefactor, who had been replying to Pendelshape. So the two of them had been in contact – perhaps for some time. What had the email said again? Jack racked his brains.

Do not concern yourself with the Cairnfield workshop…

So the Benefactor knew about his father's workshop at Cairnfield. And he had also said: *Our own Taurus is complete! Yes!*

A functioning, full-scale system.

But… could that mean the Benefactor had somehow developed another time machine? Maybe there were two Tauruses? The one at the school, and a separate one – belonging to the Benefactor. That would be incredible… but already Jack felt he had seen enough incredible things to last several lifetimes. It would have been strictly against the rules of VIGIL that Pendelshape had talked about. But on the other hand, the Benefactor was a key member of the original Taurus team… so perhaps he had the brains to pull it off. It sounded like Pendelshape must have known about it… known what the Benefactor was up to. Maybe that's why the Rector was so angry with Pendelshape?

Jack tried to remember what else the email had said:

I fear that when they find out, they may take Orion… we must protect Orion.

Who was Orion? And the email had mentioned someone else too – a 'she' – 'Lynx'. A man and a woman who could not be named. More mystery.

Then, just before the Rector had stormed in on them, Pendelshape said that he had set the Taurus "so that we can travel back in time to somewhere I know and where we will be safe, before being picked up". So Pendelshape was concerned about something. Concerned enough to have already planned using the Taurus – against VIGIL rules – to carry out some sort of escape. He must have set it to send them back to the Portsmouth naval dockyards – where Jack had been transported. Maybe that made sense. Pendelshape knew all about 1914 – he had proved from the photo taken in Belgrade that he had travelled back to this time before. So he would be on familiar territory.

But Jack was still no closer to understanding why any of this had happened. Why was the Rector angry with Pendelshape? Why had Pendelshape wanted them to escape to 1914 and why did Orion need to be 'protected'? Somehow, Jack and Angus, whether they liked it or not, had become embroiled in something big – and something they did not understand. Now he was alone and he was scared. It wasn't like being on the back of Angus's bike – then you knew it would be over quickly, one way or another. But this was different. The fear Jack felt was an all-enveloping fear that seemed to suck away at you from the inside.

But Jack had always been good at thinking things through and solving problems. And he knew part of the trick was to try not to let emotion get to you. Information. He simply did not have enough information yet to solve the confusing list of questions, so he would put them to one side until he did. But there was one question he did need to answer and that was, what was he going to do now? He fumbled around for the time phone and, through the gloom, he flipped it open and read its telltale message:

Date: Saturday 20th June, 1914
Time: 11.00 a.m.
Location: English Channel

That was right, Pendelshape had also said that the phone had its own energy source, so it would continue to say where and when he was. The screen had a kind of mini SATNAV with a map. Jack noticed that both the time and location had moved since his last reading. It confirmed that they were sailing up the Channel. So he would always know where he was. That might be handy. The yellow bar was still off – greyed out. Until it went on again there was nothing he could do and the Taurus and the people who controlled it – the Rector for one – would not be able to locate him. So he should be safe. In fact, he thought ruefully, perhaps the best thing to do would be just to waltz out and… give himself up. Say he had got lost or something… and then the crew would have to look after him, until they could maybe drop him at a port. It was a risk, but if Tony and Gordon had managed to spot him and then follow him aboard *Dreadnought*, he knew he would be a lot safer in the hands of the Royal Navy. Wasn't that why they were supposed to be there anyway? To protect people?

*

Suddenly, the door of the hold banged open and light streamed in. Jack crouched down as far as he could, but it was in vain. A moment later a large pink face loomed down at him from the pile of sacks above.

"Sir – you ain't going to believe this…"

"What is it now?" A gruff voice answered. The first face was joined by a second, which was equally surprised.

"I've seen it all now. A stowaway!"

"What's your name, son. How did you get in there?"

Jack stared back at the two faces and calculated that politeness was the best policy.

"Sorry, sir, I mean, I was with the loading gang, er, and kind of fell asleep…"

The two men looked at each other, and then guffawed loudly.

"Someone's going to cop it for this! Come out of there for a start. What did you say your name was?"

"Jack Christie."

"Well, Christie, we will have to report you; it's lucky for you that we're just on exercises. Better get you tidied up. And then, I'm sure we can make use of you." Jack thought the man looked like a cook. He laughed again, nodding at the sacks around him, "There's this lot to sort out for a start."

And with that, he was marched from the hold and soon found himself seated at a small table outside the galley.

"You stay there."

The cook went off, but the sailor, with the pink face, looked at him sympathetically. "Don't worry lad… Navy has a fine tradition of young men at sea. Nelson himself. We'll get a signal home to let them know you're safe. You look famished – tell you what – one of the boys will get you something…"

The sailor hurried off but reappeared with a large plate of stew and potatoes.

After a while the cook reappeared.

"Your lucky day, my lad! Seems that you have an audience in the chart house. Captain wants to know your story, exactly. Security breach and all that. Jones will take you up. And then…" he pointed back up the corridor, "we'll get you to work."

The sailor led Jack through a maze of metal corridors and up and down a series of ladders.

"We'll take a short cut through the Admiral's lobby," he said.

As they moved on, Jack saw two figures ascending a ladder ahead of them. They were dressed in sailor's garb, but had packs on their backs. Jack's worst fears had come true – Tony and Gordon had followed him aboard *Dreadnought*.

Cannon Fodder

" **W**e've been asked by the Bridge to take him from here," Tony said with authority to the young sailor.

Jack turned to run, but in an instant, Gordon had his arm in a vicelike grip. "Not so fast, Master Christie. You need to come with us."

The sailor looked bemused but shrugged and wheeled round leaving Jack alone to his fate.

Jack smelled Tony's stale breath as he whispered sneeringly into his ear, "Any noise, any tricks and you are dead meat. You've caused us a lot of trouble."

Gordon parroted, "A lot of trouble."

"Right then," Tony said, "we are hoping to have a Taurus signal in the next few hours. But you never can tell. In the meantime, we've got to find somewhere to hide on this floating dung-crate until we can return to civilisation."

"So we don't draw any attention," Gordon added.

"That's right, Mr MacFarlane, attention is bad. Tell the boy why attention is bad Mr MacFarlane," Tony said.

Gordon looked at Jack sardonically, "Attention is bad, because it can lead to interaction with the 'istorical environment."

"And why is interaction bad, Mr MacFarlane?" Tony asked.

"Because, Mr Smith, interaction can cause stuff to happen."

"That's right Mr MacFarlane. What stuff might that be?"

"Consequences, Mr Smith, in your space-time continuum."

"Continuum, Christie. Do you hear that?"

"You don't want to mess around with your continuum," Gordon said.

"Or to be more precise, a small change now might have significant repercussions for the future," Tony added. "And that's where we come in… we're here to help VIGIL sort out problems – like this one. Sort of tidy up any unfortunate mess."

"Time travelling bin men if you like…" Gordon gave a little shrug.

Tony gave his colleague a sidelong glance, not sure whether he approved of this particular description of their important role.

He turned to Jack, "Do you understand, my friend?"

Jack didn't. He was very scared, "But… I…"

Tony interrupted him, "So, to be sure we have no more interaction than we possibly need, we are going to ask you to help us… Mr MacFarlane?"

Gordon unzipped his rucksack. Jack could see that it was stuffed with all sorts of equipment… not least the carefully packed weapon. Gordon opened a small plastic case. It contained an array of medical equipment and Gordon removed a rather large syringe together with a small bottle of fluid. Carefully, he placed the needle into the top of the bottle and sucked up a small quantity of the liquid.

Jack suddenly realised what they were going to do.

"Sleepy time…" Tony said mockingly.

Jack tried to run, but Gordon grabbed him again.

"Now, now… let's all behave, shall we? Mr Smith – may I ask you to restrain the young man while I attend to the business at hand."

Gordon momentarily relaxed his grip, expecting Tony to take hold of Jack so that the injection could be administered.

Jack had his chance. Without thinking, he lashed out with his forearm. It was more out of self-protection than intent to harm. But his arm cracked straight into the bridge of Gordon's nose. Gordon was more surprised rather than hurt. But then he wobbled – like a large building just after the demolition button has been pressed. To steady himself, he instinctively reached out with his hand. But he only managed to grab a handful of Jack's blonde hair. It was not sufficient to prevent Gordon from finally losing his balance and with one hand still clutching a shock of Jack's hair, he tumbled onto the ground, taking Jack with him.

Jack's instinct was to escape. He was breathing very hard and he knew that with his weak lungs he might not last long. Out of the corner of his eye he saw Tony leering down at them on the floor, a look of mild amusement on his face, as Gordon struggled to get Jack under control.

Jack pawed his pocket instinctively for his puffer. His fingers scrabbled desperately as Gordon twisted him this way and that looking for a way to insert the syringe. But then Jack's fingers encircled something else in his pocket. It wasn't his inhaler. It was the lance head! In one movement, Jack whisked it from his pocket. It flashed briefly in the dull light as he lashed out and down in a violent stabbing motion. It cut through the air and into the black leather of Gordon's boot, before slicing through the flesh of his foot. Gordon screamed with pain as blood spurted from his boot. He clutched it with both hands. Jack picked up the syringe that Gordon had dropped. Tony's look of amusement turned to alarm and he moved forward. But Jack was too quick – he stabbed the syringe into Tony's thigh and pressed home the plunger. Tony fell to one knee, groping his leg. Then he reeled backwards, his eyes flickering as he tried to fight the anaesthetic.

Jack stood up shakily, wheezing and coughing in equal measure. He felt a brief moment of triumph as he surveyed his two assailants groaning on the floor... then, he ran. The door from the Admiral's lobby exited straight onto the starboard upper deck, just below the forecastle. He had to find help or at least a hiding place – but where? He looked around and spotted the squat grey steel outline of a turret positioned a third of the way down the ship's starboard side. Its giant twin fifty-eight tonne gun barrels loomed only a couple of metres above his head. Between where the twin gun barrels protruded from the turret was a short ladder that lead on to the turret roof for access to the two smaller twelve-pounder guns. Without thinking, Jack vaulted over the angled breakwater and clambered up the ladder. He was only a few metres from the deck, but he kept low to avoid over-balancing on the gently rocking ship.

Now Jack did something that he would later reflect on as being both inspirational and complete madness. He lowered himself gently from the lip of the turret roof onto the left-side gun barrel. The gun seemed to stretch endlessly towards the bow. He started to shin his way along the top of the gun towards its tapering end.

In a minute, he was there. He looked down over the end of the barrel. A couple of metres below, the starboard deck yawed as the ship moved through the water. Jack turned round on the gun so his back was now facing away from the turret and towards the bow. Balancing dangerously, he inserted first one foot and then the other into the barrel and pushed his body carefully into the end of the gun. It was a tight squeeze, but he was small for his age and he just made it. As long he kept his blonde head down, nobody would ever know he was there.

But he did not have much time to enjoy his new hiding place. Suddenly he felt a slight vibrating sensation around him coupled with a low, grinding sound. Imperceptibly at first, the giant gun barrel in which he was encased, slowly started to move. The massive gun swung its way from its position parallel with the starboard deck out towards the sea. As it moved laterally, it also rose upwards into the air. Below, in the gun turret itself, he began to hear muffled voices and the commotion of men preparing... for what? Jack, whose head had been flush with the end of the barrel, pushed himself up a little and sneaked a look. He was shocked at what he saw. His gun was now pointing well out over the starboard side of the ship and ten metres below all he could see was the grey water of the sea churning to white as *Dreadnought* drove through it at a mind-spinning twenty knots.

Emerging from a light mist on the distant horizon, he spotted first one, then two and then three ghostly shapes. They were not ships – they seemed to be stationary – although it was difficult to tell. He remembered what the sailor had said: "exercises". Were they on some naval drill? The gun rose a little further into the air, and he realised with sickening fear that *Dreadnought* was about to open fire.

For some reason, Jack remembered very specifically what Pendelshape had explained about the awesome firepower of *Dreadnought*. The shell from a twelve-inch naval gun of the sort used by the ship weighed about three hundred and eighty kilograms –

combined steel and explosive. When the gun was fired, the shell would leave the muzzle at about two thousand eight hundred kilometres an hour. In a few seconds, Jack was going to get one up his rear end. He started to panic.

The angle of the gun was nearing its thirteen and a half degrees of maximum elevation. Before he could take any further action, Jack started to lose his grip and, slowly at first, began to slip down the inside of the dark barrel. Bizarrely, the sixty rifling grooves etched on the inside of the gun, designed to spin the shell to achieve greater stability in flight, started to act on him – but in reverse. His whole body twisted, round and round, inside the barrel like he was on some crazy waltzer at the fair. The circle of daylight from the end of the gun rapidly contracted – it was like looking out from the rear of a train after it had entered a tunnel. Then, almost as soon as the uncomfortable ride had started, with a rather painful 'bang' he came to rest. There was a mechanical whirring sound and suddenly, as the breach of the massive gun was opened, he tumbled out, landing inside the turret.

The operators watched and stood like statues, their faces blank with amazement. Realising that he had not been hurt, Jack clambered up and, not knowing what on earth else to say, announced, "Clean up – ready for use – carry on…" marched purposefully to the side entrance of the turret, and left.

*

There was no sign of Tony and Gordon. Jack suspected that Tony was sleeping like a baby, given the anaesthetic that he had pumped into him. Presumably Gordon was playing nursemaid, as well as tending to his own wound. Regardless, he needed to try and put as much distance between himself and any potential pursuit, then find somewhere more sensible to hide… and think. He sneaked around another turret towards the stern and the port side of the ship. Tethered to the port side was a vast observation balloon. As he got closer, Jack realised that it didn't look like the observation balloons he had seen in books – the kind they had used on the Western Front for artillery spotting – 'kite balloons'. This one looked like a more modern design – it even had its own gas burner. Jack could make out the large passenger basket, which was just touching the aft deck area on a small raised platform, ready for flight. A single cable was holding the balloon precariously to the ship and four crew members manhandled long hooked poles to control the basket, which wobbled in the wind. Jack could make out a man's head peaking over the side of the basket – the observer. He was agitated, and rushed from one side of the basket to the other, shouting orders at the crew on the deck.

Jack crept slowly towards the platform. He turned to look back up towards the bow of the ship. Still no sign of any pursuit. What should he do? As he considered his options, he spotted a strange red dot on his white trainer. At first he thought it might be some blood from Gordon's wound, and he leaned down to wipe it off. Then he noticed it was wobbling around, even with his foot still. Suddenly, it dawned on him what it was. He glanced back along the side of the ship. A stubby black barrel was poking surreptitiously from a porthole attached to what looked like a large zoom lens. Gordon was hidden from view, but using the unique characteristics of the Corner Shot APR, he had Jack nicely in the cross hairs of its laser sight. Jack wasn't going to hang around to find out what would happen next. There was only one thing for it.

He raced towards the balloon crew who were still struggling to control the huge gas bag that rocked back and forth in *Dreadnought's* draft as she powered through the waves, her twin funnels belching black smoke. Jack heard a muffled 'crack'. Gordon must have fired! There was a loud 'twang'. Jack, with a hop, skip and jump that would have made Belstaff, the games teacher, proud, leaped from the deck of *Dreadnought* and onto the gantry, which secured the balloon's winding gear. With both hands, he grabbed the rope ladder attached to the side of the balloon basket. He knew that he could not hold on for long. The basket was swirling dizzily just off the deck and it felt much more unsteady than it first appeared. Over the side of the balloon basket the observer's head appeared. He stared down at Jack with a mixture of amusement and confusion. He was wearing a strange leather skullcap from which wispy shocks of yellow hair escaped and blew around in the breeze. He also wore aviator's goggles placed over small round spectacles. He looked ridiculous.

Suddenly, there was a second loud 'twang', and a mechanical whirring noise. The basket, with the rope ladder attached, shot upwards. Jack could only just cling on. The bullet from Gordon's APR had split the mooring cable and the balloon had broken free. There was consternation from the crew. One of them still had his tether pole hooked to the basket and as he clung onto it, he found himself being lifted right off the deck of *Dreadnought* and out over the sea. He could only hold on for a few seconds until he let go, plunging into the churning wake below. His head bobbed up above the water a few seconds later – but it was already way behind *Dreadnought's* stern.

Jack screamed up to the observer who appeared just above him in the basket, "Please… help!"

The observer stretched down, leaning out dangerously as he did so, but Jack was still too far down on the rope ladder for the observer to reach him. Paralysed by fear, he was unable to move further up the rope ladder so instead, he wrapped his limbs around its rungs as the balloon powered upwards.

"One step at a time, young man!" the observer shouted. "Don't look down!"

Only with a supreme effort was Jack able to cage his fear sufficiently to take a single unsteady step from one rung to the next, then unclench one hand and slide it up to the rung above.

"Very good!" the observer shouted encouragingly. "You can do it!"

Jack gritted his teeth, and repeated the manoeuvre. Finally, the observer was in reach and he grabbed the shoulder straps of Jack's rucksack.

"One more step my friend!" he called.

Jack swallowed hard and pushed up once more. Using this momentum, the man leaned down precariously and, placing a hand under each armpit, gave Jack an almighty heave and he finally slithered into the basket. Jack stood up but had to quickly grab the side of the basket as it swayed in the air.

"Well done my friend!" the observer said giving him a hearty slap on the back.

Jack peered down nervously – he couldn't believe how far up they had already travelled. Maybe fifty metres, and the wind had already taken them way aft of *Dreadnought*, which already looked like a toy ship. He could make out the specks of the crew, and all the features of the ship – the guns still pointing starboard in the direction of the targets – and the wide white wake. The unfortunate seaman who had fallen from his tether pole was bobbing around in the water like a champagne cork. He had been thrown a lifebelt – but would have a job to swim to it.

Jack slumped back down onto the bottom of the basket. He was panting, and reached into his pocket for his puffer. He glanced up at the balloon observer standing over him. He wore a full-length, weather-beaten, brown leather coat with a high collar. His neck was wrapped in a bright red scarf. The leather skullcap was placed on his head at a slight angle. He pushed up his aviator's goggles onto his forehead and peered curiously at Jack with piercing blue eyes, as if examining some sort of botanical specimen.

Then, he smiled warmly, thrust out his hand and, in a surprisingly high somewhat accented voice, said, "Professor August Pinckard-Schnell... delighted to meet you."

Gas Bagging

Jack said the first thing that came into his head, "Are we going to die?"

"Well, we may die or we may not. But one thing is for sure, there is nothing that either of us can do about it," the professor paused, "so we might as well enjoy the ride."

"Great," Jack said sarcastically.

"I shouldn't worry. We will soon be over land and hopefully we will be able to come down safely. Of course, if I am wrong we may plummet like a stone and our bodies will disintegrate as we hit the earth at terminal velocity. Our guts will be spread around Germany or Holland like cow manure…" he paused again, thinking to himself, "or alternatively we may hit woodland, in which case, assuming a good wind, we will be ripped from the basket and dismembered limb from limb as we crash through the canopy…" he shrugged. "Or maybe we will hit a town and be slammed into the side of a tall church just as a family wedding is taking place below. Or…"

"Stop!" Jack pleaded.

The professor paused, still enthusiastically contemplating the apparently limitless scenarios by which they might meet their demise. "Indeed, that is what makes it so very interesting, all these possibilities."

"Fantastic…"

He stared back at Jack for a moment and then guffawed loudly. It was a high-pitched intermittent wheezing – quite unlike any laugh Jack had heard before. "Very good. Very good. I never tire of the English sense of humour. Most excellent…" But suddenly his voice trailed off self-consciously as he realised that, judging from Jack's pale face and trembling hands, he did not share his own blasé nonchalance about their predicament. "I apologise, my friend. One forgets that it can be quite frightening the first time... but I assure you, we are reasonably safe. I speak from experience. Please... allow me to show you." And with that, the professor confidently stepped over to Jack's corner of the basket, placed his hand sympathetically on Jack's arm and encouraged him to get up.

"It takes a little bit of getting used to, and it's no good if you are afraid of heights... but tell me, where else on earth would you get a view like that...?"

The professor opened both arms, preacher like, out into the sky. Jack rose gingerly to his feet and, gripping the side of the basket tightly, reluctantly peered into the void.

"Look. We are over the North Sea and there ahead is the Dutch coast."

The view was breathtaking. Below, the English Channel merged into the broad blue-grey of a calm North Sea twinkling in the strong afternoon sun. There was no roar in his ears – they were travelling with the wind. In fact it was very peaceful.

The professor smiled at the look of wonder on Jack's face. "Beautiful, don't you think?"

"... bit scary."

The professor grinned broadly and slapped him on the back, "Well, let's see if we can't find something to make you feel better."

He moved over to his bags. He seemed very well equipped and soon had Jack wrapped up in a thick woollen blanket in one corner of the basket. Next, he produced a large flask of steaming coffee and then some hard, bitter chocolate, which crumbled dryly in Jack's mouth.

"Main course later... we might need to ration ourselves a little..." The professor's English was perfect, but he had quite a strong accent. Jack began to warm up... and he felt a little more confident.

"Are you from England?" he asked.

The professor looked back at him from his own corner of the basket as he cupped a tin mug brimming with coffee. He pretended to be offended, "Certainly not. I'm German. Well, by nationality anyway. I'm a scientist. Or more an inventor, really."

"How does a German get to be aboard a British battleship? Particularly when war is about to break out."

The professor looked puzzled. "War? I don't think so." He frowned. "The European powers certainly have their differences, but war – I doubt it… Our diplomacy is too good. Many crises have been averted over the last few years – Agadir, the Balkans. Surely nobody wants war – certainly not between Germany and England."

"Even so, how does a German get to be aboard a British battleship?"

The professor shrugged. "As I said, I'm a scientist." Jack was none the wiser. "This," he gestured proudly to the huge balloon above their heads, "is my invention. The navy are interested in using it for spotting at sea. We were about to conduct a test, but then something went wrong with the winding gear."

"You can say that again."

"It's very exciting."

"What is?"

"Well… obviously the navy is paying me for my new design, but I had planned that, once perfected, I might use the balloon to set a world record. Your navy and I are helping each other, if you like."

This was getting better and better, Jack thought. "A world record for what?"

"Distance travelled by air – of course."

Jack's heart sank. "Oh no. And now you think you might have a chance?"

"I admit not quite in the circumstances I expected…" the professor peered out over the basket, "but, I must say, the conditions look most favourable."

"Why would the British employ a German scientist on one of their most important battleships?"

"Well, of course *Dreadnought* is not as state of the art as she once was… and I have helped the navy out on various bits and pieces. Anyway, they know my politics."

"Politics?"

"I have none. Well… I'm a pacifist. Don't approve of politics."

He shrugged. "But if you need your research funded or your balloon tested, there are limited options." He gave another apologetic shrug and there was a pause before he looked across at Jack curiously, "Well I have given you my story," he said, "perhaps you should tell me how you come to be here…" Jack started to feel nervous as the professor's blue eyes drilled into him. "You seem maybe a bit young to be a regular sailor in the king's navy. And the escapade back down there might suggest that you are maybe, shall we say… in trouble?"

Jack weighed up his options. Should he tell the truth? He said the first thing that came into his head.

"Oh that's easy. I'm Jack Christie. I'm a time traveller from the future – and I'm being chased by time police who want to kill me."

For a moment, there was silence as the balloon cut through the sky. Then the professor shook as he let out a second wheezy, high-pitched laugh, "Excellent, excellent!" he cried. "Jack Christie – you and I are going to get along very well. Very well indeed…" He then scrabbled inside his bags again, chortling to himself, long after Jack's remark ceased to be remotely funny.

"More chocolate?"

Professor August Pinckard-Schnell might be as mad as a March hare – but at least he was making Jack feel better.

"Thanks professor."

*

Soon, the professor became distracted. He rose once more from his position, sniffed the air, looked about and then moved around the basket from one corner to the next. "Now, we need to make sure we prepare ourselves properly… it is all about optimising our chances." He checked the burner, which had not yet been used, and ensured that all the gas cylinders were properly secured. He looked up towards the gas bag above, which completely overshadowed them, inspecting it carefully. He glanced several times at the afternoon sun, narrowing his eyes, and then scribbled in a scruffy notebook. This went on for a full ten minutes while Jack hunkered down in his corner of the basket.

When the professor finished he announced, "We seem to be

maintaining our height. Still going east, or more south east, really. Fast, we are travelling fast. Maybe eighty kilometres an hour. Although it does not feel that fast." He pondered what all this might mean, "If we keep going at this rate, well…" he grinned, "a world record! Easily. A world record for manned flight!"

"I'm very happy for you."

"We should maybe try to increase our height a little… what do you say, Jack? Would you like to try the burner?"

Jack was not quite sure what he meant, but then the professor pointed at the large metal burner in the middle of the basket.

"It's easy, quite safe," the professor said. "You just do this." He pulled a lever and there was an ear-splitting whoosh as a large flame licked up towards the aperture underneath the balloon, way above their heads. The professor smiled reassuringly and gestured for Jack to have a go. Jack put his hand on the lever and repeated the procedure. Again, there was a roar as the flame from the burner shot skywards. He jumped back and watched as the flame receded, soon replaced by the silent sky as they sailed on. Reassured that the procedure had not resulted in the balloon going up in a ball of flames, Jack gained a little more confidence, and took a second opportunity to inspect the breathtaking view from their vantage point. Soon his remaining fear melted away – replaced by a surging exhilaration. The air was like crystal and you could see a hundred and sixty kilometres in every direction.

"Funny," Jack remarked. "No vapour trails."

The professor looked at him oddly, "No what?"

"You know, vapour trails. I was just thinking, professor, it's funny that you can't see any vapour trails from all the jets… there's usually loads…" Jack suddenly realised what he had said and his voice trailed off self-consciously, "even where I live…"

The professor looked puzzled. "'Jet', 'vapour trail' – these are English expressions I have not heard before…"

Jack grimaced, "Sorry professor, doesn't matter, it's just where I come from… we have some funny words for stuff – there's a bunch more I probably need to teach you as well, like 'Google', 'iPod', and

'Global Warming'. That kind of thing." He shrugged, "But you won't need to worry about any of them."

The professor frowned, "I see… oh well… you must, er, tell me what they mean… sometime." He put his notebook back in his bag and began to busy himself with retrieving some more provisions. Soon he had laid out quite a feast. Sausages were produced, bread and some cheese.

"I hope this is OK…" the professor said airily.

They ate and the professor probed again.

"So, come Jack – the truth now… what were you really doing aboard the ship… Had you stowed away? Maybe trouble with your family – at home? Maybe I can help?"

Jack considered his options again. It was going to be difficult to brush off the truth, however unbelievable. And his earlier blunder about there being no aeroplanes in the sky could easily be repeated. More importantly, he knew he was still in danger – he had escaped Tony and Gordon once – but with all the technology they seemed to have at their disposal, they could easily turn up again. Maybe the bizarre Professor August Pinckard-Schnell was right and he could help in some way. He seemed kind, if eccentric. Honesty, however unbelievable, was probably the best policy. He glanced at the professor, toying with a piece of cheese, took a deep breath and launched into the incredible events of the last few hours. As he did so, the professor studied him with a look of amused scepticism.

After he had finished, the professor put his hand over his mouth to hide a doubting smile, "Well it's an impressive story, Jack, but I'm not sure it is quite believable…" He clearly thought that the strange waif he had inadvertently rescued either had an over-active imagination or had escaped from the local lunatic asylum. To be fair, Jack could see his point.

Then he had a brainwave. He reached inside his rucksack. It was still there: the history book. In triumph, he tossed it over to the professor and it landed at his crossed feet on the other side of the basket. It blew open and the crisp white pages ruffled provocatively in the breeze.

"Well – if you don't believe me – take a look at that."

The professor took the book gingerly in his hands and leafed slowly through the pages. As he did so, the expression on his face changed.

Jack looked at him smugly, "It might be difficult for me to make all that up. Published in the year 2006 for a start… a few years from now I think you'll find. It would be hard for me to create the detail in there – the whole history of the war… all the horror… the pictures…"

The professor's amused scepticism evaporated and after a while he raised his head and looked at Jack with ashen-faced incredulity. He tried to say something, making a couple of false starts in the process, "But…", "How did…?" and finally, he muttered, "So this war of yours, this 'Great War', it really happens?"

"Oh yes, Professor, it happens alright."

"It's incredible. It cannot be true."

"Incredible. And true. Either that, or it's a complete nightmare. And I've fallen asleep in Pendelshape's class…"

The professor was concentrating intensely, his brow deeply furrowed, as he thumbed the book with increasing fervour. He began to speak to himself in a quick-fire stream of German as his brain tried to come to terms with Jack's revelations. "Well, I suppose, the new physics; of course I am familiar with this. Einstein, Planck – relativity, quantum mechanics. The new physics has incredible conceptual leaps. Few understand it, and probably none can comprehend the implications. But nothing like this, surely… surely not…"

The professor shook his head in awe as the enormity of it all started to sink in.

"The consequences of this are… profound… and this war, you say it kills, how many?"

"I'm not sure. I think around eight million… over sixty million are mobilised." Jack reached over and located a table at the back of the book that he remembered seeing. He showed it to the professor – statistics of the dead by country. The professor gawped at the numbers.

"In fact, I believe your own country, Germany, suffers greatly. Nearly two million dead. And Germany loses the war, and takes the blame for starting it."

A shadow crossed over the professor's face.

Jack shrugged, "But if it's any comfort, my history teacher says that people are still arguing about the causes of the war." He continued gloomily, "But that's not all. That book tells you all about the war... but what I haven't told you is that this war leads to another, even more horrific war. The Second World War, twenty years later."

The professor shook his head, "Sorry Jack... this... book, your... story. It is so incredible. I find it hard to believe..."

Jack fished around in his pocket again. He'd started now, so he might as well go the whole hog. He produced the time phone and presented it to the professor.

"Here, the time phone I told you about. It links to the Taurus, which sends people backwards and forwards through time – when it decides to work, that is. It's a bit dodgy. Look..." He flipped open the device showing the professor the mysterious blue light, screen, SATNAV and buttons. "You're a scientist, Professor, but I bet you've never seen technology like this."

The professor studied the time phone in wonder. Jack imagined that he had the same stupid expression of shock on his face that he and Angus must have had on first hearing Pendelshape's revelations back at the Taurus control room.

All the professor could say was, "Incredible... incredible..." He repeated the words to himself trancelike, over and over again.

As they stared into the time phone, Jack noticed that the grey bar inside was starting to flicker. Gradually, the grey was replaced by a yellow light, which was soon burning brightly. Jack's heart leaped.

"A signal! Professor! We have a signal!"

He grabbed the phone. Suddenly a message appeared on the display.

"Someone's communicating with us!" Jack could scarcely contain his excitement.

"Look! Look!"

You have one message from Taurus:

Day of the Assassins

My dear Jack - you are in great danger - your
trip through time threatens us all.
You must give yourself up to VIGIL's agents -
Tony Smith and Gordon MacFarlane - as soon as
possible. They are trying to locate you and
bring you back. You must do what they say.
I love you - Mum

Jack was gobsmacked, "Mum? A message from Mum… on the time phone… but?" He couldn't understand it… how could his mum possibly be involved?

"What does it mean?" the professor asked.

"I don't get it. The yellow light is on… that means we are now being tracked and that's why we can receive messages from the Taurus. I also think it means that we could travel back to the Taurus…"

"Astonishing. But this message, it's from your mother?"

Jack grimaced, it wasn't making any sense. "Yes… it seems so. Or maybe Tony and Gordon or the Rector are playing a trick."

"Maybe she is with them?" the professor added.

Jack was dumbfounded, "It can't be… can't."

He tried to think back through the recent course of events. How was his mum involved in all of this? And why hadn't she told him? He felt a sudden twinge of anger – it was as if she was always keeping things from him.

He had an idea, "I know!" he said triumphantly. "I could send a message back! Pendelshape explained how to do that. I can ask them!"

He scrutinised the time phone once more, trying to recall how to create and send a message. But as he stared into the device, the bright yellow light flickered.

He groaned, "No! Please not again! I think we're losing it…"

The yellow light went dead; the grey bar took its place.

"Stupid thing!"

He shook the device in disgust and then sank back into the corner of the basket, dejected. The professor moved over to him and pulled the blanket over his shoulders. He gave Jack a reassuring pat on the back. "Don't worry, my friend, I don't understand either... but I'm sure we can work it out."

Jack looked up at the professor and tried to squeeze out a smile. It wasn't easy.

*

After a while, he fell asleep – the nervous energy from a tumultuous day had finally taken its toll. In silence, on the opposite corner of the balloon, the professor studied Jack's history book. It was beyond belief. His logical mind strained to identify an alternative, more plausible explanation. But as he worked his way through the pages, his natural cheerfulness evaporated and his expression became grim. Occasionally, he glanced across at Jack, shook his head and murmured something to himself as he tried to absorb the dramatic revelations from the future. Once or twice he stood and gave a blast on the burner and then gazed from the balloon as it moved steadily southwards, pushed on by a relentless tailwind.

The sky was finally beginning to darken in the east as the midsummer sun set. Way below, the European canvas spread out from the English Channel to the Russian steppes. Far away, for the first time, the professor spotted that the horizon had an irregular, jagged outline and exuded a faint, pink glow.

He mumbled something – half to himself, half to Jack – who slept soundly on in the opposite corner. "The Alps."

Revelations

" **W**ake up!" The professor shook him hard. Jack woke shivering. He raised his head above the woollen blanket and unfolded himself from his foetal position in the corner of the basket. Every bone ached. Although it was light, the temperature had dropped dramatically. He peered gingerly over the edge of the balloon and was staggered by what he saw. Mountains. Everywhere. The balloon was scarcely clearing the peaks – vast rock outcrops, many snow tipped, interspersed with verdant pine-clad valleys. Wedged into the north-facing bowls, snowfields and glaciers still clung on, stubbornly resisting the summer warmth.

The professor seemed to be very excited. "The Alps! Mountains! Isn't it beautiful? Austria. Incredible!"

"Are we going to land?"

"No doubt about it… out of gas… we're going down. Fast! We may even crash. Isn't it marvellous?"

Jack wasn't so sure. Wasn't there supposed to be some procedure for this kind of event?

"Don't we need to fasten seatbelts, stop serving hot drinks… that sort of thing?"

The professor wasn't listening. He was now staring out from the basket concentrating hard on the mountain terrain, "I think you should wrap yourself up in the blankets… and hold on tight. We are descending quickly… let's hope we get lucky… some of those peaks look, well, they look high."

"Why didn't you put us down safely, before we ran out of gas?"

"What's that my boy?" the professor shouted back over his shoulder.

"I said… why wait until now to land?"

"In the dark? Suicide! We reached the mountains faster than I anticipated. The wind speed was even greater than I expected. I have been looking for a safe spot since first light. No luck. We'll have to take our chances."

The professor had scarcely finished his sentence when there was a loud grating as the underside of the basket made contact with a craggy peak and scraped along it for nearly twenty metres. Then, the mountain dropped sharply away and they were again suspended above a green 'U'-shaped valley with a kilometre drop to the valley floor.

*

The balloon swooped up the side of the next mountain as it caught a favourable updraught from the valley. It cleared the next ridge, but the basket suspended beneath was less fortunate. They hit a snow-covered arête between a double peak very hard and were both slammed face first into the inside of the basket. The professor groaned and blood started to stream from his nose. Then, a great slab of snow fell into them as the cornice on the opposite side of the arête collapsed onto the basket as it was dragged on by the balloon.

Breaking free from the cornice, they found themselves swinging high above the next valley. The weight of the snow in the basket forced the balloon downwards alarmingly. With only their bare hands, Jack and the professor desperately shovelled snow out of the basket to reduce weight. Ahead, they could see that they were now heading for a large expanse of snow and ice, spread wide on a plateau resting below the next ridge. A glacier. They made contact – hard. The basket bounced once and the snow, deep frozen from the night before, exploded into a sparkling cloud of icy vapour. Their journey wasn't finished. The balloon still had momentum and it continued to drag them at speed across the rising plateau of the glacier. They were now lying on one side and Jack and the professor were pressed into the wicker floor by snow rapidly accumulating inside. They were helpless. But finally, the angle of the glacier pitched upwards and the balloon decelerated. The momentum of the balloon began to slow and they came to a gentle rest.

Jack was encased in snow. He couldn't believe the weight of the stuff – he could hardly move. It was in his ears, his eyes, his mouth. He pressed his legs into the bottom of the basket, and with a momentous heave managed to wrench himself free. He tumbled out onto the glacier and lay on his back, panting heavily. A moment later, the professor managed to do the same and they both lay – prostrate and exhausted – staring up at the Alpine sky. They looked back at the tangled mess of the balloon and the trail of material their landing had sprayed onto the pristine ice shelf. The professor managed to lift his head a little further to inspect the damage.

"I hope the Royal Navy don't want their balloon back," he said, and promptly dropped his head back onto the snow. Jack was too bruised and drained to respond, but just for a second, he smiled.

*

Way above them on the same mountain, two men watched the spectacle of the balloon's crash landing and its occupants' fortunate escape. The men were well equipped and wore skis. Quietly, they slid from the shoulder of the mountain and started to carve regular turns in the slope of deep powder snow. The steep slopes at the top of the glacier, in the early morning, even at this time of year, made for outstanding powder skiing. They put in neat regular turns, to control their descent.

Towards the bottom of the initial descent the slope levelled out and gave way to the main glacier field. The men made their way to where the balloon and its contents were strewn over the glacier. In minutes they arrived where Jack and the professor still lay. The glare of the morning sun was intense and Jack was only able to open his eyes into a thin slit. But the two figures who now appeared in his narrow field of vision were unmistakeable – Tony and Gordon.

*

Tony stared down at them both, surrounded by the wreckage of the accident.

"Well you've made a bit of a mess of this little lot, haven't you son?" Tony said. The moisture on his breath instantly condensed to vapour in the freezing air.

"Bit of a mess…" Gordon parroted.

Jack could only stare back at them defiantly.

"Aren't you going to introduce us to your friend?" Tony said.

The professor got to his feet, shakily, but still managed a smile. "Professor Pinckard-Schnell – delighted to meet you." He thrust out a hand, "Are you here to rescue us? You've been very quick."

Tony and Gordon looked at each other and laughed.

"You could say that, professor, you could say that," Gordon replied.

Tony turned to Jack who still lay prostrate on the snow. He leaned down and Jack flinched.

Tony put up his palms defensively, and said, "Whoa lad – let me help you now." For a moment, Jack was taken aback – his tone was almost… kind. He helped Jack into a sitting position, dusted down the snow and then started to examine him – looking into his eyes for symptoms of concussion and checking for other signs of injury.

Soon he pronounced himself satisfied, "A bit battered and bruised – but you'll live." He turned to the professor, "What about you my friend? Looks like you could do with something for that nose."

The professor was holding his hand under both nostrils and they were still bleeding profusely. "Thank you."

Gordon took some cotton wool from his rucksack and started to wipe the blood from the professor's face. "Not as bad as it looks, Professor. It's not broken anyway. A lucky escape."

Tony shook his head, "Yep – it looked quite a heavy landing from up there. You had us worried for a moment…"

He turned his attention back to Jack, who was regaining some composure, "Now, son, first things first, we've got very disappointing news for you… It appears, under strict orders from VIGIL, that no harm is to come to you… and we are to take you back to base – safely."

"It's disappointing, because my foot still hurts from where you impaled it…" Gordon added.

"Never mind that. Anyway, rules, as they say, is rules. So we'd better get going." Tony looked up at the sky, "At least the weather doesn't look like it will turn."

Jack didn't understand why, having tried to assault him back at the control room and aboard *Dreadnought*, Tony and Gordon were now attempting to be nice. He frowned suspiciously, "So you're not going to harm us? No more injections? What's happening?"

"You're safe, son. That's all you need worry about. The Rector will explain everything."

A million questions rushed into Jack's head. "The Rector but… ? How did you get here anyway? And where are we going?"

Tony tapped his breast pocket knowingly, "With time travel you can go anywhere… any time."

"When it decides to work…" Gordon added grumpily.

Tony ignored him. "Save your energy lad. You'll need it." He half turned, and gestured down towards the glacier and the wilderness beyond. "Let's just concentrate on getting off this mountain, first." Then he shook his head and said, "Oh, I nearly forgot. I'm afraid that you will need to hand it over."

"Hand what over?"

"The time phone, of course. Can't have you gallivanting around space and time. No end to the trouble you'll cause. Have caused. Once you're debriefed, we'll get you back home…" he added with a rueful smile, "Safely. Don't you worry about that." He put out his hand, "If you please."

Jack rummaged in his pocket and fished out his time phone. He clutched onto it for a moment, then reluctantly dropped it into Tony's vast leathery hand.

"Thank you, lad. We will put that one safely away with ours."

*

Tony and Gordon roped Jack and the professor together and they made their way down the edge of the glacier. Eventually, it gave way to steep moraine fields. They picked their way through until they reached the tree line. A gentle breeze hissed through the fir canopy as they followed an old trapping trail. Later on, the forest opened onto a large expanse of high pasture, an *Almen*, and for the first time the group was rewarded with breathtaking views of the valley far below. It was a pristine wilderness of dark green firs interspersed with pasture land, guarded by towering granite walls. Along the valley sides they could see the shimmering silver threads of at least three plunging waterfalls.

Jack had been in the mountains before. Last year his mum had let him go on the school skiing trip. But that had been nothing like this. It had been busy: lots of people, the mechanical whirring of lifts, barging in queues, the slopes dotted with people in ant trails all competing to find the best way down. But here, there was nobody. The air was champagne clear; the greens were somehow greener and the sky bluer – beyond empty and beyond silent.

*

They had been going for five hours, and even with regular breaks and provisions from Tony and Gordon, Jack was exhausted. At last, they emerged onto the broad valley floor. Ahead of them was a river that wound its way lazily through the fields. It looked quite deep in places, even though the spring thaw was well past. About three kilometres away they could see a small town, with the rounded spire of a chapel peeking above the tiled rooftops. Slightly beyond this, a craggy outcrop jutted out from the side of the valley, rising to perhaps two hundred metres, maybe more. A castle had been built high up on the exposed lump of black rock. It had narrow windows like slits and at least three sub turrets with conical roofs projecting from high stone sides. It dominated the valley.

As Jack wearily craned his head up at the castle, it slowly dawned on him that he could not see any possible way to approach it. Perhaps there was a route from above, where the rocky outcrop joined the main cliff face? Or perhaps there was a winding track that approached the building from the rear – currently hidden from their view? Then he spotted it. Rising silently from the village ahead of them, a red box magically appeared and rose at a steep angle upwards towards the castle: a cable car. And sure enough, he could just make out the thin wire that looped gracefully from the village right up to the castle. The village was strangely deserted when they finally reached it. They entered the small cable car station. After a short wait, they boarded the return cable car, which transported them smoothly upwards and gently delivered them on to the precipitous landing gantry, high up in the castle wall.

*

Tony and Gordon led Jack and the professor from the landing gantry, down a stone staircase honed from the rock, and into the small courtyard of the castle. Jack followed, zombie-like, fatigue overwhelming him. Out of the corner of his eye, he spotted an occasional dark figure, high up on the battlements, peering down at them. The place was eerily quiet. It had been a fine day, but the high, dark walls shielded the sun and the courtyard was left in gloomy shadow. On reaching the opposite side of the courtyard, they entered the main keep of the castle, and were led into a hall. By contrast to the austere exterior of the castle, the inside of the hall was magnificent. Tapestries and paintings adorned oak-panelled walls and chandeliers hung from a high-vaulted ceiling. At one end, a large open fire crackled away. They were invited to sit on one of several sofas and armchairs that surrounded the log fire. In front of them, refreshments were already laid out on a low table. Jack barely made it to a chair before his legs gave way and he collapsed into it. His eyelids drooped as the physical exertions of the day and the gentle warmth from the fire took their toll. In a moment he was fast asleep. Two minutes later, the professor was also snoring loudly.

Jack didn't know how long they had been asleep when they were woken by the creak of the door opening. A man with two burly guards on either side marched in. The tall, stooping frame and the wisps of silver hair adorning his balding head were unmistakable. Just the gown was missing. It was the Rector. The last time Jack had seen him was in the control room, directing Tony and Gordon to set about Angus and Pendelshape, just before Jack had made his daring escape using the Taurus. Now, here he was with them – in an Austrian castle in 1914. The Rector marched forward and the two guards quietly peeled away to take up positions elsewhere in the hall. Then, he did something that took Jack completely by surprise. He opened his arms warmly and said, "Welcome!" He moved over to where they sat and gestured for them to stay in their seats, "Please, please, stay where you are. I know. You have had a very tiring and traumatic day. Mr Smith has already briefed me.

"You've certainly given us a run for our money!" He turned and called back towards the hall entrance, "More food! Our guests are hungry!"

The Rector's friendliness was unsettling.

"Time travel – it creates a bit of an appetite, don't you think?"

Jack was confused. He couldn't work out why the Rector was being friendly. Unable to control himself, he blurted out, "What's going on? Where are we? What have you done with Angus and Dr Pendelshape?"

The Rector tried to soothe him, "Please, Jack – calm yourself. You are quite safe. And we owe you an explanation. You are one of the school's better pupils, after all," the Rector smiled at the professor, "he really is, you know." The Rector nodded, "Yes – we have much to discuss and much to explain. But first, some proper introductions. The Rector thrust out his hand to the professor. "John Blanding – Rector at Jack's school, back at, er, home. Pleased to meet you, Professor. My men have told me all about your miraculous escape in the mountains."

The professor half rose from his seat, "Pinckard-Schnell, at your service. I must thank you for arranging our rescue so quickly… and thank you for allowing us to be guests," he looked around, unsure of himself, "in your, er, house."

"A pleasure. I understand from Mr Smith that you were taking an unexpected opportunity to set a new world record, Professor?"

"Yes…"

"Well, as you are no doubt aware, you have landed in the Southern Tyrol, so as you departed from HMS *Dreadnought*, somewhere in the North Sea, I think you will have more than achieved your objective. Congratulations are in order."

The Professor blushed self-consciously, then his expression turned to one of puzzlement, "You seem to know a surprising amount… sir, how exactly…?"

Jack piped up, his voice a little unsteady. "Professor – I don't think you quite understand – this is the Rector from my school, the head teacher, the one I told you about." He turned to the Rector, "I told him what happened, sir, I had to really, although I'm not sure he quite believes me."

The Rector smiled, "Yes, of course. I quite understand. Well, now we are all here safe and sound, I think you deserve to understand the full picture." He turned to the Professor, "Both of you."

*

"... You can see, then, how the technology we are dealing in, time travel technology, is extremely powerful. Those who use it can potentially change the past and therefore change the future. The people who are in charge of it have a huge responsibility. Sometimes we have to take difficult decisions – and we have to take them quickly."

Jack and the professor had sat back in their chairs whilst the Rector paced backwards and forwards in front of the log fire. The professor was engrossed in what the Rector had to say. Jack, however, refreshed after his short nap and the food, was impatient for answers.

"Have you killed Dr Pendelshape?" he asked.

For the first time, the Rector's warmth evaporated, "Pendelshape! That idiot! Jack – do you have any idea how dangerous Pendelshape's actions could have been?"

Jack shook his head sheepishly.

The Rector took a deep breath, "For your information, no, we have not killed him. Not our style, although he has been severely reprimanded. I don't think he will make the same mistake twice." The Rector, calming himself, explained Pendelshape's sins in more detail, "Pendelshape was collaborating secretly with the Benefactor in his quest to build a separate Taurus. We had no idea. Not only is this quest exceptionally dangerous, but it is against VIGIL rules – the VIGIL Imperative that he signed up to – and what's more, it's a personal betrayal to all his colleagues – including myself."

They looked at the Rector blankly. The Rector sighed, "I think I need to explain to you both exactly what we are dealing with here."

He stooped down to place another log on the fire, "The scientific team that developed the time-travel technology decided that using it would be too dangerous. Making interventions back in time might have unforeseen consequences for the present. We had developed very good computer-modelling techniques to predict how changes in the past would alter the future course of history. But despite this, we believed it was just too risky. We decided instead to mothball the technology, and we founded the school as a cover for what we were doing. VIGIL was set up and we agreed to be bound by its rules. In the end there was really only one dissenting voice – the Benefactor. He could not agree that we should never use the technology – he honestly believed that it could be used as a power for good. The argument became very heated. Eventually, we agreed to part company with the Benefactor. It was very sad in a way. He was one of our most brilliant scientists and one of the architects of the Taurus. But he left the Taurus team seven years ago and we heard nothing from him until yesterday."

"Until you intercepted the emails between him and Pendelshape."

"That's right, Jack. We were carrying out a check, as we do on all the team members from time to time, without their knowledge. We have to. What we found was extremely alarming."

"The Benefactor had built a separate Taurus."

"Exactly – we were staggered by this. We could not believe that he could have done it on his own." The Rector stared into the flickering flames. He shook his head and added grudgingly, "You have to admire him. Now, there are two working time machines, and suddenly, the Benefactor has the ability to time travel and, potentially, to make his own changes in history – just as he always wanted."

"And you can't do anything about it?"

The Rector turned back to Jack. "Well, of course, as we also have our original Taurus at the school, if the Benefactor made a change in time, we could go back and try to reverse that change. In fact one of the reasons we kept the Taurus intact and even tested it was in case somehow, someone developed similar technology in the future. We had considered that scenario but believed it to be highly unlikely. But science moves quickly…"

"Two time machines? Sounds like things could get really messed up. Dr Pendelshape said something about the 'Armageddon Scenario'."

"Yes – a theoretical possibility. You could get into a series of interventions and reversals in history… anything could happen.

It's unpredictable and very dangerous."

The professor removed his round glasses and started to polish them energetically on a napkin, as his mind spun in wonderment at the potential consequences of time-travel interventions.

"A kind of time war," he said – probably with more enthusiasm than he intended.

"If you like, Professor, but we don't even want to contemplate that. We must stop the Benefactor from doing anything at all."

"But you can't do that – you don't know where he is – he has his own Taurus – he can do whatever he wants… whenever he wants."

The Rector stared down at Jack. His expression had changed – he now had a sympathetic, even sad, look in his eye, "Of course, you would be right, but for one thing."

Jack cocked his head, not sure what the Rector meant.

"Sorry – I keep calling him 'the Benefactor' – old names, old habits, I'm afraid. You of course know by now, who the Benefactor is?"

"Some nutcase – sounds like." Jack glanced over to the professor and smiled nervously.

"He's your father, Jack."

A Gilded Cage

Jack heard the words but they made no sense. For a second, he just stared blankly at the Rector.

"What?"

"The Benefactor – he's your father…"

"But… how…?"

"Jack, I know this is hard…"

Slowly it started to become clear. "…the library at Cairnfield…"

"Yes – your father's workshop."

It all made sense. All the First World War memorabilia they had found there. Then there was the present of a history book and his strange flashbacks of the trip to the First World War battlefields and cemeteries – no doubt driven by his father's interest in history – maybe his desire for Jack to share the same interest, and share his horror at the slaughter. And then there was his early childhood near Geneva – where his father had worked with the rest of the Taurus team. And his father never being at home – always working – which wasn't surprising given the importance of what he was doing. And, of course, the separation from his mum. It was obvious now why that had happened. The stress must have been unbearable. Jack couldn't believe that he had not realised it before.

"But why wasn't I told… why didn't Mum say…?"

"To protect you. Knowledge of the Taurus, and the people involved with it, is strictly controlled. Carole, your mother, is aware, she has to be… but she is on our side. Your father pleaded with her desperately for you both to join him when he left. But Carole was determined that she should try to give you a normal life… not to have you caught up in all… this. And anyway…"

"Anyway what?"

The Rector turned away again, rubbing his hands by the fire. "Sorry Jack... your father could be... difficult."

"So, this explains the message we received from Jack's mother on the time phone in the balloon," the professor said.

"We managed to send a temporary signal from our Taurus to your time phone. We told Carole immediately what had happened, and we sent the message from her, we thought you would trust her, to try to warn you that we would be bringing you in. Not to resist. We would have tried to get you back right then – but there was no signal."

"So why send a couple of thugs?" Jack said crossly.

"MacFarlane and Smith?" the Rector raised his eyebrows, "This is not a game, Jack. The fight you witnessed at the school was... unfortunate. But we were desperate – we had to act very, very fast."

"But on *Dreadnought*... they were going to inject me with some stuff, then Gordon shot at me with that weird rifle thing when I managed to get on the balloon."

"No. It might have appeared like that to you. You were under intense stress. They had strict orders to sedate you if necessary, but to bring you home, safely, as soon as we had a signal. I understand that Mr Macfarlane's shot at the balloon was an attempt to free it from its moorings before you boarded it. It was the shot of a marksman... He was certainly not aiming for you. Those two are utterly trustworthy." He added under his breath, "Although sometimes they become a little over enthusiastic."

"But you still have not explained why this young man is so important to you – why he needs to be mixed up in all of this?" the professor said, glancing across at Jack sympathetically. "Surely it is Jack's father you want, not Jack?"

The Rector sighed, "Don't you see? I'm afraid, Jack, in a way, you are a kind of hostage. If we have you, then the Benefactor, your father, has his hands tied... You are the only person in the world that he cares about. He even thinks Carole has betrayed him now. The only way we can stop him using the Taurus is by threatening to harm you if he does."

Jack suddenly realised the terrible logic of his predicament and thought back to the email from his father that he and Angus had read in Pendelshape's store cupboard: *I fear that when they find out, they may take Orion... we must protect Orion.*

Orion. At last he knew who that was. Orion was himself. His father had wanted Pendelshape to make sure that Jack was safe, so that his father would be free to use his own Taurus, without the Rector and VIGIL stopping him by threatening to harm his son. It explained, too, why Pendelshape had taken them into his confidence so suddenly and taken such a risk in showing them the Taurus and its control room. Pendelshape had been working secretly with his father all along. Before the Rector had arrived with Tony and Gordon in the control room, Pendelshape was about to take Jack somewhere so that the Rector could never find them. In fact, as he had guessed, Pendelshape had been planning to use the Taurus to hide Jack in time. In 1914. Then, his father could use his second Taurus to locate them and rescue them – so they would be permanently free from the clutches of the Rector and VIGIL. But the Rector had arrived too soon and had upset the plan. Ironically, Jack had been so frightened by the sudden arrival of the Rector and the VIGIL guards, he had panicked and used the Taurus to escape anyway.

But the email had also mentioned someone else: Lynx.

There is nothing we can do about Lynx now – she has gone over to the other side.

Jack looked at the Rector, "So if I am 'Orion', who is 'Lynx'?"

"Carole – your mother."

Of course. "So, what you're saying is that I'm a kind of pawn in a battle between you and my dad?"

"I'm afraid so, Jack."

"And while you have me... you can threaten my dad that you might kill me... or... or torture me... then you know he won't do anything. Anything silly – with the second Taurus – to change things in the past. To change the course of history..."

"Yes. But you are more than a pawn. You are much, much more important than that. In fact, I would say, right now, until we can track down your father, and bring him under control, you are possibly the most important person in the world. It's only the threat to harm you that prevents your father from acting. We are all involved in a deadly high-wire balancing act... It's not how we want it to be. But it's the way it is."

*

Jack felt confused at first... then he started to feel angry. Angry that these men, with their intellects and ambitions had created a technology so powerful and so potentially lethal that it could scarcely be discussed, let alone used. Angry that, for some reason, it was in him that the precarious balance of power between these two enemies was maintained. Angry, that his mum had not found it possible to explain any of this to him before. Angry that it was the battle to control this great power that had torn his own family apart.

*

Later, with the night upon them, they were led through a series of spiral staircases and passageways to their rooms. Separate rooms. Jack's seemed to have been cut straight from the massive stonework of the castle walls. The door closed behind him and he heard a key turn in its lock and a dull clunk as two bolts on the outside were slid into place. It was like being in an underground bunker. The air was completely still and there was no sound. Although it was small, some attempt had been made to make the place comfortable. On the floor, a thick rug covered the grey flagstones. There was some simple dark-oak furniture and a pair of maroon curtains. There was a made-up bed with pillows, sheets, blankets and a richly embroidered gold and red bedspread. It looked like it must have taken months to hand sew. It was nothing like his blue-and-white striped duvet at home that had probably spun off a textile machine in China in five seconds.

Jack peered through the small window. It was getting late and the ragged outline of the mountains was darkening against an indigo sky. The window was set solidly into the one-metre thick castle wall and could not be opened. For the time being, he was caged. Of course he now knew why. He was being held hostage from his own father, the Benefactor, in case he was, in some way, able to find out where his son was located and was then able to mount a daring rescue mission.

He remembered the awe he had felt when he discovered that the extraordinary workshop beneath Cairnfield actually belonged to his own father. He had been proud to be associated with somebody so brilliant – his own flesh and blood. Now, he realised just how powerful his father was, and therefore how important he himself was, his feelings were agonisingly mixed. There was pride in feeling 'special' but at the same time he was scared and confused. He didn't know who to trust – the Rector, VIGIL and his mum, or Pendelshape and his dad. He didn't know who was really right and who was really wrong and he didn't want to have to choose.

Rescue

It was still dark outside. Jack had been dreaming again of the visit to the First World War graves – the endless sea of white crosses, the grassed-over outline of old trench networks, then running along for shelter from the storm and opening the door and seeing his mum and dad… crying… and then his mum whisking him back to his bedroom. He was relieved when gradually the curtains lightened with the arrival of a bright mountain dawn.

*

Breakfast was set out on a white-clothed buffet table at the end of the hall where they had met the Rector the night before. A fire had already been started and was crackling away merrily. The professor had been up early and sat alone at the long breakfast table nursing a cup of coffee. His head was still buried in Jack's history book. Occasionally, a figure would scurry silently into the hall from an ante-room to clear a plate or bring fresh coffee. As Jack entered, the professor raised his head in acknowledgement and waved absent-mindedly at the food. Having helped himself, Jack settled down opposite the professor, unfurled a napkin and was about to tuck into two large poached eggs and several rashers of bacon when he noticed a rather strained expression on the professor's face.

"OK, Professor?"

The professor looked to the left and to the right as if to make sure that they were alone and whispered across to Jack conspiratorially. "It's not right."

"What do you mean?" Jack asked loudly.

The professor winced, "Keep your voice down!"

Jack looked around him and shrugged as if to say 'why?'.

The professor manoeuvred a prune around his bowl with his fork. "Were you locked in your bedroom last night?"

"Yes. But the Rector explained, they can't take any chances, can they? They have to protect me. But they don't want to harm us. It's just the threat of being able to harm me that gives them power over Dad. I don't like it either."

The large oak doors swung open and the Rector strode purposefully towards them.

"Good morning, gentlemen! I see you are making yourselves at home... excellent! I trust you both had a good night's sleep?"

The professor continued to prod the prune. The Rector inspected the fare on offer at the buffet.

"Not bad at all considering the short time we've had to set this place up." He started to load his plate and was soon sitting beside them at the table.

"Is there a plan, sir?" Jack asked. "Will we be going home soon?"

"Well, your priority should be to have a good breakfast... you've had a traumatic time." He filled a large cup from the coffee pot, "And then, for the rest of today, you will stay in the castle. As you can see, we have taken over this place because it affords us a number of obvious advantages – isolation, security... But I think you will find the main courtyard a pleasant place to while away a few hours." He glanced over at the high-arched windows that dominated the far end of the hall, "Looks like it'll be a fine day."

"And then what?"

The Rector thought for a moment, "Well, as soon as we finally achieve a reliable signal connection, we shall send you back to the twenty-first century. Simple as that, really, Jack. The small VIGIL team we have here will follow, using our time phones, once we have, er, done some tidying up. Closed this place down in an orderly manner for a start. This might be today. It might be tomorrow. It's a little difficult to tell. But our plan is that you should arrive back just after the point that you made the original trip from the Taurus." His face tightened, "It will be hard, Jack, but at that point you will need to continue your life as if nothing had happened. We will be there to guide you. As I explained yesterday, our aim will be to ensure that you lead a normal life… of course, we will need to keep you protected…"

"From Dad?"

"Yes. I'm afraid if ever he gets hold of you, then, well, we will have very little hold over him. There will be nothing to stop him."

"Is there no way of finding out where he is? Dad, I mean. Negotiating or something?"

"We have no idea where your father is or where the second Taurus is, but of course it is something we are working on. As for negotiation – I'm afraid we're well past that stage."

The Rector took a slurp of coffee and then turned his attention to the professor. "As for you, Professor, you will be free to go, with your world record for the most distance travelled by balloon intact. But we must ask you not to speak of the events you have experienced. I am sure you understand."

The professor looked up from his prune and nodded half-heartedly. Something was bothering him.

*

Later, they sat in the small courtyard of the castle, sipping lemonade at a table, awaiting instructions from the Rector. The castle was very quiet although occasionally a VIGIL guard could be seen moving along the crenellated outline of the upper walls. The afternoon sun cast a sharp, diagonal shadow midway across the courtyard.

The professor continued to be engrossed in Jack's book. Occasionally, he would raise his head and contemplate the bright reflection of the sunlight on the cobblestones, or ask Jack some question about the war or the future. Nearby, water from a stone fountain gurgled into a flat earthenware basin. It was surrounded by a well-trimmed hedge. Presumably, this place still existed in the future. Jack vaguely thought about scratching his name or something, surreptitiously on one of the walls, to see if it would still be there nearly a hundred years in the future. He sighed. He'd only been away a couple of days but he missed home. It would be good to talk to his mum about everything that had happened. Properly this time. No more awkward silences or changing the subject. He could speak to her as an equal: this time they would both know the truth about Dad.

*

"You've been reading that thing for hours."

"It nearly didn't happen," the professor replied.

"What?"

"The war."

"Sorry?"

"There have been several Balkan crises before now... in fact, the Balkans is always in a crisis of some sort. Do you know what I'm talking about, Jack?"

Jack tried to tune in to what the professor was saying, "Yes, Professor, I think so, Pendelshape was always going on about it. When the Ottoman Empire's power declined in the Balkans, it kind of left no one in control."

"Yes. Well, it's not just the Ottoman Empire; the Austro-Hungarian Empire has also struggled to impose itself over all the different nationalities within its borders. There have been many crises and wars there. The point is, though, they have mostly been successfully sorted out by the diplomats. In fact, Europe has been at peace since 1871. Problems in the Balkans have happened before... and have been successfully worked out... or at least, have not led to a wider war – like the one in here." He held up the book and tapped its spine vigorously with his index finger, "A world war."

"So?" Jack said.

"But 1914, now, this time, my time, is somehow different. This time the great European powers – Germany, France, Russia, Britain, Austria-Hungary – don't work it out... But they could have!" he said triumphantly. "And then things would have continued as normal! In fact, it was all just a silly mistake... there was no need for war at all! And this silly mistake... is responsible for the deaths of millions of people! People just like you and me..."

The professor stared at Jack through his round spectacles with his intense blue eyes. He looked around the courtyard furtively and whispered, "Jack – to be honest – I think maybe your father might be right about all this – if I understand properly what he is trying to do.

113

Maybe it is right to use this amazing time machine of his to go back and try to change things so that they are better. Maybe even… maybe we have a responsibility to… stop it. Stop this war… and maybe, I, as a German, living now, maybe I have a special responsibility to stop it…"

Jack didn't like where this was going, "Professor, I'm not sure…"

The professor spoke with an intensity that he had not heard before.

"I am not like you. I am of this time. For you, this is the past. For me, this is the present. I have a responsibility…"

Jack shook his head slowly, "I'm not sure that's how it's supposed to work… you heard what the Rector said…"

"But think!" the professor pleaded. "We have the power to stop many deaths. Why wouldn't you do that… if you could? If you had that power."

Put like that, Jack could see his point. But he had also heard what the Rector had said – about the unknown consequences of fiddling with time, with things in the past. Anyway, he didn't want to get involved in this conversation. He just wanted to go home.

"But if we try to change things it might make them worse, we don't know…" he strained to order his thoughts… "Maybe the war is supposed to happen; maybe it will happen whatever we do…?"

The professor was unconvinced, "Many lives will be lost Jack. With your father's help maybe we could find a way to save them… to save them all."

The suggestion hung provocatively in the air. When the Rector had explained everything to him, it seemed that VIGIL and its leaders were right. He had even started to believe the Rector when he'd said that his father was a dangerous fugitive. But, with the professor's unexpected plea, suddenly he was not so sure. Maybe his father was right?

Their troubling conversation was interrupted by the sound of heavy footsteps coming down the stone stairs in the block behind them. Tony and Gordon entered the courtyard, closely followed by two other VIGIL guards and the Rector. They marched over to where Jack and the professor sat.

"Gentlemen, I am so sorry to disturb you but we have rather worrying news," the Rector said. He stroked back wisps of his silver hair nervously. He was sweating.

They looked up pensively.

"It appears that Dr Pendelshape's collaboration with your father was closer than we first thought – and their plans are well advanced."

"What do you mean?" Jack asked.

"I am not sure we explained to you. All time phones, including the one that you used, are linked to our Taurus back at the school. We had not previously considered a situation where there are in fact two time machines. Two Tauruses." The Rector's brow furrowed, "It appears that Dr Pendelshape may have passed the identification code for your time phone to your father."

Jack and the professor looked at him blankly.

The Rector sighed impatiently, "This means that, assuming a reliable signal, your time phone can be tracked by your father's Taurus, as well as our own."

"So if the yellow bar is on in my time phone, Dad knows where I am?"

"He knows *when* you are as well."

"So – he could..."

"Yes – he could try and mount some sort of kidnap attempt."

Jack suddenly had a brainwave, "Hold on! If he's got the codes for my time phone... then can't we use my time phone to find out where he is?"

The Rector smiled, "Good thinking, Jack. You're a bright lad. But in that case we'd need the codes for his Taurus..."

"Which you obviously haven't got..." the professor added.

"No. And we have now destroyed your time phone so it can't be tracked. But that's not the only thing. We are now receiving a good signal from our Taurus."

"But that means..."

"Yes – we have an opportunity to get you home before we lose the signal again. However, we must act quickly – there is a real possibility that your father managed to get a space-time fix of this location before we destroyed your time phone, in which case..."

"He could time travel back... to the castle – right here."

"Exactly. We must act quickly."

The Rector, with Tony and Gordon in close support, ushered Jack and the professor from the courtyard.

They were not quick enough.

In the shadows of one corner of the courtyard there was a sudden disturbance. It was as if the air had gone strangely liquid. There was a flash of white light. In an instant, the shimmering of the air stopped. Where previously there had been nothing, there was a figure – just standing there. He had a thin face and his straight black hair flopped below his ears. Jack couldn't believe it. Angus. But it was not the Angus that Jack knew from school. He was dressed like a member of the SAS. On top of that, to Jack's amazement, he was carrying a weapon so heavy, even he was struggling to hold it level.

Angus screamed over to them, "Hit the deck!"

Freefall

Jack dropped flat to the cobblestones as the whole courtyard erupted into a maelstrom of ricocheting heavy machine-gun bullets. The Rector, Tony, Gordon and the other guards dived back into the main block, taken by complete surprise. Angus's weapon dispatched heavy calibre rounds and, as he was unable to control it properly, he was soon spraying bullets everywhere and in the process dislodging great lumps of stone and mortar from around the courtyard. In ten seconds it was over. The fountain had been levelled, the hedge stripped bare and the table vaporised.

Angus dashed over to Jack and helped him to his feet.

"Come on, we've got to get out of here…"

"What? What about him?"

"Who?"

"The professor – there!" Jack pointed at the professor who was still on the ground next to him. "Professor, are you OK?" Jack asked, trying to pull him to his feet.

"Come on, there's no time – just leave him," Angus said.

"I can't!"

Angus rolled his eyes. The professor rose shakily to his feet, ashen faced.

"Right – he's fine – so let's get on with it," Angus said.

"Why?" Jack asked.

"What do you mean, why?" Angus said desperately. "There's no time to explain. You are in great danger. We all are. I've been sent to rescue you."

They heard the Rector shouting. "Make safe your weapon. There is no escape. We will not harm you. Give yourself up."

Angus screamed back, "Everyone stay where you are!" And as if to make the point, he opened up again with his machine gun, spraying the stone wall of the castle accommodation block with bullets and smashing a number of windows in the process. As the gun fired, Angus reeled backwards with the force and the nose of the barrel veered upwards dispatching rounds in a random pattern up the side of the old building.

"Put that thing down before you kill someone," Jack said desperately.

Angus ignored him. He lowered the gun and looked into his own time phone, which hung around his neck.

"No! The signal's going… I was told this might happen… it's over."

"What do you mean?"

"We can't time travel out. We'll have to run for it! Come on!" And to make his point, he unceremoniously poked the smoking barrel of his gun at Jack.

"Hey! Watch where you're pointing that thing."

Angus pleaded with his friend, "I'm telling you, stay here and we're finished. Trust me. There's a lot you don't know."

In the background, they heard the Rector's voice again, booming orders.

"The others should be here by now to help me. But something must have happened. We've got to get out of here." Angus was starting to panic. He knew something that Jack didn't. If they could escape, maybe there would be some time to think.

"How?" Jack said.

"You're the brain box. You tell me. I've never been here before."

"There's only one way down. And that's on the cable car," the professor said.

"Well let's move."

Jack had the layout of the castle in his head and they were soon racing up the other side of the courtyard to the cable-car. Angus waited briefly at the bottom of the stairs and fired some final rounds randomly into the courtyard to deter any immediate pursuit. The red cable car was waiting snugly in its arrival gantry. Jack opened the door to the small control room directly behind the gantry. There was an array of switches, gears and dials. They were labelled in German and they all looked dead. The boys turned to the professor.

"Well, Professor?"

"I am a scientist not a cable-car operator," the professor said pompously. Then he surveyed the control room and smiled mischievously back at the boys, "Which means, for me, it won't be that difficult." He manoeuvred himself in front of the main control panel. "I have always found that, in the case of technical difficulty, the best thing to do is to press the biggest button you can find…" The professor poked an index finger at a large green button and then, reading a few of the other labels, made a number of further adjustments. A bell rang above them and he pressed another button. The machinery sprang into life.

The professor jumped up in excitement, "Let's go!"

They moved across to where the cable car waited. The professor slid open the door and they piled in. He inspected the control panel inside the cable car.

"Here goes!" Suddenly, the car moved away from the gantry and began its descent into the valley below. The castle was soon receding into the distance.

"What happens when we get to the bottom?" Angus said.

"They'll telephone down… someone will be waiting for us there."

"Unless we can find some way out," the professor said.

Angus laughed, "Be serious, we're suspended several hundred metres up in the air."

The professor moved over to the large metal bench at one end of the car. It had a small hatch in the side. He slid open the cover.

"Just as I thought. Nothing overlooked."

They peered into the chest. There was a medical kit, a tool bag, some harnesses and an array of other equipment. But there was also rope. Lots of rope.

Angus said, "Well that's a fat lot of good. What are we supposed to do – suspend it from the bottom of the cable car and abseil down…?"

Jack and the professor looked at each other, and then Jack said quietly, "Angus, I think that's exactly what the professor has in mind."

Angus turned white, "No way. There is no way that I am climbing out of this sardine can and dangling myself on the end of a bit of thread two hundred metres up in the air... I've already risked my life to time travel back a hundred years to rescue you..."

Jack smiled at him slyly, "Not scared are you?"

The professor was already unloading the rope from the chest.

"Is it going to be long enough?"

"Should be. Otherwise someone has made a stupid mistake."

"How do we get down it?"

"Here," the professor handed Jack a small metal object. "It's a friction device. One end attaches to you. The other to the rope." The professor was busy securing an end of the rope to the anchor point inside the car. He leaned over and slid free the bolts on the trapdoor, which was built flush into the floor of the car.

"Stand to the side and hold on!" the professor said. And with that, he released the trapdoor and flipped it over on its hinges so it landed with a crash on the inside of the car. There was now a large square hole in the floor of the car. Cold mountain air blasted up through this gap as their descent continued. Jack stole a glance through the hole – far down, a landscape of firs, rock and alpine grass flitted silently past as the cable car floated downwards.

Angus was staring out of the front window, "I think you'd better hurry, Professor."

They looked up and spotted the cause of Angus's concern. Soon they would be at the mid-point of their journey. Still quite far below, but approaching fast, was the return cable car – making its way up the other cable to the castle just as their own cabin descended. Even at this distance, the trio could make out a number of figures eyeing them from the on-coming car.

"What do we do now?"

"We keep going. What can they do?"

"They can shoot us for a start," Angus said.

The professor dropped the rope through the trapdoor. It rapidly uncoiled and trailed freely from the cabin until it started to drag along the ground way below.

The other cable car was approaching them rapidly. The professor looked towards it. He was working something out in his head.

"Let's get ready," he said.

They attached the friction devices to sections of the rope, ready for descent.

"Angus – you go first." He pointed at the gun, "And you'll need to leave that thing."

"Great. Just as I was beginning to enjoy myself."

The professor showed them how the friction devices worked. That bit seemed straightforward. The problem was going to be launching into the abyss in the first place.

Angus's face was white. Jack didn't look much better.

"Fun isn't it?" said the professor enthusiastically.

Angus nodded in the direction of the professor, "Where did you get him from, Jack?"

The professor ignored him, "Right. I apply the brakes. Then you go. Then it's my turn. Then Jack, you wait a little, and then you go." The on-coming car was closing in on them fast. They waited, poised above the open trapdoor, the air still rushing in and the earth racing by, way below. They gripped their friction devices anxiously. The professor held his hand over the red emergency stop lever. And waited.

"OK...?"

Jack and Angus nodded. They were getting so close to the approaching car now, that they could see the whites of the VIGIL guards' eyes. The professor pulled up the lever. The cable above their heads decelerated. As it did so, the cable driving the other car also slowed. Their forward momentum caused their whole car to arc upwards alarmingly as they held on tight. The car swung back on its pivot point. Out of the window, they could see that the men in the other car had all tumbled over – unbalanced by the surprise halt of the cable cars.

"Go!" The professor shouted.

Angus froze. Unable to move. He just stared blankly into the abyss.

"Go!" the professor shouted again.

But he still couldn't move. The professor gave him a sharp kick up the backside. One moment he was there. The next he was gone. He just had enough presence of mind to apply the friction device to control his descent.

"Sorry about that," the professor called after him. "Right – my turn." He leaped through the hatch with what Jack thought was an unnatural degree of enthusiasm and slid down the rope, just as Angus had done seconds before. The car continued to sway as it slowed and it was all Jack could do to remain on his feet. Both cars were nearly side by side. Peering down, he could just see the white smudge of Angus's face as it craned upwards to the two cable cars way above. He had made it.

Suddenly, Jack noticed that the roof hatch in the opposite car had been flicked open. A VIGIL guard was crawling up onto the roof with a grappling iron. In a moment, he had tossed the device over to Jack's car before crawling, monkey like, across the precipitous divide that separated them. There was a loud scraping on the roof hatch of Jack's car, as the guard started to prise it open.

Jack wasn't about to find out what would happen next. Swallowing hard, he plunged out through the floor hatch, just as the others had done moments before. Initially, he closed the friction device too hard, so he barely moved on the rope. By gradually loosening it he gained speed. He glanced downwards. The professor and Angus had made it to the ground and both seemed to be safe.

Suddenly the speed of the rope through the friction device accelerated. It didn't feel right. Instinctively, Jack locked the device and waited, swaying in the light wind, suspended from the rope, the Austrian Alps all around. And then, slowly, he felt himself being pulled… up. There was no doubt about it… he was being pulled back towards the cable car. He felt a wave of panic as he realised what was happening. The guard above had started to yank the rope up… with Jack suspended on the end.

He had to make a decision. Angus and the professor had made it to the upper bank of the river that meandered down the valley, but as the cable car had continued to move before finally coming to rest,

Jack was now suspended directly over the river. It was quite wide and he could spot one or two black pools that might cushion a fall. But there were also rocks, and he had no idea how deep the water was. He felt another violent tug on the rope as he was dragged upwards. The adrenaline gave him a moment of clarity. It was all he needed. As the rope was tugged up once more, he took a deep breath and flicked open the friction device.

Fishing for Answers

Jack was staggered at how fast he accelerated. He closed his eyes – tight. If he was about to be splattered onto some piece of granite – he didn't want to know about it. Three seconds later, he hit the river, feet first, and the freezing water exploded around him in a plume of spray. His speed forced him down. Finally, his feet hit the bottom. It took an eternity for him to rise but then he broke the surface with nearly the same speed as he had entered. He gulped down air. He'd made it. But then the cold from the river hit him like the left hook of a heavy-weight boxer, and took his breath away a second time. He started to swim, desperately, to the bank. Soon his breast stroke disintegrated into a flailing doggy paddle. Exhausted, he pulled himself up onto the grassy bank and collapsed in a soggy heap.

From the other side of the riverbank he heard the voices of Angus and the professor. The professor was waving and jumping up and down excitedly, a broad grin on his face.

"Bravo! Bravo!" he shouted. The professor had clearly been impressed by Jack's decision to jump. Jack pulled himself up onto his feet, still breathing heavily. It was at this point that it dawned on him. It was bizarre. As he gulped down air, his lungs were… working. He felt no wheezy emptiness, no panic that he was about to suffocate, no familiar craving for his puffer. He took deep breaths and it felt – completely normal. He began to feel stronger and stronger and soon this feeling grew into a tingling elation.

He looked at his friends and noticed that to their left, on the far riverbank, was a small cabin built right on the edge of the water. It was dilapidated and overgrown – well camouflaged, unless you were actually viewing it from the river itself. He waved, pointing out the cabin to Angus and the professor. They followed Jack's line of sight. When the professor spotted the small wooden building he became even more excited. It was a boat house.

From the opposite bank, Jack saw Angus and the professor clamber up to the rear of the boat house where they disappeared from view. They had been gone for a few minutes when two wooden doors at water level gradually opened out on to the river. Soon, Angus and the professor emerged triumphantly with a rather dishevelled-looking boat. They boarded the boat and with the professor at the twin oars, it glided across the water towards him. It looked like they might have an escape route. Soon the boat had nosed onto the bank where Jack stood shivering.

Angus beamed smugly from the bows. "All aboard! All aboard!" he shouted. "Next stop, er, down there somewhere!" He thumbed in a general downriver direction. Jack jumped onto the boat. The professor reversed and then pointed the craft downstream.

They were off.

*

Jack shifted into the rear of the boat in front of the professor, who gingerly manoeuvred the craft back into the centre of the river where they soon caught the best of the downstream current. It was larger than a standard rowing boat, and in the back it had a low metal frame attached to each side. It looked as if you could assemble a canvas sheet on the frame and maybe even sleep in it.

The professor concentrated on the rowing, but it took a bit of getting used to and initially, they zigzagged uneasily.

"Any sign of them?" asked the professor. Nervously, they scanned each riverbank. There was no movement and all they could hear was the lapping of the water and the late afternoon chirrup of birdlife rising from the dense woodland. Way above, they could still see the gossamer thin threads of the cable car – but both cars had vanished.

"Seems quiet. But it won't take them long to catch up."

The river narrowed and they could feel the current speed up

a notch beneath them. Up ahead, perhaps a half kilometre away, they saw that the banks heightened dramatically as the river passed through a deep mountain gorge.

"We may have a chance – the river will be the quickest way down – and we have a good head start. Soon it will be dark too…" the professor said. "Jack – you need to get out of those things – otherwise you'll die of cold. The professor nodded towards a compartment behind Jack's legs at the back of the boat. "Anything useful in there?"

Jack rummaged, "I don't think this boat has been used for a while…"

There were a couple of dusty blankets and also the canvas sheeting that fitted over the metal awning. He shook out one of the blankets. It was dry enough but smelt dusty and moth-eaten.

"I've got some spare bits and pieces with me." Angus opened his small rucksack, pulled out a T-shirt and fleece and handed them to Jack, "Try those."

Jack was grateful for the dry clothes and wrapped one of the blankets tightly around himself in an attempt to ward off the chill. Warming up, he scratched around some more in the compartment. He then yanked out a long, thin canvas bag. He undid the ties at either end, and out slid three sticks.

"Eureka!" the professor exclaimed. "A rod. Maybe there's a reel."

Sure enough, hidden in the back of the compartment was a reel with a line and, next to it, a small cigar box. Jack opened the box and inside were eight fishing flies carefully pinned to the bottom of the little box.

The professor had now developed a more reliable stroke and the blades slopped rhythmically in the water. Pushed on by the current, the boat made steady progress. There was still no sign of pursuit and they all began to feel a little less edgy. Soon, they were listening to Angus's remarkable story.

"… I need to tell you what happened after you escaped, Jack, by the way, pretty impressive that… particularly the bit where you squashed Belstaff," Angus grinned at the memory of their games teacher who had been impaled by the blast screen. "Never liked him anyway."

"What happened to him?"

"In pain. But OK. Unfortunately."

"Thought he was dead."

"No – I tell you these VIGIL-support guys are tough. Anyway, I was pretty frightened. Particularly after Gordon had knifed poor old Pendelino... and then attacked me... I ask you – I'm even captain of the rugby team!"

"The Rector explained all that... he said they had to act quickly..."

Angus looked at Jack blankly, "Don't know anything about that... but after the Rector, Tony, Gordon and the others had made their plan to bring you back from 1914, the next morning two guys rescued me and Pendelshape – right from under the nose of VIGIL. There was a short fight, quite scary but no shooting, just karate and stuff, and then these men just bundled us straight into the back of a van and we shot off."

"Where?"

"Away from the school. And fast."

"But..."

"Wait – I haven't told you the rest. We drove on for a bit – but not that long. I was trying to keep tabs on the time, but it was tricky. I was rolling around the back of this van being driven at high speed, and getting really scared about what we'd got ourselves into."

"Tell me about it."

"So anyway, this journey went on for a bit longer – I don't know – maybe an hour, maybe more. We stopped a couple of times... I think we changed cars or vans. I needed a pee. They wouldn't even let me do that. Whatever. Eventually we stopped. I was led out of the van and it was quiet, and dark, but I could tell we were near the sea. I could smell the salt air, and hear waves lapping against concrete. Then we were in a boat. It was rocking. The engine fired up and we were off, jiggling along through the waves, at a fair old crack. And then we arrived somewhere, the boat was moored up and I was taken up some steep stairs. I thought I was on another boat – but bigger. It was all pretty weird."

The professor was listening, but because of his central position at the oars, he had his back to Angus. He gently eased the boat into a shallow pool off the main current and then pulled in both blades and let the craft drift for a while so he could rest and listen.

"Then what?" Jack said.

"The blindfold came off... and there I was!"

"Where?" Jack asked. "Where were you?"

"Well, here's the strangest thing. You know when we were with Pendelshape that afternoon down in the control room and he was telling us all that strange stuff, and I don't know about you, but I wasn't sure I was really believing any of it, and it was like, when are we going to get out of here...?"

"Yeah..."

"Right. So the room I ended up in looked just like the underground control room at the school with the Taurus. Then basically, I found out it was a second time machine – another Taurus! But I tell you – it's much bigger. You could fit a tank in it."

"So it's just as the Rector told us," the professor said, nodding to himself thoughtfully.

"You haven't heard the half of it, Professor. It was then that I met him."

"Who? You met who?" Jack was sitting on the edge of his seat.

Angus's eyes glazed over. He spoke in a hushed, reverential voice. "Him."

"Who?" Jack could hardly contain his curiosity.

"The Benefactor of course. The inventor of time travel. The man with the biggest brain ever." Angus looked at Jack in awe, "Your dad, Jack. Your dad! I always wondered where you got your brains from."

Jack shrugged, "Right. I thought that's who you meant."

"Is that all you've got to say?" Angus's cheeks suddenly flushed red with anger, "You don't get it, do you? Remember, he rescued me and Pendelshape then he sent me back using his Taurus to rescue you. I don't know what has happened to the others who should have come with me – maybe they got caught out with the time signal. Anyway, you should be grateful... and, and you should be proud of him. Your father is a great man. And he has sent us on a mission. Us! Don't you see?"

Jack felt himself getting angry now, "Not really. I haven't been sent anywhere. I pressed a random button to escape some people who were about to kill my history teacher, and then you, and who looked like they were about to kill me as well. Then I find out they're chasing me half way across Europe. We turn up here and they tell me that they're trying to protect me from, of all people, my own dad. Why? Because if he gets hold of me then there's apparently nothing to stop him playing God with history – with consequences too awful to imagine…"

There was a tense silence.

"Sorry," Jack said finally. He sighed, "To be honest I'm not really sure who's right and who's wrong in this whole thing. I feel like a pawn."

Angus replied sheepishly, "Yeah – I'm sorry too, Jack. Maybe it's a bit more complicated than I thought."

The professor pulled on an oar to steady the boat and keep it from drifting into a sandbank. "We'll get through this, boys," he said. "With my looks and your twenty-first century brains, we can't fail." Looking at the professor's dishevelled yellow hair, his muddied clothes, his round glasses, now with one cracked lens, and two bits of cotton wool still stuffed up each nostril to stop any more bleeding from the balloon crash, the remark sounded ridiculous. Angus and Jack looked at the professor and then at each other and laughed.

The professor took up the oars again and rowed them out to the main channel. A fat orange sun was melting into the rocky horizon. In an hour it would be dark.

"Probably time to try to find somewhere to rest for the night," the professor said. As they moved slowly down the gorge, they scanned each side for a suitable landing spot. The river was quite low at this point and twisted through a maze of large boulders, rocks and the occasional gravel bank. There were quite a few places where they could pull in and be well protected by the towering granite walls above. In some of the darkening pools off the main current, fish were starting to jump lazily at insects, which buzzed above the surface.

They rounded the next bend in the river and spotted a large, deep pool to the left, where another low sandbank rose gently towards the cliff wall. The professor manoeuvred the boat towards the bank and they alighted, yanking the boat as far up the slope as they could manage. The professor then scrambled back into the boat to retrieve the rod they had discovered earlier.

"Shall we give it a go?" he said as he looked at the pieces of rod and the reel and then at the box of flies. He had no idea what to do next.

"Allow me," said Jack. He quickly assembled the three pieces of rod, attached the reel and threaded the line through the eyes in the rod. Then he opened the box. "Which one do you reckon?"

"Don't ask me – you know I'm rubbish at all that stuff," Angus replied.

Jack picked a fly at random and threaded a leader, which he had attached to the line, through the narrow eye of the hook.

"Ready." He looked at the professor, "Fancy a go?"

"It's not one of my skills, I'm afraid."

Jack took the rod confidently and marched out to the edge of the sandbank, surveying the pool as he went. There was an occasional 'plop' followed by telltale concentric ripples in the water as the trout fed in the fading light.

"Here goes."

He flicked the rod once, and then repeatedly, until a large loop of line was whooshing back and forth through the still air of the gorge. Then, he thrust out his arm, pointing the rod towards the last set of expanding circular ripples he had seen in the pool. The whole line raced forward across the river. The tiny fly, invisible in the gloom, presented itself just above the rippling water. There was a sudden disturbance and a brown fish leaped up from the surface with a splash. Jack was taken by surprise, but took the strike. He felt the tug on the line as the trout struggled to free itself. Slowly, he reeled it in.

Angus danced on the sandbank shouting, "You got him!" several times over.

"Hey, first time… what do you think of that? Never done that before!" Jack half-turned to Angus and the professor, delighted with his success. He plonked the medium-sized trout at their feet.

But he had been lucky. It took him a further forty minutes to land another fish – losing two flies and having to rethread several leaders in the process. The professor busied himself with lighting a small fire from some driftwood on the bank and improvising a cooking grill. He piled up some stones on either side of the fire and looked around for something that they could use to suspend the precious fish above the flames. In a minute, he emerged from the boat waving two metal pegs. With these, they skewered the gutted fish and then balanced them neatly above the fire, with either end resting on the stones. It wasn't perfect, but it did the job and soon the fish were sizzling away. After twenty minutes, Angus removed one and cut it open on a flat stone.

"Prof?" he offered a piece of the moist, pink flesh to the professor on the end of his penknife. The professor popped it into his mouth and immediately started to gurgle appreciatively. In five minutes it was all gone.

Afterwards, they wrapped themselves, mummy like, in the blankets and canvas canopy. With the security offered by the gorge, their stomachs at least partly full and the fire still giving off a modest warmth, their spirits were lifted. Although only just dark, Jack was astonished by the number and brightness of the stars that twinkled down from the Austrian night.

The professor gently urged Angus to complete his story. They listened intently. Angus leaned up from his canvas bedding on one elbow. The dying flames from the fire flickered across his face, creating lines and shadows where none existed – making him look older than he really was.

"In the short time we had together your dad told me a lot, Jack. I don't want to upset you, but I really think you would be proud of what he's done. I'm not really sure I understand all this stuff... But after I had met him, for the first time in my life I was sure of one thing. A hundred per cent sure."

"What's that?" Jack asked.

"I agreed with him and Pendelshape on what they want to do."

"What do they want to do?"

"Change the course of history – stop the assassination of the Archduke in Sarajevo and stop the First World War. Now we're here, well, maybe we can help them do it."

Jack had never heard Angus talk about anything so seriously – it didn't sound like him at all.

"It's just what the Rector told us back at the castle," the professor said.

"Did he?" Angus was surprised.

"Yes," said Jack. "We should tell you what happened to us too."

He explained what the Rector had said. He explained how the Rector and VIGIL had been astonished to learn of the creation of the second Taurus and how alarmed they all were about the possibility that his father might use it to make changes in history. He explained why Pendelshape had taken them into his confidence – and how his attempt to snatch Jack to safety, away from the Rector – might have succeeded if the Rector had not arrived in the Taurus control room with Tony, Gordon and the others.

"… So you see, it is not as simple as you first thought. When you came to rescue us, I suppose we panicked, and followed you… but maybe the Rector and VIGIL are right and Dad and Pendelshape are the ones who are wrong about all of this…" Jack struggled to remember what the Rector had actually said about making changes in history, "It might mean that we would make history different – possibly worse." Yes that was it, "And maybe the war would happen anyway, maybe it's even supposed to happen. Have you thought about that?"

But Angus was having none of it, "Jack – your dad and Pendelshape are right. I'm certain of it. Your dad talked all about how this war leads to the Second World War and how the whole of the twentieth century is a complete nightmare – and it all starts this Sunday in Sarajevo."

"This Sunday?"

"Yes. This Sunday coming – 28th June 1914 – in Sarajevo. That's when the assassination happens."

"Today is…"

"Monday 22nd June," the professor said. "So – only six days to go."

"Right," Angus continued. "You know I never paid much attention in Pendelino's classes – but the way your dad talked about it – it was real, I can tell you. And what is also real is that he has now made a way of changing it all and, well, making it better. If you talked to him, I think you'd get it." Angus shook his head and then lay back on the ground, exhaling slowly, "I think we need to help him do this. Your dad called it our destiny."

There was silence as they thought about the significance of what Angus was saying. In the short time that he had known him, Jack's father had obviously made a big impression on Angus.

"Why did he send you – why not come himself? Did he have any message for me?"

"Not really. He sent me, I think, 'cos he knew that you would trust me. As I said, I was supposed to be supported by a couple of others – the guys that rescued us from the school – but something must have happened during the transfer. Your dad hasn't got as big a team as VIGIL, or guards like Tony and Gordon. Pendelshape stayed with your dad – kind of in reserve – in case something went wrong. As for instructions… It all happened very quickly. We had one chance to rescue you. Your dad's Taurus was powered up, we finally got a signal and a fix on your time and location and, of course, we were going to travel straight back again. We weren't supposed to hang around here. But the signal went…"

"Not very reliable these time phones…" Jack said. "What does it say now?"

Angus sat up again and rummaged in the breast pocket of his fatigue jacket. He unzipped a padded pouch and took out his precious time phone. He cupped it in his hands carefully and flipped it open. Just in the same way Jack's had done, a very faint blue light illuminated the device from the inside and they inspected the glowing read-out.

Date: Monday 22nd June, 1914
Time: 11.33 p.m.
Location: Southern Tyrol

"The yellow signal bar is still off," Angus said. "So we still can't use it. No surprise there."

"Did Dad or Pendelshape say anything else? You know – that might help us decide what to do… or where to get help… now we're stuck here?"

"Not really – although he confirmed what Pendelshape said to us – remember? That when they did the final testing of the Taurus at the school, Pendelshape, and I think your dad too, made some test trips back to 1914. Pendelshape chose the year himself – made some excuse that it was a period of history he was interested in."

Jack rummaged for the photo that was now in his pocket. "Yes – I think I've still got the photo that he showed us." Jack produced the black-and-white photo of the four young men of the Black Hand standing next to Dr Pendelshape. They could just make out their gaunt, grey-washed features by the light of the flickering flame.

"There they all are. Pendelshape and the assassins…"

"Funny to think in the time we're in now, 1914… this photo can only have been taken a few weeks ago, months at the most."

There was a pause before Angus continued, "Yes. And by choosing 1914, Pendelshape and your dad were actually starting to put their plan to change history into action. Pendelshape infiltrated the Black Hand – the assassination cell – and gained their confidence. They always planned to return…"

"… and somehow disrupt the assassination in Sarajevo."

"Right," Angus continued. "I think Pendelshape and your dad's plan was to kind of infiltrate the group and support them – but then sabotage them at the last minute. You know – stop the assassination…"

"And so stop the countdown to the war," the professor added. "Incredible."

"But then the final bust up must have come, VIGIL was about to do away with your dad, but he escaped. As far as VIGIL was concerned the tests were complete and the Taurus was shut down. Without your dad to guide him, Pendelshape, must have just hunkered down at school, got on with his life, and continued to pretend he was loyal to VIGIL."

Jack shrugged, "Well, that's all very interesting... but we're still nowhere nearer deciding what to do."

"Well, I know what your dad would want us to do – now we're here: help them complete their plan."

"But it's like the Rector said – that could have unexpected consequences..." Jack said with alarm.

The professor weighed in, "Jack, I think your father is right. It's what I was trying to explain to you back at the castle..."

"What?"

"As I said, Jack – it is a bit different for me. I am from this age. I am part of it. As a civilised person, living at this time, I should do everything to prevent the war that is threatened. I think if I know about it, I must act. I have a duty. Remember – nothing has actually happened yet." He shuffled nervously inside the canvas, "It sounds as if my own nation has an important part to play in the whole matter... and it sounds as if my nation will suffer – terribly..."

Jack shook his head. He didn't know what to do. The embers in the fire were dying and the last warmth of the evening evaporated into the twinkling Austrian night. They lay silently staring at the sky for a while longer. While Angus and then the professor gradually slid into a chilly slumber, Jack's head continued to buzz with unanswered questions and the choices he would yet have to make.

Anna

They were up early, chilled by a dawn mist shrouding the river like a damp net from a lonely trawler boat. The fire from the night before was just a pile of soggy ash. Inside the canvas covering, Jack's bones ached. It was good to get moving and pack the boat ready to leave. Soon, they were pushing the boat back into the river. The professor took position at the centre of the boat, manned the twin oars and manoeuvred them back out across water. As the boat rotated into the current, the mist unexpectedly parted and the gorge brightened for a moment in the morning light. Jack saw two birds, possibly birds of prey, circling way above them at the top of the gorge, where the green pine forest fringed the cliffs. As he slowly shook off the fatigue from a restless night, he sensed a slight vibration in the heavy air of the gorge.

"Hear that?"

"Probably my stomach – that fish didn't have much impact," Angus moaned as he scratched sleep from his eyes. "When are we going to get some decent food?"

"Maybe not for a while," the professor said. "We have no choice but to keep following the river downstream."

Angus snorted grumpily and folded his arms around himself to ward off the chill.

Jack looked over the professor's shoulder, downstream, but the view of the main river was well screened by the maze of boulders and rocks. The vibration in the air seemed to be getting stronger and he was sure that the current beneath them was increasing in strength. As the boat began to sway a little more in the water, occasionally a plume of white spray would whip up from the bow and spatter them.

"I hear something now too, Jack," the professor said, his brow furrowed. "Ahead of us maybe."

The vibrating sound was becoming louder – amplified by the canyon walls. The boat, now moving at a pace, rounded a large boulder on a wide bend in the river and, to their horror, they were suddenly presented with the source of the noise. Rapids. For most of its course the river had meandered through a network of boulders and pools. But just a hundred metres ahead, it steepened and descended angrily in a white-water torrent that threw vapour high up into the gorge. The vibration in the air was now a deafening roar.

Jack and Angus braced themselves. The professor grabbed the two spare paddles from the bottom of the boat and tossed one each to the boys, just as the river dropped into the rapids. At the stern, Jack thrust his paddle into the heaving water. The force of the torrent nearly levered Jack clean of the boat. He snatched the paddle back before trying a second time. His efforts made little difference, but miraculously, the current guided the boat between the large boulders, which peppered the rapids.

Somehow the boat stayed upright, and as they progressed they developed an uneasy technique for avoiding the worst of the rocks and the white water – with the professor in the middle, balancing the boat with the two large blades, and prodding the occasional rock to avoid collision, and Angus and Jack trying to guide them with the small paddles from either end. Then, just as their confidence was starting to build, the gorge suddenly opened out and the river washed over a wide downward-sloping platform of glass-smooth rock.

The boat came up on to the lip of the precipice and then accelerated downwards, water spraying from the bow. They could hear the hull scraping as the stone beneath tore into it. The boat slewed left, then right. Then they were airborne. The rocky outcrop had given way to a sheer cliff where the waterfall cascaded down into a smooth expanse of blue water. The boat took off from the edge of the outcrop and twisted high in the air, propelled by the momentum gathered on its downward slide. They were flung free and wide from both the waterfall and the rotating boat. If it had been Olympic diving, none of them would have scored highly for technique as they plunged into the lake

Angus belly flopped badly onto the water's surface with a loud 'smack'. He was quickly followed by the professor, who entered the water on his back, and finally Jack, who went in head first. Then, in the same order, the lake released them from its icy depths – bruised and confused – but otherwise unhurt. A moment later, their battered boat also emerged – like a whale coming up for air. Astonishingly, although the boat had a bad list to port, it was otherwise intact. They made their way towards it and, with the occasional groan and grunt, helped each other back in, before collapsing in a wet, panting heap. After a while, the professor eased his way, shakily to his knees. He looked down at Jack and Angus.

"Great ride," he grinned from ear to ear.

Jack looked across at Angus, and promptly threw up.

The lake was large – a couple of kilometres long. Behind them the waterfall cascaded unremittingly from the gorge above. The mountains to one side of the lake dropped dramatically towards the far end, where there looked to be a small village. To their right, the land was flatter and heavily wooded, but it appeared as if there might be a decent landing spot. Leaning over the battered sides of the boat, they used their hands to paddle to shore.

At last they pushed the boat up onto a small stony beach where the lake met the wooded shoreline. A quick search of the boat indicated that almost everything had been lost in the final plunge into the lake. Angus nervously fingered his breast pocket – the time phone was still there. He whipped it out and flipped it open. The yellow bar was still defiantly greyed out, but the distinctive lettering of the read-out was glowing steadily:

Date: Tuesday 23rd June, 1914
Time: 8.17 a.m.
Location: Achensee, Austria

"Looks OK," he muttered to himself with relief, placing the device carefully back in the zipped pocket. Jack and the professor were busy ringing out their clothes. The professor stopped for a moment and gazed across at the lake and the mountains beyond. He sniffed the air and said, "I think I know where we are…"

"Achensee?" Angus asked.

The professor's face lit up, "Exactly! Achensee! How did you know?"

Angus tapped his head, "As you said, brains, Professor, twenty-first century brains. We have silicon chip implants you know."

The professor looked at him oddly, and chose to ignore the comment. He seemed excited about where they had ended up, "Yes – we used to come up this way quite often on holidays… I know the spot well. It hasn't changed at all."

"So does that mean you know how to get us some food?"

"Better than that, I think. Nearby is the Mueller estate. I'm sure of it. It's been a while, but they used to be good family friends. I met Mueller when he worked in the diplomatic corps. The family were quite big landowners round here." The professor scanned the oak woodland which fringed the lake, looking for an entry point or pathway.

Then, some way down the narrow beach, they spotted two figures emerging from the woods… and marching towards them purposefully. The larger of the two, a round portly man with a red face, was shouting loudly in German. He was wearing some kind of strange hunting uniform. It included a homburg hat adorned with feathers and a green high-collared jacket from the belt of which were suspended a dagger and, incredibly, a full-length sword. The outfit was completed with breeches and riding boots. His companion was a great deal shorter and thinner, dressed more modestly in a felt jacket, and was struggling to carry a large shotgun in one hand and a brace of rabbits in the other.

The portly man strode confidently towards them, down the shallow bank and on to the pebble beach. The boys had little difficulty guessing what he was saying:

"You cannot land here – no trespassing! No fishing. No hunting…

No anything! This is the Mueller estate…!"

The man got closer and his eyes narrowed as he focused on the group. Then, suddenly, the angry red face lightened a little.

"It cannot be… surely not?"

He advanced a little further. The professor also moved forward, his hand out-stretched, smiling, "Herr Mueller?"

"Pinckard-Schnell? I don't believe it."

The two men shook hands warmly and Mueller, who was a daunting figure close up, immediately peppered the professor with questions.

"How on earth do you come to be here? It's been, how many years? Perhaps five? Why did you not tell me you were coming…?" Then he paused for a moment, looking at Jack and Angus, "And who are these young men… and, my, you are wet, what has happened to you?"

The professor thought quickly, "My dear Mueller, we are so sorry to, er, surprise you like this… we, well, these are my cousins from England and we are, well, the family is touring, yes, touring in the Alps. Well, we thought we would come up here for a couple of days. Show them my old holiday haunts. Left the others sightseeing in Vienna. Yes – Vienna. We thought we'd do a spot of early morning fishing, then maybe surprise you… I'm sorry – but we had a bit of a disaster with the boat… I was never much good at sports and that kind of thing, unlike you Mueller…"

Angus and Jack winced at the professor's story. He had to make it up on the spot – and it wasn't very convincing. But the truth would have been even less so. Mueller looked at the three of them for a moment in exasperation and then broke into uproarious laughter. In fact, he found the whole thing so funny, he nearly fell over. Meanwhile his servant just stood there and, a bit like his brace of limp rabbits, continued to look miserable. Mueller's laughter was infectious and soon he had the professor going as well. Between the professor's high-pitched wheezing squeal and Mueller's booming guffaw, it was quite a contest. Mueller wiped a tear from his eye.

"Come, my friends, come. No time to waste. Oskar – your jacket, please. At least one of these fine fellows can be kept warm. Now, you must come up to the house at once and we will get you all sorted out. What about your things?"

"At the bottom of the lake…"

Mueller laughed again, "Dear me, dear me. Well, that's too bad. Come now, Marta will be so excited to see you all…" And with that they plunged into the woods, following Mueller and the long-suffering Oskar, while Mueller chattered away happily, barely pausing for breath or for anyone else to get a word in edgeways.

*

Mueller's house was an impressive wooden chalet set in its own grounds, surrounded by woodland and overlooking the southern end of the lake. Larger-than-life Mueller and his diminutive wife, Marta, lived well now that Mueller was retired. Any children had left home, but there were a number of servants around and by all accounts the Muellers had an active social life among the upper class of the Achensee valley.

The most interesting, and Jack thought, rather gruesome, aspect of the chalet, was the stuffed wildlife. Everywhere you looked there were stags' heads, chamois and ibex heads and other, more exotic stuffed beasts. There were even two hollowed-out elephant hooves near the front door, and a pair of giant elephant tusks adorning the entrance. Jack had read that this kind of slaughter was not thought unethical at the turn of the twentieth century, in fact, it showed sporting prowess. According to Pendelshape, Franz Ferdinand himself had bagged thousands of game in his lifetime – not to mention hundreds of stags. It looked like most of them now hung from Mueller's walls. Jack realised the irony that in only five days' time, Franz Ferdinand and his wife Sophie were going to be similarly butchered in Sarajevo.

After some loud introductions, they spent the day recuperating. Marta managed to locate some of her sons' old clothes, and now Jack and Angus looked ridiculous in traditional Austrian garb, which would not have looked out of place in *The Sound of Music*. Marta inspected Angus's fatigues and trainers closely and remarked that she had not seen anything quite like them before, but assumed they were some sort of English fashion of the time. The professor faked a call, using Mueller's recently installed telephone, to Vienna to inform the 'family' that they would be back a little later than they had originally planned. Despite Mueller's protestations, they managed to decline his invitation for the fictitious family to travel the long way to Achensee to join them for an extended house party.

By late afternoon, they were sitting in Mueller's grand conservatory overlooking the lawn that led down to the lake. It was very beautiful; the grand chalet with its flower-laden window boxes was surrounded by its own woodland looking onto the pristine lake with the white-capped mountains in the distance. Jack wondered what would have become of the place in the twenty-first century. Maybe it was a ski chalet, or a rehab clinic for ageing celebs.

The professor and Mueller were trading stories on what had happened since they had last met. The professor had been working briefly on behalf of the German military in a research job at the time and Mueller, before he retired, had been an attaché with the Austrian diplomatic service. Mueller was now onto one of his favourite subjects – the 'problem' of the Southern Slavs and the Balkans. His small and patient audience was more than happy to nod and listen, whilst picking freely from the large plates of cakes, sandwiches and biscuits that had been laid before them.

"...Of course, we had no option but to annex Bosnia–Herzegovina in 1908, although in so doing we added a million Slavs to the empire – most of them peasants..." Mueller puffed on a large pipe as he held court. "We had to show that we could still act as a great power... and we couldn't be doing with a strong Serbia on our doorstep. You know it's not easy for us – a patchwork of so many nationalities – if we show weakness to one group the whole Austro-Hungarian Empire could collapse... and that would be tragic." Mueller turned to Angus who had just taken a large bite of cake and boomed, "Do you know how long the Habsburgs have ruled, my boy?"

Angus's mouth was filled with cream cake. He tried to say, "No" but it came out as a sort of 'Ooarg' sound, and bits of saliva and cake spluttered out onto the tablecloth. Angus blushed and covered his mouth. "Er, sorry."

Mueller looked bemused, but pressed on, "Since 1273... 1273

I tell you! You English talk about the British Empire being the empire on which the sun never sets... but that title first belonged to our mighty Habsburg Empire – we stretched across Europe to Spain and even South America!" Another large smoke ring wafted up into the air as Mueller exhaled. Jack nearly gagged.

"You're a true Schwarzgelb, Mueller," the professor said.

Mueller snorted in acknowledgement, "But we need to watch out! Now, after the Balkan wars of a couple of years ago, of course, Serbia is much stronger... Turkey has lost most of its possessions in Europe, you know, Professor?" The professor nodded, not wishing to question Mueller. "We have so many Serbs within the empire. Serbia is becoming stronger by the day, egged on by their wretched students and revolutionaries and those damned Russians – they have their eye on Bosnia and Herzegovina next. A direct threat to our empire..."

Mueller took another long puff on his pipe and then exhaled a curling wisp of blue smoke, adding sinisterly, "No, there's no doubt, we will need to teach Serbia a lesson sooner or later..."

Mueller paused and without warning turned to Jack and Angus, "Politics, I'm afraid, my young friends, a bit boring for you, I think. Anyway, let us change the subject. Tell me now, what did you think of Vienna – isn't it a jewel?"

Jack and Angus had not anticipated this. Contrary to the professor's story, they had never been to Vienna in their lives. Jack looked at Angus nervously and blushed – he was stumped.

"Well? Has my friend the professor not shown you the Belvedere, Schönbrunn Palace, and all the other wonderful sights? Don't be shy. Come on what did you think of it?"

There was a pained silence, then Angus suddenly blurted out, "It was cool."

Jack nearly fell out of his seat.

Mueller frowned, "Cool? At this time of year? I don't think so. It is typically very warm in June..." He turned to the professor with a confused expression on his face.

"Professor? Was it cool?"

"Er, yes Mueller, in fact it was unseasonably cold the day we arrived, but, er we did not stay too long as we were so keen to visit the mountains. We are saving the sights for our return."

Mueller eyed the boys with a puzzled expression for a moment, but then accepted the explanation and moved on.

"Oh, I see. Well, you have much to look forward to." Distracted, he withdrew a large chain watch from his breast pocket and grunted in satisfaction.

"Professor – I think it might be that time. How about a brandy?"

The professor sighed in relief, "Most kind, Mueller."

"Excellent! Anna – if you please?"

At the entrance to the conservatory, for the first time, Jack noticed that a young woman, a servant, had been waiting patiently. She had a dark complexion and brown eyes. She appeared not to be listening to the conversation – but staring straight ahead. Jack noticed that Angus was staring at the maid admiringly. But Angus's trance was broken as, with Mueller's order ringing in her ears, the maid scuttled off to fetch the brandy. Jack thought it was a bit strange to have someone else in the room who was just an ornament – except when required to serve.

The brandy arrived, and the professor had the presence of mind to excuse Jack and Angus, who gratefully grasped the opportunity. Not sure what to do, Jack stood and did an awkward little bow and thanked Mueller. He nudged Angus. Having never bowed before in his life, Angus's attempt at the procedure was faintly comical – like he was lowering himself onto an imaginary toilet. They then left the room, trying not to appear in a hurry.

Mueller looked at them with curiosity as they departed.

"Friendly young men, Professor, your nephews... interesting, er, manners."

The professor shrugged. "English... you know... what they're like..."

Mueller snorted, took a gulp from his brandy goblet and busied himself with refilling his pipe. "Anyway, Professor, talking of the English, tell me about your work with the Royal Navy..."

*

Angus and Jack made their way up the old wooden stairs to their bedroom at the top of the chalet. The room had a low-beamed ceiling and, like the rest of the house, extensive wooden panelling. There were twin beds on either side of the room and two old pictures of local hunting scenes. Inevitably, the horns of some unfortunate animal had been pinned to one wall. Doors led out to a balcony with an elaborately carved balustrade. Beyond, shadows crept through the woodland as the sun sank below the mountains.

Angus flopped onto one of the beds. "That was a near miss."

"You plonker. You could have said something better than that. 'It was cool'."

"Least I said something."

Jack removed his jacket and lazily dropped it on to the floor before collapsing in his own bed.

"Let's take a look, then."

"What – the time phone?"

"See if it's changed at all."

Angus took out the device. He flipped it open. They inspected the miniature read-out:

Date: Tuesday 23rd June, 1914
Time: 07.47 p.m.
Location: Achensee, Austria

"Five more days until the assassination," Jack said. "But still no yellow light."

"We're still stuck. No escape."

"Does that thing ever light up?"

Suddenly, there was a knock at the door. Angus quickly closed the time phone and slipped it back in his pocket.

"It'll be the Prof..." Jack called to the door, "Come in!"

But it wasn't the professor. The door opened and the boys were surprised to see Anna, the maid who they had last seen being barked at by Mueller in the conservatory.

Angus sprang from the bed as if he had received a mild electric shock.

"I prepare room for sleeping," she announced in broken English.

Angus's face lit up, "Sounds like an excellent idea..."

Jack rolled his eyes. Anna either didn't understand the remark or just ignored it.

Jack said, "You really don't have to... we can..."

"No – my duty."

She moved into the room and stooped to pick up Jack's coat from the floor. Embarrassed that she felt it necessary to do so, Jack also reached down for the jacket – trying to beat her to it. They both stooped simultaneously and there was a loud 'crack' as their heads banged together. Jack winced. Anna clutched her head. Then she giggled.

"Nice one mate," Angus said sarcastically. "Sorry – he was born in England."

"Are you OK?" Jack said.

Anna grimaced, "No – not OK – you are clumsy Englishman..."

Angus laughed, "You've got that right – you should see him play rugby."

Jack put out his hand, "Jack Christie – very pleased to meet you."

Anna smiled again and shook his hand gently, "I, Anna Matronovic."

Although she wore a maid's white smock and cap she held herself with poise and looked Jack straight in the eye with a challenging self-confidence, yet she couldn't have been more than eighteen years old. Close up, Jack could understand why she had caught Angus's attention. She had dark, hypnotic brown eyes and was exceptionally pretty; Jack stared longer than he probably should have. As he picked up his jacket a piece of paper slipped onto the floor. Again, Anna stooped to pick it up. As she did so, she glanced at the paper and a puzzled expression slowly crept over her face. She did not return it to Jack but studied it intently.

"What is this?" she finally asked. Her face was flushed.

Jack looked at the paper Anna was holding and suddenly realised what it was – the photo of Pendelshape and the plotters of the Black Hand. Jack had transferred it to the coat provided by the

Muellers. Despite the drenching in the lake, it was still quite clear and Pendelshape and his 'friends' stared back at them eerily.

"It's mine. It's just a photograph…"

Anna's brow furrowed.

"Where you get it?"

Jack faltered, "A friend…"

Anna looked down at the photo again. "You know the English teacher, Dr Pendelshape? He said he would send help soon. You and the professor, you sent by him to help us… yes?"

Jack and Angus couldn't believe what Anna had just said. They looked at each other, stunned. "Hold on, what did you say… how do you know…?"

Anna ignored the interruption and carried on quietly, urgently. "I understand now. I must talk to friends. I go now. But you in danger here. Big danger. We must go soon." She was very agitated. "I get message to friends in Vienna, Belgrade, Doboj. You say nothing. We talk later… "

And with that she left the room.

Jack fingered the edges of the photo nervously, looking back to the door that had closed behind Anna.

"She knows Pendelshape. It's incredible," he said.

"And what's this stuff about Belgrade…?"

"Belgrade. Belgrade – doesn't that tell you anything?"

"No," Angus said stubbornly.

Jack sighed impatiently. He was a step ahead, "It's where the photo was taken. Belgrade is the capital of Serbia. Remember, that's what all this is about – Austria and Serbia are enemies. Just like Mueller was saying."

"But what's that got to do with Anna, and how does she know Pendelshape?"

Jack sighed, "Keep up, Angus. 'Matronovic'. 'Belgrade'. Anna's a Serb. What she's doing in the house of a rich Austrian like Mueller, though, I have no idea." But suddenly he had a brainwave, "Of course! The name – Matronovic."

Jack flipped the photo over. The names written in Pendelshape's distinctive scrawl could still just be made out – 'Princip Matronovic'.

"Dani wasn't it? Dani Matronovic."

"You don't think…?"

"Yes, Anna has the same name, Matronovic, and recognised the people in the photograph. Pendelshape said the picture was taken by Dani's sister – Anna!"

"Incredible!"

"Yeah, incredible all right. Anna is a Bosnian Serb working here, for some reason. She and Dani met Pendelshape when he travelled back, testing the Taurus, and now she must think we have been sent by Pendelshape… to help them." Jack exhaled slowly. "Angus – it looks like you, me and the professor are going to have to make that decision we talked about."

"What?"

Jack sighed, "Come on Angus, you were the one who was going on about it. What Dad said. It's what we talked about last night – up in the gorge."

"What, you mean try to stop the assassination?"

"Yes. Anna can probably lead us to the assassins. In fact, she is expecting us to help them – because of what Pendelshape promised when he was here. If we make contact with the assassins we can probably somehow stop the assassination from happening. Just like Pendelshape and Dad want." There was a pause, before he added, "That is… if we want to get involved at all…"

"Well – you know what I think already. I think we should," Angus said. "And anyway," he grinned, "I'm happy to help Anna as much as she wants."

"Come on Angus. This is serious. Listen – I know what Dad and Pendelshape want to do. And I also know that the professor agrees with them."

"So what's the problem?"

"I'm not sure. Maybe it's not as simple as that. I'm thinking maybe we should just wait until we've got a signal on your time phone… if that ever happens… and then, we'll travel back to Dad… and work it out with him… Or, maybe just give ourselves up to the Rector again."

"NO WAY. If you do that – you're on your own. You saw what they did to me… and to poor old Pendelino."

"I'm not sure, Angus. Is it really up to us?"

"We're involved whether we like it or not. And anyway, if you'd heard what your Dad said about it, you'd know the right thing to do was to help them. I think your Dad would expect you to."

"Maybe. But see, I'm not even sure I know how we could stop the assassination even if it is the right thing to do. We have no idea how Pendelshape and Dad had planned to stop it… "

"Well I'm not hanging around for those VIGIL nutters to catch up with us again and lynch us…"

"I don't know Angus… the Rector seemed to make sense at the castle… He was OK."

"Yeah? Well, I'm sorry, he wasn't that sensible when I saw him last with his bunch of thugs back at school…"

Jack had no answer.

*

Later, Jack lay back on his bed and stared up at the ceiling. He felt very tired and slowly closed his eyes. Images from the last two days flickered randomly through his head as he fell into a light, dreamy sleep. In his dream, Angus and the professor were marching ahead of him down a muddy track. He was trying to keep up, telling them to slow down, to wait… but they kept going and going and seemed to know exactly what they were doing. Coming towards them on the same track, marched a column of bedraggled men. On the horizon, way beyond, the air lit up with white-and-orange flashes of artillery fire. The earth rumbled beneath their feet. The line of men stumbled on past them. Their uniforms were dirty, bloody, ripped and torn. Each one of them rested a hand on one shoulder of the soldier in front… and for the first time he noticed that they were blindfolded – a single grubby white bandage was tied around each head.

Without warning, as he hurried on after the professor and Angus, one of the soldiers stopped, broke from the line and squatted down in front of him. His face was dirty and lined… the pale skin hanging heavy with fatigue. Then, to Jack's surprise, the soldier put out one hand towards him and his lips curled up into a weak smile. Suddenly, to Jack's horror, the blindfold was whipped away and he found himself looking straight into two bloodied pits where the eyes should have been...

Muellered

Jack woke with a start. His sheets were wet with sweat. The room was dark. It took him a moment to understand where he was. He heard a gentle knocking at the door and then a whisper – a young woman's voice, "Jack! Jack!"

Coming to his senses, he crept over to the door and opened it a fraction. Two big brown eyes peered back at him. It was Anna.

She eased him to one side and sneaked into the room, "Wake your friend and listen carefully... I have plan."

*

Mueller had decided that he would drive them personally from Achensee to the train station in Innsbruck. He was keen to show off his new Mercedes Benz. Picking up where he had left off the evening before, he continued to chatter away, starting off by pointing out all the features of the large motor car. Somehow they had all managed to squeeze in, together with Anna. Marta had been left at home, and was a little tearful to see them go, but there was no room for her, and anyway, she was "afraid of motor cars".

The mighty machine took three hours to phutt and lumber its way down from the Achensee valley to the town of Innsbruck. They had to stop several times. Mueller's excuse was that the radiator needed a refill, or something under the bonnet needed adjusting. But his main objective was to rummage in the boot of the car for 'refreshment'. These stops proved good opportunities for Angus and Jack to surreptitiously inspect the time phone. The distinctive yellow bar remained stubbornly blank – just as it had since they escaped from the castle. On one occasion, at Mueller's insistence, they descended on a village café where their host downed at least a litre of beer. By the time they entered Innsbruck, he was somewhat inebriated, and as they worked their way towards the station, the car slewed uneasily from side to side as he attempted to avoid pedestrians, horse-drawn carts and other vehicles.

*

The station was busy. The massive black Vienna train was steaming gently alongside the platform as people boarded. Mueller had kindly supplied them with a small hamper for the trip and he had even given the professor some money to replace what had been lost in the lake. As they prepared to board the train, Mueller shook them each warmly by the hand. Anna stood a little behind Mueller, eclipsed by his massive bulk, which swayed gently from the effect of the alcohol.

They climbed aboard and found a compartment all to themselves. It was small, but comfortable and smelled of coal smoke. They spread themselves out on the neatly upholstered bench seats. Mueller was also sending Anna to Vienna with a long shopping list, but she had been banished to one of the third-class carriages further down the platform. Soon, the train was rumbling through the Austrian countryside, which looked greener than ever. It was hard to believe that this was a country on the brink of war.

*

With each kilometre that the train put between them and Innsbruck, they became more relaxed. The professor was relieved to have left the Mueller household without arousing unnecessary suspicion.

"You did well boys…"

"Funny chap, Mueller…" Jack said.

"We were lucky, he and I go back a long way. He…"

Jack interrupted, "We should explain, Professor." Jack said. "Anna, the maid, she's not what she seems. She's a Serb."

"More – a spy," Angus added.

The professor looked shocked, "What? What do you mean?"

Jack took out Pendelshape's photograph from his pocket and placed it on the little wooden table next to the window in front of the professor.

"Remember this, Professor? Well – Anna took the photograph. She told us all about it this morning."

"What?" the professor exclaimed. "But…"

Jack pointed at one of the figures in the picture, "That's Anna's brother, Dani. He is a member of the Black Hand. They are a Serb underground movement."

"Incredible!" The professor held the photo level with his eyes, "So how on earth does Anna come to be working in Mueller's house?"

"Placed there to keep tabs on him. Remember – you told us – he worked for the Austrian diplomatic service. Anna says he still has senior contacts, apparently. There is a large network of informants, like Anna. They're everywhere. But the main point is…" Jack took the photograph from the professor and held it in front of them so they could all study it properly, "Anna, and her brother, Dani, know Pendelshape."

They all looked at the photograph closely.

"Anna explained to us who they all are," Jack continued. "This photo was taken in Belgrade when Pendelshape, my dad and the rest of the VIGIL team originally tested the Taurus, just before Dad disappeared. Look – there's Pendelshape. Anyway, that one is Gavrilo Princip, the man who shoots Archduke Franz Ferdinand, this Sunday… in Sarajevo… four days from now."

"So how do these plotters come to know Anna's brother? How come he is involved?"

"Part of the Belgrade café set… but that's not all." Jack sucked through his teeth and looked at Angus nervously, "Anna and Dani's father was murdered. Anna didn't tell us the whole story, but the Austrian authorities did nothing about it."

"So Anna and her brother, Dani, don't like living under Austrian rule?" the professor asked.

"Hate them. Anyway, it seems that Pendelshape quite easily penetrated the plotter's circle by pretending to be an English academic travelling, but also with a big interest in the Southern Slavs. He pretended to be sympathetic to them, gave them money, that kind of thing. They were grateful for Pendelshape's support – being so poor and eager for any help that they could get to fight the Austro-

Hungarian Empire."

"Wait," the professor said, "I thought your teacher, Pendelshape, and your father for that matter, wanted to stop the assassination and the war... not help the Bosnian Serb conspirators who trigger it?"

"You're right, Professor," Jack said. "Angus and I talked about it last night..."

The professor raised his eyebrows expectantly.

"Using their knowledge of history, Pendelshape and my dad wanted to get the trust of the conspirators, infiltrate the group and then, at the last moment, disrupt the entire plot, stop the assassination and thereby prevent the war from starting. It's quite the opposite of what Anna and Dani think."

Angus added, "Yeah – and Anna and Dani were taken in by Pendelshape. He must have impressed them – because they trust him completely."

"Thing is, Anna also trusts us now."

"So Anna thinks that Pendelshape was a friend... and will be returning soon to help them," the professor said.

"Yes – but Pendelshape isn't a friend at all. He was going to blow the whole thing. He was going to betray Anna and Dani. But Anna thinks we have been sent by Pendelshape. She thinks our guise as English boys travelling abroad with our German uncle is a good one. Mueller thinks she is going to Vienna to do some shopping for him. But her plan is different. When we get there, she will meet us at the station and then she wants to take us to Dani. After that, she didn't say. But she assumes we have instructions from Pendelshape to help them. Her first job is to get us to the assassins."

As Jack explained it all, the professor's eyes flashed in anticipation. "Well, this is our chance!" He nodded keenly, "Yes – we now have a way in – a way to stop this horrible war happening – just as your father and Dr Pendelshape intend!"

*

After many hours, the train slowed as at last they approached Vienna – the centre of the Austro-Hungarian Empire. The professor and Angus were slumped in one corner of the carriage, the gentle movement of the train having rocked them to sleep a good hour before. Jack craned his neck – sure enough, they were rumbling towards a large station.

"Wake up – we're here!"

The professor and Angus came round, eyes blinking. The train creaked to a gentle halt with a loud hissing of smoke and steam. Doors started to swing open onto the hubbub of the platform.

Angus studied their new surroundings, "Vienna, eh? Cool."

"You said that once before – and nearly stitched us all up," Jack said.

They approached the barrier, showed their tickets, and moved quickly on.

Anna pushed through the throng emerging from the third-class carriages and greeted them with a warm smile. She had jettisoned her maid's outfit, and her long hair flowed loosely – a first gesture of freedom. There would be no return to the drudgery and humiliation of life in the Mueller household for her.

She looked around furtively. "You need to follow me," she said quietly.

But they had no time to obey.

*

At that moment, they were surrounded by five uniformed officials. Out of the shadows, a sixth man appeared. He wore a simple double-breasted suit and a straw boater. He was a thin, wiry man and he spoke English with a strong foreign accent.

"Welcome to Vienna," he said. "I hope you had a pleasant journey from Innsbruck? We have been expecting you. Please, let me introduce myself – Friedrich Kessler. I work for the Austrian government."

Schönbrunn Shenanigans

The professor started to speak, "What is the meaning…?" Kessler put his finger to his lips, "Please, Professor, no trouble now. If you would like to come with us, I assure you, you and your, er, family, will come to no harm. No harm at all."

They were marched through the station concourse causing a flurry of heads to turn in the crowd.

"What's this all about?" Angus whispered.

"Well one thing's for sure… this lot don't look like VIGIL agents – more like royal life guards or something," Jack replied.

"That's exactly what they are…" the professor said out of the corner of his mouth.

But Anna, for one, was not going to hang around for confirmation. Suddenly, she elbowed the guard next to her in his solar plexus and then bit his hand – hard. She writhed free and made a dash into the thronging crowd on the concourse. One of the guards raised his rifle. But it was too late – Anna was gone.

Kessler swore and harshly reprimanded the guards, who now gripped Jack, Angus and the professor firmly by the arm, so they could not try a similar stunt. They were bundled unceremoniously into a waiting motor van outside. The professor protested again, but was ignored, and the van rumbled off with the trio in the back with two guards.

The professor rattled the mesh that separated them from the driver's cabin.

"What's happening? Where are you taking us?"

Kessler replied evenly, "Please calm down, Professor, all will be explained shortly."

The van rumbled along and from their cramped position inside it was difficult to make out their direction through the streets of Vienna.

Jack was scared, "What's going on, Professor?"

"No idea and I don't know Vienna well, but if these are Austrian officials... there are a limited number of places they would be taking us... a police station, maybe one of the jails, maybe even the Belvedere..."

"Or maybe there..." Angus pointed through one of the slit windows. Through the narrow aperture they caught sight of the most incredible building that Jack had ever seen. In books he had seen pictures of the Palace of Versailles, outside Paris, but this seemed to eclipse even that.

The professor nodded knowingly, "Schönbrunn. It's Schönbrunn Palace. The home of the Habsburgs. This is where the emperor lives."

"Looks like they have plenty of rooms."

"One thousand four hundred and forty-one at the last count," the professor said.

"Why do they have so many?" Angus asked.

"Because they can," Jack replied.

As the modest entourage filed around the outskirts of the palace, Jack craned his neck to get a better view of the magnificent building. From whichever angle you looked, it exuded splendour. Jack had seen wealth in his own time, of course, and had heard people bemoan the gap between the 'rich' and the 'poor', but he had never seen wealth like this.

They were led into an entrance at the rear of the palace, up some stairs and then through an increasingly ornate series of passages and state rooms. Finally, they entered a vast gallery, it must have been at least forty-five metres long, and it stopped Jack in his tracks. Along one side, a series of massive arched windows displayed the formal gardens beyond. Opposite these, huge gilt-framed mirrors reflected the light to make the whole room appear even larger. Above them, the ceiling was painted with three grand frescos between which hung crystal chandeliers, which looked like oversized wedding cakes.

Day of the Assassins

"The Great Gallery," the professor muttered.

Jack was stunned by the extraordinary opulence. The place was making him feel very small indeed. Half way down the gallery, they were ushered into an unusual oval-shaped room. Lacquered compartments of varying shapes and sizes were set into white-painted wooden panels in the walls. Each compartment was framed in gilt and housed its own piece of blue-and-white porcelain sculpture. Kessler gestured to them to sit at an ornate table, and spoke for the first time since their hurried journey from the station.

"Count Sieghard will join us shortly. In the meantime, I will ensure that you receive some refreshments." He said no more and slipped quietly from the room.

"Count Sieghard…" Angus whispered, "Who's he?"

They didn't have to wait long to find out.

The guards stationed by the door barely flinched as a tall, grey-haired man swept into the room. The two guards quickly disappeared, closing the doors behind them. He was dressed in a high-collared double-breasted jacket with two columns of brass buttons and elaborate gold braid around the collar and cuffs. His trousers had a twin red braid down each side. Whoever he was, he was important.

He settled himself down at the end of the table from the three of them and they got a closer look at his face. He was perhaps in his forties, with finely chiselled features and a good head of silver hair which gave him an air of distinction. Jack thought there was something unusual about the man's face, which made him seem a little out of place… but for the moment he couldn't quite make out what it was. Then he realised. All the men he had encountered on his journey so far: Mueller, Kessler, the people in Innsbruck and at Vienna station, had moustaches. Some of them had real handlebar jobs. But this man had no moustache – which was strange – it put him quite out of place with his surroundings. In fact, he would have been much more at home in the City of London in a pinstriped suit.

The professor bravely managed to find his voice again, "Sir, I don't know who you are, or why we are here, but I am a member of…"

Count Sieghard raised his hand. It was all that was needed to silence the poor professor on the spot.

"Please professor Pinckard-Schnell," he talked smoothly in crisp English with effortless confidence. "Of course we owe you an explanation... and to you as well, Jack and Angus," he smiled. "My young time-adventurers."

Jack and Angus exchanged glances nervously.

"I'm afraid that your friend, Herr Mueller, has somewhat landed you in it."

The professor frowned, "Mueller? What has..."

"Yes, professor, I know he appears to be a complete idiot... and of course to some extent he is. But he is still a loyal idiot. Mueller didn't like what he was doing. But nevertheless felt he had to do it. I'm afraid he betrayed you. I don't think Herr Mueller really bought your story of being on holiday in the Alps, Professor. And, of course, the word had already gone out amongst our network, so we have been looking to pick up a man and two, er, younger men, with your description for over a day now. Mueller is an ex-member of the Austrian diplomatic corps... and he was able to correctly identify you when you appeared on his land. I'm afraid he had no choice but to turn you in."

"So we are being held by the Austrian government? May I ask for what possible reason? We have done nothing wrong, and may I add, I am a citizen of the German Empire..."

Sieghard waved his hand dismissively, "Yes, yes Professor, please don't waste my time."

The professor fell silent.

"I should introduce myself properly. This might make things a little clearer for you. You have probably heard my name by now. I expect my colleague, your Rector in fact, boys, may have referred to me. I chair VIGIL, and I have played a modest part in a not unimpressive scientific achievement..." He smiled for the first time. It was a little disconcerting. "The invention of time travel. And it has been my dubious pleasure, along with your Rector and the rest of our team, to try to prevent your father, Jack, from doing something completely mad.... My real name, of course, is not Count Sieghard at all, but Inchquin. Counsellor Inchquin."

Day of the Assassins

*

It took a little while for them to take in what Counsellor Inchquin had said and then it slowly dawned on them. Here was the Rector's boss: the man who chaired VIGIL and directed their whole secret operation. He was the one who was responsible for having them chased half way around Europe. He was, in fact, the man who controlled time travel.

"Yes, I know it must all seem rather confusing… so perhaps I should explain. First of all, you've probably gathered that you are at Schönbrunn Palace. The home of the Habsburgs and the centre of the Austro-Hungarian Empire. The current occupants might be alarmed to find that in our time, nearly a hundred years from now, seven million tourists a year tramp through the palace and its gardens. But anyway, how do I come to be here?" he nodded as if to say 'good question' to a point that they had not even raised.

"Well, with the significant benefit of hindsight and VIGIL's encyclopedic knowledge of history, it has proved quite easy to insert myself into the apparatus of the Austrian bureaucracy – acting as a visiting foreign diplomat. Although I have no executive role here – that would be far too intrusive in terms of my impact on the future course of history – I have a temporary position that allows me to know what is going on. Call me a special agent if you will. And of course knowing the personal history of some of the key players makes it a little easier for me to influence, if I must, and tidy up any damage that your journey might cause. Hindsight is a wonderful thing," he paused. "Yes, I have access to them all: the Austrian Premier, Count Sturkh; the Hungarian Premier, Count Tisza…" He shrugged, "And, if I were to need it, an audience with the Emperor Franz Joseph himself, is easily arranged…" He sighed with satisfaction, "Now we understand what Pendelshape and your father are up to we have had to put in place contingency plans. Thus my rather unusual presence here. But currently, we have no need to do anything. Everything seems to be moving along quite nicely. Just as the course of history intended. And that is exactly how it should be."

Inchquin now looked at them more gravely, "This war will happen despite the antics of my old colleague, Christie, and Pendelshape…"

The professor spoke up bravely, "Counsellor Inchquin, I think I speak for the boys here as well as myself. We have no wish to become embroiled in something we do not understand. We have become involved in this simply by chance. We are innocent victims. All we wish, is to return to our lives."

"Do you really think there is such a thing as 'chance' Professor?" Inchquin snapped. "History is determined. There is a required course of events and we meddle with them at our peril. Although you protest to be innocent bystanders, I am afraid that you are involved whether you like it or not. We must therefore consider very carefully what we do next. I think the Rector explained the VIGIL Imperative and the delicate role we in VIGIL must play in terms of preventing and controlling interventions that are made in history. And this is not helped by fools like your father, Jack," he added bitterly.

The professor tried to stay calm, "Counsellor Inchquin, we have no desire to interfere with your plans…"

Of course, Jack knew what the professor really thought, and that this was a lie.

Inchquin shrugged, "Sometimes, desperate times call for desperate measures. We are dealing with matters of utmost importance and now we must take executive action…"

"What does that mean?"

"It's just as the Rector explained to you. While we have you we can protect you from your father. You are the only hold that we have over him. I'm afraid that you will be incarcerated here until we can get a time signal to send you back home where you will need to be protected at all times from him. Until we can get you home we must limit your contact with the outside world, but…" he added with a little more warmth, "we will try and make your stay as comfortable as possible."

"You're going to lock us up again?" Jack said.

"It is for your protection."

"What about the war?" the professor said, his voice rising in agitation. He immediately wished he hadn't.

Inchquin looked at the professor, "What about it? When Princip pulls the trigger in Sarajevo on Sunday, four days from now, then the cogs of history will grind inexorably forward and we will have our war. I will stay here to ensure the diplomatic process is smoothly executed. And you will stay here, Jack, to ensure that neither your father, nor Pendelshape for that matter, do anything stupid. If they do I fear your father may find himself without an heir."

Inchquin's words hung ominously in the air. There was no emotion, no histrionics. There didn't need to be. He held all the cards.

"Ah. One thing I nearly forgot. Your time phone, Angus," Inchquin held out a hand, "If you please."

Angus reluctantly removed the precious device from his pocket and slid it over the table. Inchquin eyed the time phone in his hand.

"Thank you," he nodded. "I must say, very impressive of your father, Jack, to recreate all this. And he was certainly taking a risk by giving this to you, Angus. He must have known it might fall into our hands. But that's just like him. Brilliant – but impetuous. A risk taker. He hasn't changed. But now, finally, I have a time phone that is linked to his Taurus. We can use it to give him a little surprise." He flipped open the time phone and peered at the display, "As I thought. No signal. But there will be at some point, and then we'll be able to locate your father and his Taurus and get rid of this whole annoying problem once and for all."

*

Inchquin got to his feet. The meeting was over. He clapped his hands and the guards re-entered the room to usher them back towards the Great Gallery and into the bowels of the palace to begin their imprisonment. Inchquin stopped by the door to acknowledge their departure. The professor and Angus were escorted away by the guards and a third guard was about to take Jack when Inchquin unexpectedly touched him on the shoulder, causing him to wait for a moment.

"Jack, one last thing. How is your mother?"

In the circumstances, Jack felt this to be the strangest of questions and did not really know what to say, "She's fine. I hope."

Inchquin smiled. It was an odd smile – there may have even been a hint of warmth there, warmth that had been absent from the earlier conversation. But it also hid a tinge of embarrassment, perhaps guilt.

He said quietly, "That's good, Jack, that's good. She has been loyal to us and she and I, well, since Geneva and through all this turmoil, we have become good… friends." He paused and grimaced slightly. "This is not easy. Not easy for any of us. But I want you to know that we are doing the right thing. We are not monsters. I just hope your father sees sense. I really do… Jack… I really do."

*

The words lingered briefly in the air. But Jack had little time to consider their meaning before he was marched off with the others. As they made their way from the Great Gallery a small group crossed from room to room ahead of them. Their escorts suddenly halted and gestured for Jack, Angus and the professor to follow suit. In unison, they dropped their heads in a bow. In the centre of the group ahead was an old man. He was dressed a bit like Inchquin; he had the same double-breasted jacket with brass buttons, high-braided collar and gold-braided cuffs. An insignia of some high office dropped from his neck and a number of impressive medals hung from his left collar. He was balding but had a fine white moustache and white mutton-chop side burns. Although the man was old, he was tall and had the straight back of a horseman. He carried himself with an air of superiority. Suddenly Jack realised that he was gazing upon the emperor himself – Franz Joseph.

As the entourage crossed their path, the emperor glanced round and, for a split second, Jack caught his sharp blue eyes. Through those eyes, he was suddenly looking into a different era. An era where God gave power to the few, who in turn took on the responsibility of ruling. He realised that, although he and the emperor were both human, they were a whole world apart. And in a way, this pending war would be the very thing that made Jack so different to him. It was going to be the great watershed between the 'old' and the 'new'. The emperor turned his head away again. He had not even registered the rather odd presence of Jack and his friends, chaperoned by Inchquin and his helpers. He was not to know that in only four days' time his own nephew would be assassinated in Sarajevo, triggering a chain of events that would lead to the end of his mighty empire.

Incident at the Orangery

Jack, Angus and the professor were led back into the depths of the palace. The building was endless. You could have fitted a hundred Cairnfields inside this place, and still have room for the garden.

At last they were deposited in rooms close to the servant's quarters at the rear of the palace, on the ground floor. There was a small bedroom, with two bunk beds, and a larger living room furnished simply with a table and four wooden chairs. There were no windows, only a couple of metal grilled skylights. Two guards had been stationed outside the door. This was to be their home, until… well, until they were told otherwise. Jack took the chance to wash in the small bathroom that adjoined the bedroom. A strange array of early twentieth-century bathroom accoutrements had been supplied and although he was unsure what a number of them were for, he did identify some soap, which took an age to lather.

He peered into the mirror. Somebody stared back – but it didn't look much like him. His eyes seemed to have turned a dullish grey and his blonde hair was greasy. He rubbed his eyes tiredly, as if tuning an old TV set, trying to improve the image before him. He remembered what Inchquin had said about his mum… they had become good friends. It hadn't really registered at the time, but now the remarks combined uneasily with his mum's guarded attitude towards his father and her unwillingness to trust Jack with what she had known all along. He frowned; was there something else his mum hadn't told him? Jack felt a sudden stab of despair. He sat on the edge of the bath. Here he was stuck nearly a hundred years in the past, with no obvious way home. He was a pawn in a battle in which he was unsure which side was right and which side was wrong. It was a battle that had torn his own family apart. It meant he had to grow up without a dad and with a mum who felt she couldn't tell him the truth. Jack put his head in his hands. But he didn't cry – he just bit his lip.

He emerged from the bathroom. The professor had his head propped up on two pillows on one bunk and continued to read Jack's history book, which he had somehow managed to hold onto. Angus sat at the table fidgeting with a splinter of wood, trying to remove some dirt from under his fingernails. There had been no discussion since the meeting with Counsellor Inchquin and the naïve excitement that they had shared on the train journey from Innsbruck was long gone.

As they slowly prepared for bed, they heard muffled voices from the servant's quarters outside their rooms. Then, the door to their living room swung open. A small posse of life guards marched in followed by Inchquin. He was holding a time phone.

"Sorry to disturb you, gentlemen," he announced. "However, we have our time signal – much sooner than we anticipated. This is our chance to send you home, and, for us to pay that little visit I promised to your father, Jack. Come – we must get down to business immediately."

Inchquin took a step over to the table, gesturing for them all to gather round. But one step was as far as he got.

*

There was a deafening explosion and a powerful shockwave hit them like an express train. Jack was propelled backwards and landed awkwardly on the stone floor, a cloud of dust and plaster fragments spraying over him. He spluttered uncontrollably and raised his head, trying to peer through the swirling dust. The brick wall on the far side of their room had collapsed. It was now just a smoking heap of bricks and masonry. Jack pulled himself shakily to his feet. Angus and the professor were in front of him, shouting and pointing. But all Jack could hear was a loud ringing in his ears. He tried to shout back, 'I can't hear you!' but his words came out as a muffled booming in his own head. They pointed again and Jack could see the shadow of two figures appear in the large hole that had been created in the wall by the explosion. Beyond the figures, Jack could make out the palace grounds and the vague shape of trees in the moonlight. The two figures were gesturing wildly at them. They were being rescued!

He rushed forward, following closely behind Angus and the professor who had already made it out into the garden. As he moved through the living room he spotted Inchquin. He had caught the full force of the blast and was lying on the floor, moaning. He was hurt – hit by a piece of flying mortar – and his face was white with dust and plaster. Dark blood, oozing from a wound on his forehead, was starting to mix into it. Lying next to Inchquin, seemingly untouched and still open and glinting on the stone floor, Jack spotted Angus's time phone. He snatched it up, then rushed onwards clambering over the debris that was strewn across the floor and through the ragged hole created by the explosion. From out of the shadows, two more rescuers dashed forward. One was a man – large and stocky. As they approached, Jack could see they were both carrying rifles. The second figure was smaller, slimmer – a young woman. In the moonlight, he could just see her smile and she put out her hand to greet him.

"Nice to meet you again, Jack Christie. Sorry about our bomb. We want little bang – but we make big bang. This is my brother, Dani... and friends – Vaso and Goran. We thought you need help... So we come. "

The big brown eyes and wide face were unmistakable.

"Anna? But how did you...?"

But as he spoke, she stopped smiling. There was shouting as the guards regrouped in the room behind them. A shot rang out and whistled past Jack's temple. Then, in one fluid motion, Anna raised her rifle and, aiming over Jack's shoulder into the room, closed one eye and squeezed the trigger. The rifle bucked violently in her slender hands and the gunshot exploded right beside Jack's ear. Instantly, she slipped back the bolt, released the used cartridge and smoothly re-filled it with a fresh round from her belt. She fired again, without hesitation. The life guards dived for cover.

Having halted the guards, Anna and Dani hurried the three of them onwards.

"Quick – this way!"

Jack's head was ringing like a fire alarm – first from the crude bomb that their rescuers had used to blow a hole in the wall and now from Anna's rifle that had just discharged right next to his ear. Another shot rang out and whistled over his head. One thing was certain, if they hung around, in all this confusion, one of them was going to get killed. Anna and Dani dashed off into the palace gardens. They had no choice but to follow. There was a flash of white light and, close in front of them a VIGIL guard appeared. There was another flash, and another VIGIL guard appeared.

Jack groaned – he couldn't believe it – Tony and Gordon.

Tony leered at them through the gloom. "Evening all," he said and readied his APR. "Let's just all hold our horses, calm down and not try anything silly."

Tony and Gordon were not alone. Soon the garden outside the palace was alight with blinding flashes as guard after guard appeared – each armed and each dressed in VIGIL's telltale flak jackets. There must have been at least ten guards fanned out in front of them. Inchquin must have planned for reinforcements to travel from the Taurus, each using their own time phones, as soon as there was an available signal to secure and protect Jack once and for all, before executing the raid on his father's base.

Inchquin had dragged himself to his feet and was issuing orders. The life guards in their bright uniforms and plumed hats emerged from the hole in the wall and approached them from behind. With Tony, Gordon and the other VIGIL guards in front, they were now trapped. Jack looked round at his friends. Angus was standing there – his fists clenched defiantly by his sides. The professor, yellow hair messy as ever, was following the proceedings with a detached curiosity as if he were observing a strange experiment. Anna was grim faced; the reckless confidence she had shown a moment before had vanished. She lowered her rifle, realising the hopelessness of their situation. Her lower lip was trembling in fear. She knew what the Austro-Hungarian Empire did to traitors. Jack suddenly felt a pang of sorrow for her, and as they stood there, he did something that surprised him. He took her hand and gently clasped it in his own. She looked at him a little oddly and opened her mouth to say something.

But his tender gesture of solidarity was short lived. A single gun shot rang out from the group of guards behind them and, at almost exactly the same time, Jack felt some sort of warm substance splatter the side of his face. Beside him, the professor's legs just seemed to give way and he collapsed on to the ground in a heap. They heard Inchquin scream an order, "No shooting!!!"

Too late. Jack looked down at the professor uncertainly. Dani dropped to his knees and held the professor so his face was turned upwards, his open eyes staring unblinking at the moon. The side of his head, where once there had been that distinctive, curly yellow hair, was just a dark mess.

Jack had read about death, seen it on TV and experienced it a million times on a hundred different computer games. This was horrifically, gut-wrenchingly different.

Next, they heard Inchquin commanding them to put their weapons down and their hands up. They had no choice. One by one, Dani, Anna and their two companions placed their weapons on the ground and reluctantly raised their hands. Jack was about to raise his own when he realised that he was still clutching Angus's time phone in one hand. Through the dark mist of his despair, a pinprick of light suddenly appeared. Of course! Jack peered down at the time phone and flipped it open. Sure enough, the bar was still lit up in an intense yellow light. In his hand he had a time travel device. It had a signal and it was linked to his father's Taurus. Maybe, just maybe, he could use it, somehow, to bring the professor back. With one finger he started to tap out a message. Behind them, Inchquin and the guards were now cautiously approaching their little huddle. Jack hurried.

VIGIL attacking. Need help. Hurry. Jack

He pressed a button and the message was gone. Inchquin was nearly upon them and he continued to bark orders to the VIGIL guards beyond and to the palace life guards. He was furious that a lack of discipline had resulted in the professor's unseemly death... More mess in the space-time continuum that they would have to clear up later.

There was a sudden 'bleep'. Dad had replied!

Rescue imminent; hold tight.
Proud of you. Dad.

"Yes!" Jack hissed. As Inchquin approached, he flipped the time phone shut and slipped it back into his pocket. He didn't have long to consider what form his father's rescue attempt would take, because off to their right, there was another flash of light. For some reason, this flash was brighter than those that had signalled the arrival of the VIGIL guards. Everyone turned to see what had caused it, but they could only make out the outline of the bushes and trees of a large thicket, some way off, silhouetted by the moon. For a moment everything was still. Then, they heard a loud mechanical grinding. The earth shook. The grinding got louder and soon they could hear the roar of an engine. A very large engine.

Suddenly, the bushes at the front of the thicket collapsed and a huge dark object emerged, crawled half way across the moonlit lawn in front of them... and stopped. The distinctive shape of the metal behemoth was so clear in the moonlight, Jack knew at once what it was, and understood exactly how his father proposed to expedite their escape. Their little party at Schönbrunn Palace had a gatecrasher. But this was not any old gatecrasher. It was a Mark II Tiger tank of the German Wehrmacht. The biggest, heaviest and deadliest tank from World War Two. And it wasn't there for the lemonade and cream buns.

All hell broke loose. The 7.92 millimetre forward machine gun on the Tiger opened up and bullets ripped across the lawn and into the band of massed life guards, who leaped for cover. At the same time the muzzle of the Tiger's massive 88 millimetre main gun flashed and a shell whistled over their heads, narrowly missing the VIGIL guards and embedding itself in the nearby wing of Schönbrunn, which promptly collapsed in a pile of rubble as the high explosive shell discharged.

The VIGIL guards returned fire, but their APRs were useless against the armour of the seventy-tonne Tiger. Its machine gun continued to rattle away as the main gun found its range. The muzzle flashed again and a second shell pumped straight into the melee of VIGIL guards.

Jack's father had been one step ahead. Inchquin had been about to use the time signal to send them home and then to carry out some sort of assault on his father's base using the assembled VIGIL guards and the location codes on Angus's time phone. But Christie had got there first. Even before Jack's message, he must have anticipated that help would be needed and, when the moment had come, had taken advantage of the available signal to send help in the form of a tank. But now this wasn't looking like the best of plans. Jack, Angus and Anna were caught in the middle – they had Inchquin and the Schönbrunn life guards behind them, Tony and Gordon and the VIGIL guards in front of them, and a Second World War tank off to one side. The professor already lay by their feet – dead. It wasn't looking good.

Next Jack spotted two of the VIGIL guards fiddling with a large device – some sort of bazooka. One of them hoisted it onto his shoulder. The weapon bucked and its shell fizzed like a firework as it shot across the lawn. It smacked plumb into the side of the Tiger and there was an ear-splitting explosion. The 180 millimetre frontal armour of the Tiger was holed and the machine gun abruptly stopped. Yet someone in the tank had survived. The gun turret swivelled towards the two VIGIL guards who were desperately reloading the bazooka. The massive gun aimed downwards across the lawn towards them, but just as the muzzle flashed and recoiled, releasing a third shell, a second round fizzed from the bazooka towards the Tiger. It was too late for the VIGIL bazooka crew who were vaporised as the shell exploded just in front of them. But almost instantaneously the second bazooka's round ripped open the Tiger's armour and buried itself in the engine compartment. The rear of the Tiger erupted in a huge orange fireball. In a moment, the turret hatch swung open and a figure emerged, briefly silhouetted against the fierce flames rising from the Tiger. Even at a distance, the portly figure was immediately recognisable to Jack and Angus.

"Can't be," Angus said.

"It's Pendelshape. Dad sent Pendelshape back," Jack confirmed, awestruck.

"In a tank," Angus added unnecessarily.

Pendelshape leaped from the turret into the gloom and was gone.

"Come on!" Anna shouted.

As one, they dashed further into the gardens. Jack's eyes had adjusted to the moonlight, and he could now make out the elaborate matrix of Baroque-style pathways and hedges. Anna pushed them on at a heart-burning pace. He had a nagging feeling that, with his lungs, he would be unable to keep up. But they stayed strong... and he found himself breathing deeply – actually managing to keep pace with Anna. Suddenly, Jack felt a tremor in the earth. He glanced round and made out some large shadows behind them. Lancers from the palace – on horseback. They hadn't wasted much time. Anna shouted to her brother.

"Dani – what do we do?"

"Split up – as we planned. You and I take the English boys. Vaso and Goran split off."

The lancers were already only ninety metres away and bearing down on them.

Dani and Anna whisked Jack and Angus off the main path and into a narrow, hedged passageway. Vaso and Goran disappeared in the opposite direction.

Behind them, the horsemen came to a sudden halt, in a maelstrom of dust, scraping leather and metal. They had been temporarily caught out by the split of the group – but it wouldn't be long before they were back on their trail. Dani led them out through an archway in the hedge. Ahead of them was a wide, grass bank, which rose gently to a long, low building with a series of archways built into the walls. It was a strange structure and it was not clear what it was for.

Anna egged them forward, "Come on!"

Behind them, one of the lancers had managed to force his horse through the narrow passageway and was hot on their heels. Anna raced towards the low building – Dani, Jack and Angus following closely behind. Anna took her rifle and thrust the butt hard into the large glass window of one of the arches. It shattered instantly.

Anna jumped through the gap and they followed her through and started to run. Inside, the faint grey moonlight washed through the arched windows. The building was so long that they could barely see from one end to the other. It was mostly empty, although there were some large tables set in rows and, bizarrely, a section of manicured trees in large boxes. The atmosphere was different in here – it was warmer than outside and more humid... there was a fragrance in the air – a citrus smell, like oranges. That's where they were: inside a massive orangery – although most of the trees had already been moved to the gardens for the summer. But before they had a chance to gather their wits, there was another loud crash. They wheeled round. A tall figure sat astride a large black horse. One of the pursuing lancers had burst through the broken window and skidded to a halt in the central aisle of the orangery. His steel helmet glimmered and the long, feathered plume quivered in its crest. The horse bucked, and the horseman wheeled round expertly to face them. He was balancing his lance, a gossamer-thin pole in his right hand. At one end, Jack could make out a small metal spike. In a flash, the lancer dug his heels hard into the flanks of the black horse. It reared... and then charged.

They could feel the paving beneath them rumble as the four hooves pounded forward. The horseman skilfully manoeuvred the lance so that it pointed at a slight angle down to where Dani and Anna stood, between Jack and Angus. In seconds he would be upon them. Jack and Angus dived for cover. But Dani was too slow. Jack twisted round and, as Dani fell, he saw the lance pierce his chest. Anna screamed in horror as her brother slumped to the ground. The horseman withdrew the lance from Dani's body. He steered the horse back and it snorted as the lancer turned round for a second attack. Anna climbed, catlike, onto one of the long banquet tables. From her elevated position, she leaped out at the horseman landing plumb on his horse's rump. The horse reared up in surprise, its front hooves kicking out wildly. First Anna, then the lancer tumbled backwards onto the stone floor. The lancer landed awkwardly on his head. He didn't move. His lance spun from his hand and its metal tip shattered free from the wooden pole as it hit the stone floor. Jack and Angus rushed over to Anna who groaned, opened her eyes and shakily pulled herself up into a crawling position. She crept over to where Dani lay, and cradled her brother's head in her hands. But it lolled uselessly and his eyes stared out into the darkness.

First the professor and now Dani. Dead.

In the dim moonlight, something caught Jack's eye. He peered down and the metal lance head glinted up at him. It lay in a pool of Dani's blood. It was exactly the same size and shape as the lance head he had discovered in his father's workshop at Cairnfield. The Schönbrunn raid was not a historical myth. Jack knew now – because he had been part of it. In fact, his trip back to 1914 had caused it.

*

Anna turned from her brother and stared up at Jack and Angus. She had a strange, questioning look on her face. Then the shock of her brother's brutal death hit her and she started to rock violently back and forth cradling his head, sobbing uncontrollably. Anna was in a place beyond comfort, and for a moment Jack and Angus just stared down, not knowing what to do.

Suddenly they heard voices from outside. More guards.

Angus looked at Jack, desperation on his face. "What do we do now?"

Jack fumbled in his pocket, "Time phone! Maybe we still have a signal… maybe we can get out of this mess, once and for all."

He held the device in his hand and flipped it open, but the yellow bar had turned grey. The signal had vanished.

"No good," Jack groaned.

At the far end of the orangery, the guards were starting to scramble through the shattered window. Soon they would be upon them.

"What's this?" Jack had noticed something else in the time phone's read-out. "Another message! Must have been sent just before the signal was lost."

Sure enough the read-out was blinking.

Message 2...

Jack tapped a button.

Have lost contact with P-shape. Rescue may have failed. Can only help when we have a signal. If P-shape alive - he will help you.

In frustration, Jack snapped the time phone shut.

Next to them, Anna kissed Dani lightly on one cheek and rested his head on the stone floor. She looked back down the orangery where they could now see the shadows of the guards approaching. Then she got to her feet. She had stopped sobbing. She was suddenly cold and emotionless. There was steel in her voice. "Now I want one thing... only one thing: justice."

*

It took them two hours to creep from the grounds of Schönbrunn and make their way cross-country to the pre-arranged meeting place. They worked their way through thick woodland, where shards of moonlight ghosted through the canopy above. Eventually, they arrived at some farmland, where a rustic timber barn nestled between the edge of the wood and the fields beyond. The crude structure was raised from the ground on four wooden stilts and in the grey light Jack saw that a large stone rested on each stilt, supporting the barn – the smooth surface of the stones deterred rats and mice from the barn's contents. Gingerly, Anna approached the wooden ladder that led to the elevated doorway. She climbed up and levered open the door. Soon all three of them were safely inside. It was clear that this was to have been the rendezvous point with Vaso and Goran. But worryingly there was no sign of them. They had no idea what had happened to Pendelshape either, following his escape from the burning Tiger. They were alone and they would not be able to stay long.

Through cracks in the crude wooden walls, the moonlight washed eerily into the barn. Anna curled up in a corner and for a while remained motionless – brooding. Finally, seeking comfort from distraction, she pulled some bread and cheese from her bag and shared it out. They sat and tried to eat, but Jack's mouth was dry and the bread and cheese rolled up in his mouth in a papery ball. When Anna finally spoke to them, her voice was strangely calm, "So – you will help us – as we planned, yes?"

It was clear what she meant. They had not staged the rescue from Schönbrunn for fun. Dani's death was not to be in vain. They were still expected to travel to Sarajevo to help in the assassination attempt and help Anna find justice.

Zadok the Priest

"**D**oboj, eh? I tell you what, they've got some daft names around here..."

Jack could not summon the energy to respond to Angus. The night in the third-class railway carriage had exhausted him.

Anna scanned the thronging crowds from the steps of Doboj's main railway station. "There!" she whispered.

Further up the street stood a pony and hay cart. A dark-skinned boy – he couldn't have been more than ten years old – was perched high on a wooden seat at the front of the cart.

"Our transport..."

"It just gets better and better," Angus groaned.

Soon they were slumped on the hay in the back of the cart and the contraption rumbled off.

*

Jack reflected on their escape from Schönbrunn the day before and their six hundred and fifty kilometre journey from Vienna to Doboj – one hundred and sixty kilometres north of Sarajevo. It had been long and exhausting. On Thursday afternoon Anna had managed to get them aboard a train from Vienna to Belgrade and then on to Doboj. The Bosnian Serb underground network was proving to be remarkably pervasive and efficient. Jack had lost count of the times Anna had started a sentence with the words, "I have a friend who...", or "I know someone who...". The valuable train tickets had been procured from just such a source – a young train porter who was part of the network, and also, as Jack was starting to notice, one of Anna's many male admirers.

Since Schönbrunn, and the final message from Jack's dad, the time phone had gone back into hibernation and the telltale yellow bar had remained stubbornly unlit – making any pursuit by VIGIL very difficult. It also meant that there had been no communication with Pendelshape. There was still the risk, however, of being picked up by the regular Austro-Hungarian authorities – but so far they had avoided this fate.

Jack had begun to understand more about Anna as they rumbled south. Her desolation over the loss of her brother became buried under a brooding and renewed hatred of her Austro-Hungarian masters. Jack had persuaded her to tell them how she had orchestrated the daring rescue from Schönbrunn.

She had explained, "We are planning raid in Vienna for long time. It is heart of Austrian Empire. We have plans already. After I meet you, and realise you are sent by the English teacher, Dr Pendelshape, I know we must protect you... get you to Zadok to help us in Sarajevo. After capture at Vienna Station, we activate the Vienna cell. We know where they take you – so we organise raid."

"You took a big risk to save us," Jack had said.

"We must. You sent by English teacher. You will help us." Anna's eyes had softened, just for a moment.

Anna had not explained, however, what form this 'help' was supposed to take, and exactly how he and Angus, in particular, could possibly bolster the cause of the Southern Slavs. Clearly Pendelshape had mightily impressed them on his visit and any connection with the 'English teacher' meant access to great, if as yet unrevealed, powers. Of course, Jack had not explained to Anna the strange history of Pendelshape, and how they really came to be there. They had also pleaded ignorance about the battle at Schönbrunn. In the moonlight, it had been confusing, and only Jack and Angus knew what had really happened. But even using the extraordinary powers of VIGIL, Inchquin and the Rector would surely have their work cut out to minimise its historical impact.

Anyway, Anna was only interested in one thing. There was no question in her mind as to the righteousness of their mission in Sarajevo. Nothing would persuade her to deviate from her chosen path. Now she was doing it for her brother... as well as her family and her nation. To have this certainty, Jack thought, must be good. It would make everything so... simple.

Jack recalled the conversation that he and Angus had had with Anna on a sleepless moment on the long journey from Vienna.

"Anna, why do you hate them so much? Why do you want to kill the Archduke?" he had asked. There'd been a pause. A shadow had passed across her face and her eyes had moistened.

"You need to understand who I am... where I am from." She had spoken softly – in monotone. It was almost as if she had been trying to distance herself from the words that came out of her mouth. "My family is poor. Some years ago my father had argument with neighbour. One day there was knock at the door... my father was murdered..." Anna wiped a tear from her eye, "in front of me... and Dani." Jack was speechless, but he heard the bitterness in her voice. "To the authorities, it was just another peasant dispute. They do nothing. This 'great power'. And for this we could never forgive. Then they take Dani. And now I want justice."

*

They lay down in the hay and the gentle rocking of the cart finally put them all to sleep. Jack woke up as one of the cart wheels hit a pothole. He didn't know how long they had been going... but it must have been some time, because the dust and smell of the coffee shops of Doboj had long since gone and now they were surrounded by verdant woodland. The road had changed to a rutted and bumpy track.

Jack now pulled himself up from the hay and the grubby-faced boy at the front turned and flashed him a toothy grin. They were in hill country and occasionally through a gap in the trees Jack spotted the ragged outline of the mountains. He breathed in the fresh air. Anna and Angus still slept soundly in the cart and, Jack noticed, that one of Angus's arms had fallen across Anna's waist as they lay side by side. Jack rolled his eyes.

"So how long now, Anna?" Jack said the words deliberately just loud enough, almost shouting, to wake his two companions. Both Anna and Angus jerked up their heads, disorientated and confused. Then Angus's face turned red and he snatched his arm away from Anna. Anna giggled.

It was the first time Jack had seen her smile since Schönbrunn. She pulled herself up onto her knees scanning the track and surrounding country. Content with their progress she leaned over to the boy, ruffled his hair and said something they didn't understand.

"We are nearly there..."

Sure enough, they rounded another bend, and the woodland abruptly thinned out leading into a small valley surrounded by gently rolling hills.

"That's it."

They followed Anna's eyes to one side of the valley where there was a raised plateau. Then they saw it.

"The church?" Angus asked.

"Monastery," Anna confirmed.

As the old wheels of the cart creaked onwards, the monastery came into full view. Jack had visited a couple of famous ruined abbeys near home – Dryburgh, Melrose. Their ruins suggested something much grander than the building in front of them now. The whole structure was enclosed by a large, circular outer wall. Built into the front, was a large bell tower with a pyramidal roof and an arched gateway leading into a main courtyard, with overgrown gardens and a small orchard beyond. On either side of the tower, were simple two-storey structures built into the curved outer walls. The white stone had turned grey in many places, and some parts of the outer wall had collapsed completely. There was a large hole in the sloped roof of one of the buildings, exposing the beams within. The place may have once deserved the label 'monastery' but now it was a ruin and probably deserted. Nevertheless, surrounded by the hills and woods, and with the tower glinting in the late morning sun, it possessed a peaceful beauty.

Just as the cart approached the arched entrance gate, Jack had a powerful sense of déjà vu.

"You know, I think I recognise it... this place." Suddenly the memory was there, "Got it!" He jabbed Angus in excitement, "It's the picture! The picture of the old church – you know, stuck to the map of Bosnia in Dad's workshop... at Cairnfield – remember?"

Angus screwed up his face, "Not sure…" Then he also remembered, "You know what, you're right. Definitely. Definitely this place."

But neither of them could explain it. "Does that mean that Pendelshape… or Dad… maybe, maybe they've been here before?"

They stepped down from the cart but the swaying sensation continued to stay with them. Anna handed the boy some coins and ruffled his hair a final time.

Suddenly, through the entrance a tall thin man with long dark hair and a beard appeared. Anna squealed in excitement and rushed forward to hug him.

"Zadok!"

The man beamed and held Anna in his arms, "We received your message. We are ready…" Zadok held her away from him to look into her eyes, "But Anna… I was so sorry to hear of your loss."

Anna fought back her grief and chose not to respond to the remark. She gestured to Jack and Angus.

Zadok stepped forward and smiled, "Ahh, you are the ones we have been waiting for. Sent by the English teacher. We are honoured." Zadok then did something that completely astonished Jack and Angus. He knelt on one knee before them and kissed each of their hands in turn.

Jack was embarrassed, "It's OK, er, really, you can get up."

Zadok rose to his feet. "I am Zadok. Zadok the priest." He paused theatrically. "We were promised help. Help has come. This is a happy day. Come. You must eat after your long journey."

*

They sat at one end of the old refectory and, through the broken windows, Jack inspected the small, white stone chapel in the centre of the overgrown monastery grounds. Beyond, lay the remains of the cloister that curved round the inner wall on the far side. It was very quiet. Zadok was alone and explained that he had only come up the night before "to prepare everything", as he put it. He and Anna had cooked a simple stew with vegetables and bread and now the empty plates rested in front of them.

"Zadok is from my village," Anna explained. "But you're not really a priest are you Zadok?" she smiled.

"No?" Jack asked.

"No. When the English teacher came he seemed to think it was funny I was called Zadok. Not a Serbian name. He called me 'Zadok the Priest'. It's from the bible."

Jack looked puzzled. "When did you meet Pendel... I mean, the English teacher? What did he do?"

"Dani, Anna and I first met the English teacher – in Belgrade." Zadok's eyes twinkled in excitement, "We were not sure at first. Why an Englishman would want to help the Bosnian Serbs in our cause... We thought he might be a spy... but he knew so much. He knew everyone, he knew everything... it was incredible. On his first visit he warned us that the Austrian police had identified one of the Black Hand and were going to arrest him. He proved to be right and we were able to save him... It was almost as if the English teacher could predict..."

"The future?" Jack finished Zadok's sentence.

"Yes – Jack. Exactly."

"On his second visit, he brought plans."

"What plans?"

"Some of the others – Princip, Ilic, Apis , Grabež, Čabrinović – had an idea to organise a major blow to the oppressors."

"You mean the planned assassination of Franz Ferdinand when he visits Sarajevo – the day after tomorrow?"

"Yes – this was what was finally decided. And the plans are now in place. But the English teacher suggested that we split into two groups. We should operate separately to Princip, just in case one of the groups was infiltrated. Dani, Vaso, Goran and I would form the second group. It was a good idea." His face darkened, "But then we heard that Vaso and Goran were captured at Schönbrunn, and Dani... killed." Anna flinched at the memory and Zadok held her hand gently over the table.

"Were there any more visits by the English teacher?" Jack asked.

"Yes – one last time – only two months ago. He said we needed a base, near Sarajevo."

"This place?"

"Yes – a ruin now of course, and no one comes up in these hills."

"And help?"

Zadok looked at Jack and Angus and smiled, "You two of course..."

Angus looked at Jack again with a worried expression on his face.

"Did, er, the English teacher... well, was he specific about the kind of help that we would provide?"

"No. He had to leave urgently. It was always the case... on each visit he would arrive quite suddenly and then... just disappear. I think it was his way of not arousing the suspicions of the authorities. He just said that near the time, 28th June, the date of the planned assassination, he would send help." Zadok smiled knowingly, "We now know what he meant. He sent you. Two boys and an uncle – the professor. He must have thought that nobody would suspect you." He paused and got to his feet, "And now you are here, you can tell us how it all works..."

"How all what works?"

Zadok smiled, "The English teacher has planned well. He has only given you the minimum amount of information you require and no more. This is so that if you fall into the hands of the authorities and are questioned or tortured... the plan will still be kept secret. Come... I will show you, and then you can explain."

Zadok led them from the table, leaving the empty plates. They followed him down the cloister and past the old chapel. They took the path through the old orchard at the back of the gardens to what looked like some garden sheds. Zadok took a giant key and unlocked an old oak door. The air inside was dry and dusty. Zadok lit a small lamp and the contents of the shed were revealed in shadowy outline. At one end there was a large cupboard. Zadok took another key and turned. The cupboard door creaked open to reveal its extraordinary contents in the flickering lamplight.

Angus and Jack couldn't believe what they saw.

Arms Cache

What they saw before them was a rack of six assault rifles – but they didn't look like rifles from the First World War.

"What are they?" Jack asked.

"L85A2s," Angus replied matter-of-factly.

"What?"

"British army assault rifles. Not the old SA80s, either."

"So they're modern?"

"Bang up to date. British standard. Accurate to 400 metres. Ninety-five point six per cent reliability rating. Probably the best standard assault rifle in the world."

Jack shook his head, "And you call me a boffin."

Zadok opened a second cabinet. It was a veritable arsenal. There were two grenade launchers, two boxes of hand grenades and several ammunition clips.

"You've got enough stuff here to wage a small war... not just kill some archduke with a funny hat..."

"The English teacher has been generous... we are behind the times here, I think, we had no idea such weapons existed... and over here..." Zadok moved to the far end of the room and with an extravagant flourish swept away a mangy dust cover.

Angus's jaw dropped, "Unbelievable..."

"What are they?"

Angus lowered his voice reverentially, "Jack – before you stand two Harley-Davidson MT350Es. American army issue, Rotax engines – four stroke, 30 bhp, 160 kg, 80 mph top end, 255 mm ground clearance..." He turned to Jack. It was as if he was having some sort of religious experience, "Jack... they've even got gun carriers..."

"So…" Zadok said, scarcely able to control his excitement, "The English teacher said you would know…"

"Know what?" Jack asked.

"How it all works."

Angus smiled, eyeing the bikes, "Oh yes, Mr Zadok, we know how it works all right."

"Excellent. The English teacher said this equipment is all modern English designs, the very latest and very best. I am not a military man, so I am afraid I have no idea where to start. But I suggest that Anna and I leave you here to check everything is in working order. Then you will be prepared to carry out the English teacher's instructions. Anna and I will make preparations for the journey to Sarajevo. We should leave after nightfall."

Anna and Zadok left them alone in the dingy outbuilding with its extraordinary array of twenty-first century firepower.

Angus turned to Jack as soon as they had gone, "I hope you know what's going on – 'cos I don't."

Jack was concentrating hard, "So Pendelshape made three visits. Probably in quick succession. On the final trip, he brought all this stuff with him and set up this arms cache."

"But why?"

"It's just as we said, Angus. Pendelshape and Dad's plan was never to help the assassins. Anna and Zadok still don't know it, but the real plan is to betray them. They were going to stop the assassination."

"But why do they need all this… kit?"

Jack shrugged, "Kind of makes sense. The bikes to get to Sarajevo easily and quickly. The weapons need to be good and reliable – just in case anything goes wrong. Remember, there are several potential assassins from the other cell that make their way to Sarajevo… and a whole network of supporters. I guess Dad and Pendelshape needed to be sure if it turned ugly they would be ready. Remember, they might need to hold out without a time signal for quite a while. And not only that…"

"What?"

"Well – Pendelshape and Dad knew that they might not only have to take on the other assassins. They were probably more worried about..."

"VIGIL."

"Right. They couldn't be sure that VIGIL, the Rector and Inchquin, would not find out about their plan, and maybe even spring a trap for them in Sarajevo. So all this stuff," he waved around at the equipment, "was just in case they ran into difficulties. One thing's for sure, Pendelshape and Dad were taking a big risk bringing all this stuff back here."

"Why?"

"Like the Rector said, making any intervention in history may have unforeseen consequences. I would have thought that bringing some of this modern kit back here, even though it is hidden in these ruins, would be a risk. Someone might find them..." Jack's mind raced ahead, "it could trigger anything... the Austrian army, or, or German army, if they got hold of one of those guns, or one of the bikes... they wouldn't understand what they were at first, but they might work out a way to copy them or something..."

"Could give them an edge... a military edge."

"Yeah – these guys are not stupid. If they got hold of all this, then maybe they could win the war. The whole of history would change. We'd be living in a very different future. Did they really think about all these possibilities when they did the computer modelling of how the future might change?"

"I hate to admit it..."

"What?"

"I was wrong, Jack. And your Dad and Pendelshape are wrong. I was taken in by them."

"Got to say, Angus, I think I agree with you. It all sounds too risky. But not only that..." Jack turned to Angus, shaking his head, "ever since we've been on this mad trip, death and destruction have followed us around... it doesn't feel like we're supposed to be here. Doesn't feel right."

"I'm with you on that." Angus picked up a pebble from the dirt floor and flicked it at the wall, "And there's Anna... we can't betray her, can we?"

Jack got to his feet, dusting himself down. "No Angus, I don't think we can. In which case, Dad's not going to be happy with us."

Angus shrugged, "Just say we felt we didn't belong here – you know, none of our business." He reached into his pocket to retrieve the time phone.

"Don't tell me, still dead, right?"

Angus flipped it open. "Dead – apart the usual stuff."

Date: Friday 26th June, 1914
Time: 6.03 p.m.
Location: Ozren, Bosnia-Herzegovina

"Still on our own."

"Apart from Pendelshape."

"Yeah. If he's still out there. But we're doing the right thing coming here with Anna. Pendelshape will want to come to this place… or Sarajevo. He'll know that's where Anna will be taking us."

"Well, I hope he pitches up sooner or later – I want to hear him explain himself – properly this time."

"Right," Jack nodded at the two Harleys, "Will those things work?"

Angus looked them over. "Incredible: keys in the ignitions…" He unscrewed the fuel gauge of one of the bikes and peered in. "Full tank of petrol. They look like they've never been used." He grinned at Jack, "What do you reckon?" He continued in a mock southern US accent, "Shall I fire up this Harley – this old 'Haawg'?"

Soon they had managed to haul both bikes out of the shed. Angus deftly climbed aboard the nearest. "Here goes!"

He turned the ignition and the engine fired immediately. "Bingo!" He revved the engine, "Nice sound, better than my insect two-stroke bike back home." He revved a couple more times and then cut the engine. He shrugged, "So they work… what next?"

"Let's go back up and think about it – decide what to do."

They walked slowly from the shed returning up through the small orchard. The long grass swayed gently in the early evening breeze. At this point the circular outer wall of the monastery was much lower and you could see over it across the untended fields towards the woodland beyond. Angus paused to take in the view.

"Nice here. Bit like home. Hotter though. Look over there – they've even got sheep."

Jack cocked his head, "Miss them, do you?"

"Ha, ha – I'm in stitches."

Jack stopped in his tracks, "Hold on, Angus, what did you say?"

Angus looked at Jack blankly.

"Sheep. You mentioned the sheep," Jack smacked his forehead. "What an idiot I've been!"

"What are you talking about?"

"Sheep… your sheep farm back home… your home… your family… your dad… your great grandfather… you know on the mantelpiece… Ludwig?"

Angus was staring at Jack as if he was mad, "What are you on about?"

"Ludwig. You said that he met your Great Gran Dot, after he was captured by the Brits in the war. This war coming – the First World War."

"Yeah. So?"

"We've been going on about my dad and Pendelshape on one side wanting to stop the war and the Rector, Inchquin and VIGIL on the other side trying to make sure nothing disturbs the past and worrying about who's right and stuff. But that doesn't matter!"

"Doesn't it?"

"Well, yes, it does, of course, but there is something else, much more important – to us… in fact to you, mainly."

Angus was none the wiser.

"Let me spell it out. No assassination equals no First World War equals Ludwig doesn't become a German soldier equals he doesn't get captured by the Brits equals he doesn't meet Great Gran Dot equals they don't get married equals they don't have kids equals you don't exist equals bye bye Angus."

Now Angus got it. He had a look of panic on his face. "What will happen to me?"

"No idea. Maybe you'll go up in a puff of smoke… or be zapped by lightning or, more likely, you just won't exist."

"I don't fancy that much. I mean, I quite like existing…"

"Exactly – mind you it's tough on the rest of us."

"So…"

"So that seals it. Unless Dad and Pendelshape know something that we don't… messing with history will have consequences. And in this case one consequence we know for certain – you won't exist. I can't believe we didn't think of that before."

Angus tried to assimilate the consequences of what Jack had said. He looked thoughtfully at the scrawny sheep chewing away on the hillside, and then lowered his eyes to the trees that fringed the far side of the fields.

Jack frowned, "What's up? He followed Angus's gaze and suddenly his eye caught a glint of metal from within the woods. He narrowed his eyes. There was something there.

"People – there are people in the…" But before he could finish the sentence there was an explosion and a plume of mud erupted from the field just outside the monastery wall.

A moment later there was a second explosion. This time closer. A whole section of the monastery's outer wall was blown apart. Ahead, Zadok and Anna were pelting towards them, shouting, "Soldiers! The Austrian army's here!"

A third shell whistled overhead and landed in the refectory building, which promptly collapsed.

"They've got artillery. We've got to get out of here!" Angus shouted. "Only one option."

"You mean the bikes."

Jack's heart sank as they turned back to get their bikes. He remembered his motorbike experience back at Angus's farm. It hadn't gone well. The Harleys were bigger and heavier. And there was another difference – on Angus's farm they hadn't been under artillery bombardment.

The field gun in the woods had found its range and its crew was now delivering projectiles into the monastery with impressive regularity. The troops in the wood stayed low – they wanted the occupants of the monastery cowed into submission before moving in.

They were not in a hurry.

Angus had his bike going. Jack copied Angus but felt very precarious perched high above the ground on the saddle. It took all his strength to hold the machine at an angle so one of his feet could touch the ground. With a light push from his left foot he checked neutral and turned the ignition. The Harley roared into life beneath him.

"Let's go!" Angus yelled.

They powered back up the path through the orchard towards Anna and Zadok. Angus halted his bike expertly next to Anna and scooped her up to ride pillion. Jack realised that he was expected to repeat the procedure with Zadok.

"Angus – I can't manage a passenger!"

Angus swivelled round, "You must!"

There was another explosion, this time in the bell tower. With a muffled, distorted clanging, rubble and timber crashed down around the old bell. The whole structure swayed, but for the moment the tower and the arched entrance beneath stayed intact.

"Come on then."

Zadok clambered aboard. The extra weight dampened the suspension and made the bike lower and marginally easier for Jack. He pulled in the clutch lever, kicked down to select first and pulled back the throttle. The engine roared. Angus was already away, heading for the archway, Anna clinging on behind him. Jack let out the clutch lever, but this time far too quickly, and the whole machine jerked forward, the engine immediately stalling. He groaned.

There was a sharp whistling through the air and another explosion, so close this time that it peppered them with great clumps of dirt.

Jack was starting to panic. He could feel Zadok's heavy breathing on the back of his neck. Again, he selected neutral, turned the ignition, and the four stroke burst back into life. He stabbed down on the gear pedal a second time. Now they could hear voices. The soldiers were emerging from the gun position in the woods and gingerly picking their way across the open fields towards the burning monastery. An officer barked orders. Jack's palms were sweaty and he was having difficulty holding onto the grips. Through a supreme effort of self control he pulled back the throttle more gently this time, the engine tone increased, and he let the clutch out carefully. The knobbly back tyre slewed momentarily on the gritted path, and then, miraculously, it gripped and they were away. Jack was exhilarated. He twisted the throttle some more and the bike responded eagerly. He pulled in the clutch again and kicked up into second. They were in business.

Angus had stopped under the archway, revving his machine. It provided momentary cover from the bombardment and a temporary blind spot from the approaching soldiers. Both Angus and Anna craned round to check on Jack and Zadok's progress.

"Come on!" Angus shouted.

Soon, Jack had drawn parallel with Angus's bike and the two of them waited beneath the stone archway. They looked back at the monastery – fire was taking hold everywhere. A final shell whistled in over the heads of the approaching soldiers in the fields and slammed into the shed, which housed the arsenal. There was a moment of quiet and then the whole structure wobbled briefly before the final explosion.

"There goes the arms cache."

"And with it, the evidence that Pendelshape was here."

"You ready for this?" Angus said.

"No," Jack replied.

"Well, you'll have to be. We've only got one chance. Soon as I say 'go' let's hit it. Hard."

Angus twisted his throttle. "Go!"

Angus red-lined each gear in turn as he and Anna screamed off down the track away from the monastery gate, a plume of dust rising high into the air behind them. Jack, trying not to think, crouched low on the bike, gunned his engine and set off in pursuit.

To the right of the farm track leading to the monastery, soldiers were fanned out across the fields – about twenty of them. As soon as they saw the bikes, there was wild consternation. But Jack and Angus were quick. In ten seconds the track would lead them into the forest. They had a clear run. But suddenly, three uniformed soldiers emerged from the woods, on the track thirty metres ahead. They were staring straight at the two bikes bearing down on them and fumbling clumsily for their rifles. Jack's heart sank, but then, only ten metres ahead of him, he heard Angus drop a gear and the four-stroke MT350E wailed. Suddenly, the front wheel of Angus's machine popped high into the air and, with Angus standing proud on the foot rests, and a rather surprised Anna clinging desperately to his torso, his friend pulled a twenty metre wheelie straight at the unfortunate soldiers, who dived for cover. In five seconds it was over, the front wheel touched down again and Angus was through and into the cover of the woods, closely followed by Jack, who now sported a very wide grin. He heard Zadok behind him whoop in delight and he slapped Jack on the back as they powered on.

"Well done, my friend!"

Suddenly, there was a crack behind them, curiously muffled by the dense woodland and the roar of the bike engines. One of the soldiers had risen from the mud and just managed to let loose a single rifle shot. It caught Zadok square in the back with the force of a pile driver. For a moment, Jack didn't know what had happened. He twisted round, but Zadok was already slumped behind him, the pressure of his grip around Jack's torso weaker.

"You must go on Jack. I have done my part. You go."

With a supreme effort, Zadok, rose from the saddle and pushed himself free from the moving bike, landing in the ditch at the side of the track.

Jack looked back in horror, and brought the bike to a sharp halt. Zadok was still breathing, and looked up at him weakly, "Go!" He groaned.

The soldiers were now running hell for leather down the track towards them. One was kneeling and aiming his rifle. It bucked in his hands and Jack felt the bullet whistle past his head. Ahead, Angus had gone, leaving only exhaust fumes in his wake. Jack couldn't wait. "I'm sorry, Zadok."

Jack revved the engine, dropped the clutch and powered off down the woodland track in pursuit of Angus and Anna.

Sarajevo
Showdown

This was the day. Sunday 28th June 1914. Archduke Franz Ferdinand and his wife Sophie would soon pass right before Jack and Angus in a procession of cars on their royal visit to Sarajevo. The town of Sarajevo was set in the centre of a great bowl surrounded by mountains – the lower slopes wooded, the higher ones heath land. Jack thought he would be entering a European town, but he had been struck by the number of minarets. This really felt like a divided city. People spoke a number of different languages and they wore different clothes. Even at night their customs were varied. Anna had explained, "...the clock of the Catholic cathedral strikes at two a.m. Shortly after, you'll hear the bell of the Eastern Orthodox Church and later, the Sahat Tower near Beg's Mosque. The Sahat strikes eleven times, Turkish time. Even when everyone is asleep, the counting of the hours shows we are all different..."

*

Jack, Angus and Anna had made good their escape from the monastery. Anna knew the hills well and had found them a shepherd's hut above Sarajevo where they could spend a fitful night. Early on Saturday morning, they had sunk the two bikes in a woodland lake. As the last bubbles floated to the surface, Jack worried that Angus was going to cry. They had walked the remaining distance to Sarajevo. With the raid on the monastery and the death of Zadok, the second assassination cell, set up by Pendelshape and Jack's father, had been fatally compromised. Anna had decided to take a risk and contact the main assassination group in Sarajevo, following a pre-arranged emergency plan. Jack and Angus had little choice but to follow.

Their rendezvous was with only two of the gang – Princip and Ilic. It took place in the rundown Café Miljacka in a dusty back street. Jack had not known quite what to expect from his first encounter with the assassins, particularly Princip, about whom he had heard and read so much. Here was a man who was unknown to the world now, but within twenty-four hours would become a household name. The meeting was inauspicious. Princip was skinny and somewhat dishevelled with dark eyes and a thin moustache. He was furtive and nervous. Communication was difficult. A package was handed over at the meeting. Inside was one of the few pistols that had been smuggled into Bosnia with the gang. It wasn't clear from the meeting what Jack and Angus's role was to be... but it was obviously assumed that, because of their association with Pendelshape, if all else failed, they would intervene in a way that would ensure that the Black Hand would succeed. After only twenty minutes, the meeting ended.

*

Now, standing behind a growing crowd of people on the Appel Quay, Jack thought it incredible that he knew precisely the course of events that was about to unfold. He was already aware of every detail of the Archduke Franz Ferdinand's visit – he had seen it all in *Point-of-Departure*. In just a few minutes Franz Ferdinand and his wife, Sophie, would die.

Suddenly, in the distance, they heard a muted explosion. A ripple of consternation ran through the crowd. Voices were raised; there was confusion. A car drove rapidly down the road, then a second. There were a few muted cheers as a third car passed. Jack caught a fleeting glance of hat feathers and finery over the heads in front of him... then the Archduke and Sophie and their pursuing entourage were gone. There was a rumour in the crowd that a bomb had been thrown at the Archduke, but the would-be assassin had been mobbed by the crowd, and the Archduke was bravely continuing with the tour...

After a while, out of the corner of his eye, Jack saw the unmistakable figure of Princip furtively cross the Appel Quay and disappear into Moritz Schiller's delicatessen. The entourage had passed on its way to the presentation at the Town Hall and Princip thought that he had missed his opportunity. Bizarrely, he had decided to get some early lunch. Jack followed Princip and took up position next to the shop, just back from the road. Angus followed a few paces behind. Jack scanned the crowd. If VIGIL guards were in Sarajevo, they were well hidden.

"Jack, we must do something!" the urgent voice startled Jack.

It was Anna. She had left her position by the Čumurja Bridge. She was out of breath. Her face was flushed and her dark hair dishevelled.

"Our bomb missed, Čabrinović is captured, the others have fled. It is only us and Gavrilo left…" She was distraught.

Jack reassured her, "It will be OK."

She looked pleadingly into his eyes with the same desperate expression on her face that she had had as she held her brother's lifeless head.

The mayor's car rumbled round the corner and passed them as it turned into Franz Joseph Street. It was leading the procession back from the presentation at the Town Hall. A second car followed carrying the Archduke and Sophie. The big headlamps and fender of the Graf und Stift lumbered round the corner from the Appel Quay. It was slowing down – the driver had taken a wrong turn and was not following the route straight out of Sarajevo, which had been hastily rearranged following the earlier bomb assault. They could clearly see all the occupants, including, in the rear, perched up high, the Archduke and, to his left, Sophie. A man was leaning over to the driver telling him something.

Gavrilo Princip emerged from the delicatessen, a sandwich in one hand. There was a look of astonishment on his face as the Archduke's car ground to a halt, delivering Princip's target to within a couple of metres. He dropped his sandwich and reached into his coat pocket. He quickly looked around, and as he did so, just for a split second, his dark, wild eyes caught those of Jack only feet away. Jack felt a sudden twinge of doubt. He could stop Princip right there and now. His mind flashed back to the family holiday when he was small – the visit to the war graves. He remembered the endless sea of white crosses and in his head the image fused with the pictures of the war from his father's history book – all the horror and suffering laid out in black and white. He could feel the pistol that had been given to him the day before nestling next to his chest. He could shoot Princip now. He slipped one hand into his inside pocket and felt the cold metal. His fingers closed round the weapon…

Suddenly, from across the road, two burly police officers broke from the crowd and advanced towards Jack. They had spotted the suspicious movement of his hand to his inside pocket and, taking no chances, they were now moving menacingly towards him. Jack spotted them and quickly snatched back his hand, leaving the gun snugly in place. But Princip had ignored Jack and had already turned towards the Archduke's car. He levelled his pistol, then he fired – two shots in quick succession.

Sophie slumped onto the knee of the Archduke. For a moment, the Archduke remained upright, but then blood from his neck wound started to spurt from his mouth and he listed into unconsciousness.

*

Chaos. The crowd quickly realised what had happened and turned on Princip. Jack, Angus and Anna were engulfed by the angry crowd and Jack felt himself being jostled and harried. The officers were wading into the melee to make sure no one escaped.

"Run!" Angus shouted.

He lowered his head and barrelled through the crowd. Jack and Anna followed in his wake. The crowd thinned, and in an instant they broke free into the open street. For a moment Angus hesitated, not knowing which way to turn. Anna took up the lead. Jack stole a glance behind him and saw that two officers were hot on their heels.

"Down here!"

Anna sprinted down a dusty side street where a market was in progress, Jack and Angus still following closely behind. Quite unexpectedly, a cloaked figure stepped from the shadow of a doorway, into their path. They clattered straight into him. Without hesitation, the man somehow bundled them each through the doorway and into a small storeroom. The man checked each way up the street, and, satisfied that the pursuers had been temporarily shaken off, stepped

The Archduke and Sophie leave the Town Hall moments before they are assassinated

SARAJEVO
28TH JUNE, 1914

POSITIONS OF THE CONSPIRATORS

1. Mehmedbašić
2. Čubrilović
3. Čabrinović (throws bomb)
4. Ilić
5. Popović
6. Princip (first position)
7. Princip (second position, shoots Archduke Franz Ferdinand and Sophie)
8. Grabež
9. Jack, Angus and Anna's final position

R.C. CATHEDRAL

FRANZ JOSEPH ST.

To Museum

Miljačka River

LATEINER BRIDGE

KAISER BRIDGE

ČUMURJA BRIDGE

KONAK

To the Station & Hospital

KEY

Route actually taken by Franz Ferdinand

Route planned before bomb attack

Route planned after bomb attack

Jack, Angus and Anna's escape route

back into the room and closed the door behind him. His hair was ruffled, his face was a little dirty and his clothes creased and in places were torn. But the face was unmistakable. Dr Pendelshape.

*

Anna was breathing hard but she was also smiling and had a tear in her eye. But this time it was a tear of happiness. She rushed over to hug Pendelshape.

"We did it," she said.

Anna, of course, had no idea what horrors her friends, the assassins of Sarajevo, had unleashed. She only knew that some sort of justice had finally been done for the crimes against her family.

Pendelshape smiled, "So it would seem, my dear, but I'm afraid I arrived a little late for all the action." He looked across at the boys, who were dusting themselves down, "Well, I am glad to see that you have all become acquainted – it was just as I hoped." He gestured to some crates in one corner of the storeroom, "There, take a seat. We will be safe in here for a short while – but not for long. The police will be here soon, I'm sure. But first things first." He removed his cloak and turned to Anna, "Now my dear, I fear that the authorities will be quickly upon you and your friends. You must flee Sarajevo immediately. Now I am here, I will take care of the boys. Don't worry about us."

Anna opened her mouth to speak, but Pendelshape put up his hand to silence her.

"There is no time, my dear. Trust me Anna – you are in great danger. Look here, I have brought you some money," he presented her with a leather wallet, "please – take it. You will need to start a new life… away from all of this. I'm sorry this is so sudden, but it is the only way. You must go. Now."

Anna looked at the wallet and then at Pendelshape, not knowing what to do.

Pendelshape chided her, "Please Anna… you must go. You are in danger. They will be searching all the cafés and houses. You have done what you came here to do."

She nodded and reluctantly took the wallet, "I understand. Thank you." She smiled, turned and without looking back slipped through the door into the dust and heat of Sarajevo. Anna was gone.

*

"How did you get here?" Jack asked.

"Probably like you. With difficulty," Dr Pendelshape replied.

"We didn't stop the assassination, you know… as you wanted." Angus said.

"I know. It was perhaps too much to expect. I'm afraid I arrived too late from Vienna to help." Pendelshape reached into his jacket, pulled out his time phone and flipped the device open, "The good news is that we have a time signal. Now we are together, we can finally travel back to your father's base, get you safely away from VIGIL and then think about how we can complete our objective. We will be coming back to 1914 – as soon as we have dealt with VIGIL once and for all."

Jack felt numb. He could hear Pendelshape's words but they did not register. He could only think about the murder he had just witnessed. The wild look in Princip's eyes before he turned his gun on the Archduke, the flashes from the muzzle of the pistol, the muffled cracks as the shots rang out, Sophie slumping forward and the blood from the Archduke's neck… The sequence repeated itself again and again in his head.

Pendelshape had no idea what they had been through these last few days. The deaths that Jack had seen on their journey – the professor, Dani, Zadok and now, finally, the Archduke and his wife… it was too much. Jack glanced over at Angus. He sat on the dusty crate, just staring into the gloom of the musty storeroom. He looked pale and drawn. This wasn't like playing some sort of super bonus round of *Point-of-Departure*, where you had to get three gold stars on every level. This was real.

Pendelshape sensed Jack's unease, "Look – I understand – I know you have endured a lot. We all have." Jack stared back at him blankly. Pendelshape sighed, "In truth we don't have much time, but it might help if I tell you our side of the story… perhaps then you might understand a little better."

Jack shrugged.

*

"I was always on your father's side. Taurus gives us the chance to change the world for the better. We must be careful, but used with precision, we now have the tools to do infinite good. But Inchquin and the Rector poisoned the rest of the team against your father. They thought that it was wrong to meddle with history – even though our computer technology is highly effective at modelling the consequences of interventions. They still thought it was too risky. So as soon as we knew that the Taurus at the school worked, they closed the whole thing down. Put in place rules, protocols, all codified in the VIGIL Imperative. But they still remained suspicious of your father – they knew he wouldn't come over to their point of view. He remained a risk. So eventually..." he paused.

"Eventually, what?" Angus asked.

"They tried to get rid of him for good."

"What – kill Dad?" Jack said.

"Yes, Jack. And they nearly succeeded. So he disappeared when you were just eight and became a fugitive. I remained at the school, I had pretended to side with VIGIL, but I was secretly loyal to him. That is why your father had to leave you and your mum, Jack. I'm afraid that's why you have had to grow up without him. It's not what he wanted. Not at all."

*

"In exile, it took your father a long time to recreate the Taurus... the machine that sent first Angus back to rescue you and then me, in that wretched tank. I took risks to help your father by channelling information to him. The work took many years. But from our earlier research we had already pinpointed a moment in time where we knew we could make a massive beneficial change in the course of world history."

"Sarajevo, 28th June, 1914," Jack said. "Today."

"Exactly. The twentieth century was mankind's bloodiest and that date – today's date – was the trigger. It needn't have happened. We conducted three short expeditions – using the Taurus at the school during the testing phase – just before your father left. That's how I infiltrated the Black Hand and the assassins, met Anna and Dani and set up the second cell, led by Zadok. We were going to return, having laid the groundwork, and then disrupt the assassination to prevent the war. Of course, before we finalised the plan, we created many detailed computer simulations of the various interventions in time that we might make and how they might affect the future."

"Timeline Simulations."

"Yes. I remember when we cracked it..."

"Don't tell me – Simulation 0107. The wallchart that was missing from Dad's workshop at Cairnfield?"

"Yes. This was the scenario that optimised the future most effectively. It started with stopping the Sarajevo assassination."

"Then your plan failed because Dad had to escape from VIGIL."

"But when your father told me that he had perfected his own Taurus, he asked me to bring you to him so you would be safe. There was little time. So I decided to use the school Taurus once more to hide us in history – in 1914 in fact. The school Taurus was already configured for that period – from the earlier tests."

"You knew you had to take me with you because if VIGIL had me captive – they could threaten Dad."

"Yes. But we would escape from the school and you would be safe. Before leaving I would invoke a programme that would wipe all the Taurus's control discs after we'd gone – remove all the software, documentation and design, and wipe all the back-up devices. Without the software or documentation, Taurus is just a useless lump of metal. At that point your father and I would have the only working Taurus and VIGIL would be impotent. I had passed our time phone codes to your father – so once we had escaped he would be able to track us and pick us up with his Taurus. Nothing could stop us then. We had it all worked out."

"But then the Rector found out. He intercepted Dad's message."

"In our excitement, we made a stupid mistake. Once they knew that your father had built his own time machine they were very concerned. They thought he had disappeared. Over the years VIGIL had ceased to be worried about him – and they certainly never suspected me."

"So they moved in – just as you were about to tell us your plan in the Taurus control room at school."

"But you escaped, not surprisingly, scared to death by the Rector and the VIGIL thugs, and we were in a completely new situation. It was unplanned."

"Then you and Angus were rescued by Dad..."

"Your father knew we might need back up. Over the years he has recruited a few very loyal supporters," Pendelshape nodded proudly at Angus, "And Angus kindly agreed to rescue you from the castle."

Angus looked down sheepishly, not sure whether to be proud of his actions or not.

"Why did you send Angus alone?" Jack asked.

"We didn't! Angus was included because we knew you would trust him. He wanted to come. But the signal failed as we were sending the rest of the team. The time phone signals are intermittent. It has always been a problem. The next signal was at Schönbrunn and when we got a fix on Angus's time phone we had a second chance."

"The tank?"

Pendelshape smiled, "A German Tiger tank from the Second World War. Your father has got a little collection of historical artefacts. And it did the job – or at least it diverted VIGIL sufficiently for you to escape." For a moment, doubt flashed across his face, "Near thing though..." He leaned over so the boys could see the top of his bald head. "See... burned off the remains of my hair."

Pendelshape chortled – he seemed to think that it was quite funny – but Jack didn't, "I don't think you understand. There are people we have met here... who helped us, who were good to us. Real people..."

"Right, sir, and three of them are dead now," Angus added bluntly.

Pendelshape replied dismissively, "Yes, yes. I am not saying any of this is easy..."

This was too much for Jack. He felt anger welling up inside him. "You can't just say that. The professor, he was our friend, he saved my life." Jack shivered at the memory of the professor's death. "Don't you get it?" Jack was finding it difficult to control himself... "And Anna... she rescued us from Inchquin... her brother was murdered... right before our eyes..."

"With a lance," Angus added.

"And Zadok – who blindly trusted you – if he hadn't been there, the bullet that killed him would have hit me!"

Pendelshape snapped back, waving his time phone, "I'm afraid this time signal won't wait for us to complete this philosophical debate." Angus and Jack glared at him and Pendelshape sighed impatiently, "Sorry – look – I understand that you have witnessed some bad things... I'm sorry... and I know your father is as well. This is not how either of us had intended the mission to work out. But there is so much more at stake than one or two deaths..." Pendelshape turned to Jack, "I can see that this is difficult for you. But your father wants you to follow him. Our desire is that you join us willingly. You can help us achieve a great deal. You can help us change the world." The boys continued to look unimpressed. Pendelshape rubbed his chin. "Maybe I need to show you how much is at stake here." He was mulling something over in his head. "Indeed. To convince you, perhaps I need to show you the consequences of today's events – give you a real history lesson, if you will."

He peered into the time phone and started to tap away.

"What are you doing?"

"Well, Angus, it is quite simple, we need to return to Jack's father's base. We can't stay here. But we can make a little detour," he paused. "Yes, I know exactly where we should go..." Pendelshape murmured to himself, "I believe there was a large field hospital at that point behind the allied front line... Now, if I can just code the right space-time fix..."

Jack and Angus exchanged nervous glances as Pendelshape busied himself with the time phone.

"Sir – are you planning what I think you're planning? Because if you are, I don't think that's a good idea at all, in fact I think..."

Suddenly, the door of the storeroom flew off its rusty hinges in a storm of splintering wood. A young Austrian army officer stood in the doorway brandishing a pistol.

Pendelshape looked up from the time phone and spoke quietly, "Well boys – I am afraid whatever you think, it looks like we have little choice."

"Good afternoon, officer…" Pendelshape said. The officer seemed a little taken aback by Pendelshape's confident English voice and eyed them suspiciously. "Come on boys – close in – hands on the time phone," Pendelshape whispered out of the corner of his mouth.

The boys did what they were told but, alarmed by the sudden movement, the officer shouted an order and raised his pistol to shoot.

Mud and Guts

The shock wave from the air burst caught Jack full on, lifted him up and threw him backwards a full six metres, his body twisting in mid air as he flew. Gravity pulled him back to earth, but where there should have been churned-up mud to cushion his landing, there was nothing. Instead, he was propelled into a huge empty space on the ground. With a crunching thud, his face, and then the rest of his body, hit the sloping inner wall of a large hole. As he slid down, mud filled his ears, nostrils and mouth. He came to rest in a large puddle in the bottom of the hole.

Pendelshape's plan to give Jack and Angus an impromptu lesson in the horror of war was looking like a very bad idea indeed. With his encyclopedic knowledge of the First World War, it had sounded like he was aiming for some field hospital way behind the allied lines. But with the intrusion of the Austrian officer things had not gone according to plan. The time travel technology had placed them slam in the middle of no-man's-land during a major British offensive.

Just as they had landed, there had been an ear-splitting explosion and Jack had suddenly become airborne. He didn't even know if Angus and Pendelshape had survived the blast. And now, here he was at the bottom of some putrid hole in the ground.

Suddenly, on the other side of the puddle, Jack saw two eyes staring back at him from a mud-freckled face. The figure opposite was lying against the side of the crater, caked in dirt. From his uniform and helmet, Jack recognised immediately that he was German. But judging by his pink skin and the fear on his face it was clear that he was more a boy than a man. Above the boy's knee, Jack could make out a large dark patch. The boy-soldier was wounded. At that point

Day of the Assassins

Jack realised with dismay that within his white, fragile, boy-fingers, the soldier held a large black pistol. It was pointing at Jack.

He felt panic start to build from the pit of his stomach. The boy was as terrified as Jack was, but nevertheless, Jack could see his index finger slowly squeezing the trigger of the pistol. There was a yellow flash and a loud crack as the gun fired. Jack braced himself – but the impact from the bullet didn't come. Instead, it had buried itself in the wall of earth to his left. The boy held the pistol up again, this time both index fingers wrapped round the trigger and squeezed a second time… there was a click. The gun was empty.

At that moment, a second German soldier loomed from behind the lip of the crater. Even at that distance, Jack could see that he was stockier than the boy opposite. The soldier surveyed the scene and quickly descended into the crater moving with speed and confidence. Reaching the bottom of the hole, he bypassed his young comrade and marched directly through the puddle to where Jack lay. The soldier reached down to the bayonet hanging on his belt and fastened it to the end of his rifle, which he now lifted up and pinned under Jack's chin. Jack was helpless. This was it.

Suddenly, out of the corner of his eye, Jack detected a large, fast-moving blur descend from his side of the crater. The German soldier half-turned, momentarily distracted. The blur moved with uncanny speed. Jack recognised the figure. Angus! The soldier had no time to react. Angus launched at him with a crunching rugby tackle. Jack was first to his feet and grabbed the soldier's rifle. The tables were turned.

The soldier stared back defiantly from his prostrate position on the crater floor. Then he reached to grab something from his back.

"Don't even think about it," warned Jack, raising the rifle and inching the glistening bayonet towards the soldier's face. He thrust the bayonet forward – instinctively copying the soldier's action against himself a few seconds earlier. But Jack misjudged, and the serrated steel edge of the seven-inch blade made contact with the lobe of the soldier's right ear, slicing right through it. The soldier whimpered in fear. Jack recoiled – alarmed at the ease with which the injury had been inflicted. Angus was now up on his feet. The soldier stared, pleadingly, first at Jack and then Angus standing next to him. A moment before, he had seemed like an automaton – a killing machine. But now he was helpless and terrified. Contrary to what Jack had first thought, he could not have been that much older than either Jack or the boy soldier who still sat quivering on the opposite side of the crater. And there was something else about the soldier lying at their feet, something about the face… and now with the injured ear… Something odd. Jack waved the rifle and shouted a second time.

"Go! Go on, get out of here!"

For a moment, the soldier looked confused and stared back at them questioningly.

Jack raised his voice, "Go! Now! The British will be here soon."

Euphoria spread across the soldier's face – it was if he had been re-born and his humanity restored. He scrambled to his feet and staggered through the water to the other side of the crater. He stopped briefly to haul his young comrade to his feet. Then, supporting his friend, he clambered up the opposite side of the crater and away.

Jack was shaking, "Er, thanks Angus."

Angus was silent and stared at the opposite side of the crater.

"You OK? Look like you've seen a ghost."

"I think I might have."

"What?"

"That soldier… I'm sure…" Angus stopped mid-sentence and rubbed his eyes. "Doesn't matter… Come on, we can't hang around. It's dangerous here."

"Where's Pendelshape – did he make it?"

Angus jerked his head to one side, "He's behind me. He's OK."

They looked round, and sure enough, Pendelshape's head loomed into view above them on the crater lip.

"Come on boys – the bombardment has stopped. We need to get out of here."

"Really? I thought we might hang around and maybe do a bit of shopping," Angus said to Jack as they dragged themselves back up to the top of the crater. The smoke was clearing steadily and a weak sun was starting to wink through. They seemed to be on a slightly raised part of the battlefield.

Jack couldn't believe his eyes. They were in the middle of some sort of extraordinary lifeless moonscape of craters and mud as far as the eye could see. There were no trees, there was no grass… nothing. On either side of them in some places not more than a hundred metres apart, embankments of earth signifying the position of the two armies' front line trenches, snaked towards the horizon. Barbed wire was strung out along each trench – in some places there were gaps where it had been cut or blown apart. As Jack gained his bearings, he began to notice that, strewn haphazardly about the landscape, were dead bodies. In some cases their position was only signified by a discarded rifle or a helmet or a flapping piece of material. But they were there. And it was clear that some of them had been there for a long time. He'd been staring for ten seconds. But he'd already had enough.

"Look – they're retreating," Pendelshape gestured over to the German lines. In the distance they could make out the figures of hundreds of men picking their way from the German front line. "They're evacuating following the bombardment. Come on… we can take refuge in there."

They followed Pendelshape and careered forward thirty metres to the German lines. First Pendelshape and then Jack tumbled over the side, landing on the fire step above the bottom of the badly waterlogged trench.

"It stinks in here," Angus said.

Pendelshape glanced left and then right. The trench was deserted apart from a single corpse that lay face down in the water only metres from where they had landed.

"Quick – over there."

A small bunker had been honed from the earth on the opposite side of the trench and they stepped inside gingerly. A makeshift bed had been set up in the subterranean room and there was even a small table and chairs. There were papers strewn everywhere and a chess set lay on the table with the pieces scattered.

"Should be safe here for a moment."

Jack sat down on one of the chairs, "I've had enough. Let's see the time phones... now!"

First Angus, then Pendelshape placed their time phones on the table. The telltale yellow bar on each of them was burning fiercely.

"We still have a signal – we can get out of here. Now!"

Pendelshape seemed to hesitate, "Well, hold on..."

Jack was incredulous. "You're not seriously suggesting that we hang around?"

"Well, now we are here..."

Angus interrupted him, "Sorry, sir – you're mad if you think we're staying."

"Yes – I think we've seen enough already," Jack added.

Pendelshape replied, "Good. As you have now observed, the consequences of war are indeed horrific... so we can travel back... back to your father now?"

Jack couldn't believe it. Pendelshape seemed to be almost... smiling. It was at that moment, seeing that smile, that Jack knew he couldn't go along with Pendelshape or, for that matter, his father.

Jack spoke calmly but there was steel in his voice, "In the last week, we have been shot at, chased half way around Europe and seen three good people... friends... die and now you've brought us here. You and Dad have taken terrible risks with our lives and those of many others... for your own... ambition."

Pendelshape stood up, "But we have to change history; we have to change it so it's all better, so it's all good... don't you see? We must..."

"You might think you have to, so might Dad. But I don't."

"What do you mean?"

Jack's heart was pounding, "We don't want anything to do with this. We've got our own lives to lead. We belong in the present and we should stay there," Jack tried to steady his voice, "Look – I think what you and Dad have done is..." he shook his head, "...incredible. Really. Creating the Taurus. All that. But it's dangerous. Just one example – Angus and I worked out that if we had done what you and Dad planned – he wouldn't even exist."

Pendelshape waved his hand dismissively, "We can fix that… it would just be another variant of Simulation 0107…"

"The point is: we belong in the present. I know that puts me at the mercy of the Rector and Inchquin and VIGIL."

Pendelshape was incredulous, "What? But they might kill you!"

"No they won't. They would only threaten that if you and Dad were to use your Taurus. If you don't – they won't touch a hair on my head. So it's simple, really. If you and Dad promise not to use your Taurus, then we will be safe… We'll be left alone."

Pendelshape stared back at him goggle-eyed, "So you're going to make yourself a willing hostage to VIGIL? And stop us fulfilling our life's work?"

"It's nothing to do with you or your life's work. It's to do with us. I'm doing it because in the last few days we've already seen too much death – more than enough to last a lifetime. I don't want any more. The past should stay where it belongs – in the past."

Jack knew what he was saying was right.

"So, you set your time phone to go back to Dad's base. We need never know where it is – so VIGIL will never know and you'll be safe. I know you've also got the codes for the other Taurus at school. So you set Angus's time phone so me and Angus can travel back to school. Simple…"

"But…"

"And do it now before we lose the time signal again," Angus said.

"I can't – your father… He will never forgive me."

But seeing the expression on the boys' faces, Pendelshape knew his cause was finally lost. He leaned over the time phones and started to tap.

"Good. Hurry up."

From outside the bunker they heard a distant whistle.

"What's that?"

"The British are going over the top. They'll be here in a minute."

Angus breathed into Pendelshape's ear, "Well you'd better get on with it!"

"I'm going as fast as I can!"

Jack jerked his head at Angus to move away from Pendelshape.

Suddenly, there was an explosion further along the trench.

"What was that?"

"A shell?"

"Or a grenade?"

"The Brits must be here already."

Angus turned back to Pendelshape, "How long?"

"A minute… at most." Pendelshape was sweating.

"Go faster!"

"You're not helping."

There was a sudden commotion from outside the trench.

A British voice shouted, "Check down that end, Corporal!"

"They're clearing the trench," Jack said. "We must hurry – they won't take any chances – they'll just assume we're the enemy…"

At last, Pendelshape lifted his head and slid Angus's time phone across the table, keeping the other for himself.

He had a sad look in his eyes, "It's recoded. You can go home."

"No funny business, right?" Angus said.

Pendelshape looked resigned and shrugged, "No. I am disappointed, and your father will be too, Jack. We may not see each other again. Certainly not for double history."

Jack flipped open the time phone. The bar was still shining bright yellow.

The British voices were now very close.

"In there, Corporal! I heard someone!"

"Any grenades left, Jim?" There was a pause. "Good – just chuck it in!"

The door to the bunker flew open and a grenade rolled menacingly across the floor towards them.

Angus moved close to Jack so that they were both touching the time phone. Jack put an arm round his friend's shoulders and stabbed the time phone with his thumb. There was a flash as the grenade exploded.

Rising Son

Jack looked up at the massive dinosaur. Two eye sockets, way above, leered down at him from a large white skull. If the creature had still been in possession of its prehistoric eyes, maybe it would have winked at him, knowingly. Instead the vast skull and the huge skeleton, to which it was attached, hung there lifelessly – a monument to past glory. Normally, Jack liked this place. Particularly the dinosaur exhibit. The Royal Edinburgh Museum. He liked its open spaces and polished floors and the hushed voices that would echo through the exhibition halls. You could happily wander around for hours, lost to the world. But today, he knew there would be no time for that.

*

"So why did we end up here?" Angus asked for about the fifth time.

"I told you – no idea. Just be grateful that the grenade didn't get us before we escaped and we got back to approximately the right time and location."

"Close one. Do you think Pendelshape made it?"

"I should think so. He pressed at the same time as us."

"Wonder if we'll see him again," Angus said ruefully.

Jack sniffed, "Wonder if I'll ever see my dad again."

"Sorry Jack – you know what I mean."

"Sure. No matter."

The clock at the end of the large entrance hall struck seven p.m. In thirty minutes the museum would close for the evening.

"Where are they? They should be here by now."

*

The Taurus had dumped Jack and Angus in the toilets of the Royal Edinburgh Museum – thoughtfully the Gents and not the Ladies. It took them a little while to work out where, and when, they were.

Finally, they made it to the large marble-floored reception area. The calendar indicated 14th October. Only the day after he had made his original fateful decision to use the Taurus to escape the Rector back at the school.

The receptionist did not quite know what to think of the two mud-caked teenagers, but she allowed them to use the phone. Jack called his mum. He could tell that she was immensely relieved to hear from him, and now she and VIGIL were on their way. They waited patiently in the hall, trying, with difficulty, to look inconspicuous.

*

Jack spotted his mum first. She was running towards him, arms outstretched and soon he was in her arms. Close behind followed the Rector who was smiling broadly and then his two old friends, Tony and Gordon, who stood back at a respectful distance. Thankfully, they were in their janitor's uniforms and unarmed – assault rifles weren't generally permitted inside the Royal Edinburgh Museum.

Soon they were aboard the school minibus speeding back home. It seemed a rather modest form of transport, compared to what they had been used to. And now their lives would be one long secret – to keep the mystery of the school, the extraordinary technology within it and the powerful people entrusted with its control – carefully hidden from the rest of the world.

In the back seat, Jack and Angus were wedged between the large frames of Tony and Gordon. Angus had dropped off to sleep. As they sped along, Tony punched Jack in the upper arm, with, Jack thought, rather more force than was necessary. In fact, it hurt. He looked up at Tony and his glare was returned with a wide, yellow-toothed grin.

"Gotta tell you, son," Tony said.

"What's that, Mr Smith?" Jack replied.

"You were the best mission we ever 'ad."

Jack smiled, reluctantly, "I guess that's a compliment, is it?"

Gordon chimed in from his left, "Yeah, lad." He put out his hand in a high five, "It is. *Semper Fi*, lad, as the marines say – 'Always faithful.'"

*

Jack was surprised how quickly life got back to the usual routine. The powers that be went out of their way to try to make everything as normal as possible for them. After all, VIGIL was indebted to Jack and Angus. Tony and Gordon resumed their janitorial duties and a new history teacher replaced Pendelshape as if nothing had happened. She didn't quite have Pendelshape's passion for the subject and seemed to be sticking closely to the curriculum. But, on reflection, that was probably a good thing. It was said that Pendelshape had been taken quite ill and had moved to Switzerland, for 'treatment'.

Once or twice, as autumn wore on and the last of the brown-and-orange leaves melted away, Jack found himself lying on the green lawn at Cairnfield, staring up at the sky, thinking about all the things he had seen and the people he and Angus had met on their adventure. They had all been wrapped up in their own lives, ambitions and troubles. He couldn't stop thinking that, even though it had been nearly a hundred years ago, in a funny way, these people were the same, as, well… the same as him. Two arms and two legs, two eyes, same size of brain… they were just as clever as him, if not more so, and felt the same sort of emotions. The only real difference was that they had less history to look back on. It was only now, having seen it and smelt it, not just read it in a book, he could kind of see Pendelshape's and Dad's point of view. These people were real. The deaths of the professor and Dani had made that agonisingly clear. In unguarded moments like these Jack felt… well, responsible. He could understand his father's drive – to go back and, as Pendelshape had put it, 'make things better'. But Jack knew it was a temptation he must resist.

*

One day, a few weeks later, Jack and his mum were sitting at the dinner table. His mum seemed much happier these days.

She started to clear the table and noticed a small plastic bag on the side.

"Sorry Jack – I forgot – that's the next cartridge for your puffer – from the chemist." She nodded at the plastic bag absent-mindedly.

Jack smiled, "Thanks Mum. But I don't think I'll need it."

His mum glanced round, "Oh?"

"Think I'm cured. I think they call it shock treatment. No more puffers for me…"

His mum smiled, "Good. That's good, Jack."

He shrugged.

There was a knock at the back door and, as usual, Angus did not wait for it to be answered, but instead came careering down the corridor to find them in the kitchen.

"It's arrived!" he waved a thin package above his head, then suddenly remembered his manners, "Oh, sorry Mrs C."

"What's arrived?"

"The next *Point-of-Departure* of course!"

It was probably force of habit, but in an instant, both of them had left the kitchen and tumbled down to the cellar below. The hole in the wall that Angus had crashed through into the workshop had been repaired and was now a door to what was an empty room.

"Hey Jack, something else!"

"What?"

"Look at this," Angus passed Jack an old black-and-white photograph. It was frayed at the edges. Jack peered at the image.

"Remember?"

For a moment, Jack didn't know what Angus meant. From the photo stared a broad-shouldered man in a dress uniform. A German dress uniform. Jack studied the image closely – there was something odd about the man's face. Then he noticed it – one of his ears had no ear lobe.

Jack suddenly understood, "Ludwig… the German soldier in the crater…"

"The very same. My great grandfather. Think about it, Jack… if your bayonet had been a few centimetres further to the right…"

"You wouldn't be here…"

"But I am."

"…and the rest, as they say, is history."

Five members of the Black Hand group in court following the assassination of Archduke Ferdinand. Princip is seated in the centre.

Day of the
Assassins

BACKGROUND INFORMATION

What was the Austro-Hungarian Empire? (see page 30)
The Austro-Hungarian Empire, also known as Austria-Hungary,
was a large, powerful state in central and south-east Europe that was
broken up at the end of World War I. It was the second largest state
in Europe after the Russian Empire.

What was the alliance system? (see page 30)
By 1914, the great powers of Europe were inter-connected by a
system of alliances. The Dual Alliance between Germany and
Austria-Hungary was created in 1879 and Italy later joined them
in the Triple Alliance. Otto von Bismarck, the architect of the
German Empire, created the alliances as a defensive system.
This was largely against France, whom he regarded as the main
enemy following defeat in the Franco-Prussian war in 1871 and
their loss of the French territories of Alsace and Lorraine to the
newly created Germany.

In 1891, for a variety of reasons, Russia cooled relations with
Germany, and formed the Dual Entente with France. In the early
twentieth century, Britain moved closer to her traditional enemies
(France and Russia) – partly fearing Germany's rapid build-up of
an ocean-going navy that might challenge Britain's naval supremacy.

Day of the Assassins

In 1904, Britain settled her differences with France in Africa, establishing the Entente Cordiale, and in 1907, following defeat by Japan, Russia was eager to settle her differences with Britain in Persia and Afghanistan. This led to the Triple Entente between Britain, France and Russia.

German military strategists were required to devise a plan (which became known as the 'Schlieffen Plan') to deal with a war on two fronts – Russia to their east and France to their west. This aimed to defeat France rapidly, before Russia had mobilised her large army.

Although this alliance system was defensive in nature, when coupled with the military problem that Germany potentially faced war on two fronts, it became an important reason why a conflict, essentially between Austria-Hungary and Russia, over their spheres of influence in the Balkans (or south-east Europe), turned into a European war and then, with the entry of the United States in 1917, a world war.

What was the general mood within the Austro-Hungarian Empire in the lead up to the assassination?
A key problem for the Austro-Hungarian Empire was that it was composed largely of minorities – Slovaks, Romanians, Croats, Czechs, Poles, Ruthenes, Slovenes, Serbs and others.

The administration of neighbouring country, Bosnia-Herzegovina, was placed under Austrian control following the Treaty of Berlin in 1878. In response, the Balkan state of Serbia created a liberation movement for Bosnian Serbs with a terrorist wing called the 'Black Hand'. With Russian encouragement, Serbia also created a Balkan league with Greece, Bulgaria and Montenegro, which aimed to exclude Turks from south-east Europe. Two Balkan wars were fought in 1912 and 1913, and as a result, Serbia's territory and population doubled and she became more ambitious. This generated fear in Austria and also gave encouragement to the Serbs living within the Austro-Hungarian Empire. Tension finally boiled over on 28th June 1914 when the Archduke Franz Ferdinand (heir to the Habsburg throne) was assassinated in Sarajevo, the capital of Bosnia-Herzegovina, by Gavrilo Princip, a Bosnian Serb, trained and armed by the Black Hand.

Why did the assassination of Archduke Franz Ferdinand lead to full-scale war?

Following the assassination, determined to crush Serbia for good, Austria issued an ultimatum to Serbia that would effectively have made Serbia into a client state of Austria-Hungary. Serbia rejected the ultimatum and Austria declared war on Serbia on 28 July 1914. On 30th July, the Russians started mobilising their armed forces. The next day, Germany (Austria's ally) issued an ultimatum to the Russians to stop mobilisation, and when they failed to do so, Germany declared war upon them.

On 1st August, the French began to mobilise and by 3rd August, Germany had declared war upon them and advanced into Belgium – following the logic of the Schlieffen Plan. This violation of Belgian neutrality caused England to declare war on Germany on 4th August. Austria declared war on Russia on 6th August.

What had started as a conflict between Austria and Serbia in the Balkans rapidly escalated into a war that involved all the great European powers. Germany and Austria-Hungary were joined by The Ottoman Empire and Bulgaria to complete the Central Powers.

Countries such as Australia, India and South Africa, were involved in the Allied Forces as part of their allegiance to the British Empire. In 1915, Italy also joined the Allies, and in 1917, the United States entered the war on the allied side.

Who was really involved in the assassination of Archduke Franz Ferdinand? (see page 58)

There were many people who assisted the assassins, but the group in Sarajevo on the day were Gavrilo Princip (who fired the shots to assassinate Archduke Ferdinand and his wife), Nedjelko Čabrinović, Vaso Čubrilović, Trifun Grabež, Mehmed Mehmedbašić, Cvijetko Popović and Danilo Ilić. A key architect of the plot was the Chief of Serbian Military Intelligence Dragutin Dimitrijević (known as Apis – 'the bee'). Dani and Anna Matronovic and Zadok are fictional characters.

Is the Schönbrunn Palace real? (see page 42)

Yes – Schönbrunn Palace in Vienna is one of the most important cultural monuments in Austria and is a major tourist attraction. 'Schönbrunn' means 'beautiful well'. The palace and gardens were home to successive Habsburg monarchs. At the age of six, Mozart performed in the Hall of Mirrors before Maria Theresa and her court. Marie Antoinette grew up there, Napoleon lived there and Kennedy and Khrushchev met there in 1961. The 'Schönbrunn raid' is fictional.

What is CERN? (see page 55)

The European Organisation for Nuclear Research, known as CERN, is the world's largest particle physics laboratory and is situated near Geneva on the border between France and Switzerland. Nearly

8,000 scientists and engineers (including around half of the world's particle physics community), work on experiments conducted at CERN – using CERN's particle accelerators. CERN also has a large computer centre containing very powerful data-processing facilities.

Was HMS *Dreadnought* real? (see page 68)
Launched in 1906, HMS *Dreadnought* was the first British Royal Navy 'all big gun' battleship, and she revolutionised battleship design. She was built at Portsmouth in only fourteen months. She was also fast – adopting revolutionary steam-turbine engines which had undergone little testing at the time. *Dreadnought* gave her name to a class of battleships that made warships built before this time virtually obsolete. Germany started to build '*Dreadnought*-type' battleships following Britain's example, and there ensued a naval race between Britain and Germany, who both spent significant resources trying to out-build each other. At the outbreak of war, Britain had twenty-two *Dreadnought*-type battleships and Germany had fifteen – the later models were even bigger and more powerful than the original. HMS *Dreadnought* herself saw little action in the First World War and was de-commissioned shortly afterwards.

What is a Schwarzgelb? (see page 143)
To be a true supporter of the Austro-Hungarian regime was to be called a 'Schwarzgelb' – reflecting the colours of the Habsburgs – black and yellow. It is also a term used to refer to policies in favour of the regime.

What happened to the assassins?

Gavrilo Princip was imprisoned after the assassination. He was technically too young to be executed under law. He died from tuberculosis in April 1918 in a prison hospital. In Serbia, he became a national hero. Moritz Schiller's delicatessen is now the Princip Museum, and two footprints on the pavement outside mark where Princip stood to fire the shots.

Nedjelko Čabrinović was sentenced to twenty years in prison. He died in January 1916, also of tuberculosis.

Vaso Čubrilović received a sixteen-year prison sentence. Released in 1918 he became Minister of Forests for Yugoslavia.

Trifun Grabež was sentenced to twenty years. He died in February 1916 of tuberculosis.

Mehmed Mehmedbašić was implicated in a new assassination plot. He was imprisoned then pardoned in 1919. He returned to Sarajevo to work as a gardener and carpenter.

Cvijetko Popović received a thirteen-year sentence. He later became curator at the Sarajevo Museum.

Danilo Ilić was arrested by Sarajevo police a few days after the assassination. In the hope of avoiding the death penalty he gave the police the names of everyone involved in the plot. In 1915, he was hanged.

Dragutin Dimitrijević was arrested in 1917 and was sentenced to death for treason. He was executed in 1917.

How did the war end?

World War I came to an end on 11th November 1918 when Germany agreed to a ceasefire and signed the Treaty of Versailles in the following year. This treaty required Germany to accept responsibility for causing the war and to disarm, make substantial territorial concessions and pay reparations to certain allied countries.